S0-DPG-188

Her face told Sam
all that she was thinking

Sam sighed and spoke quietly as though answering each one of her unspoken questions. "All right, Jenny Hunter. You can run for cover. Get into your truck and drive away. Find a nice shady tree to brood under. Take a nice cool drink from the thermos you carry. Eat every bite of that lunch that shouldn't go to waste."

Jenny couldn't speak as she stared into his midnight-blue eyes.

"And think of me," he continued. "Admit we're attracted to each other. Reconcile yourself to my attentions. Because—" he punctuated these last few words with the lightest taps on her chin "—I'm—not—going—away."

ABOUT THE AUTHOR

Cara West reports that *Jenny Kissed Me*, her third Superromance, was "a lot of fun to write." A lifelong dog lover, Cara was moved to create a dog-trainer heroine when she took her own new puppy to an inspirational woman for obedience training! Cara, whose household now includes two gray weimaraners and a cat, lives in Texas with her two sons.

Books by Cara West

HARLEQUIN SUPERROMANCE

Don't miss any of our special offers. Write to us at the following address for information on our newest releases.

Harlequin Reader Service
901 Fuhrmann Blvd., P.O. Box 1397, Buffalo, NY 14240
Canadian address: P.O. Box 603,
Fort Erie, Ont. L2A 5X3

Jenny Kissed Me

CARA WEST

Harlequin Books

TORONTO • NEW YORK • LONDON
AMSTERDAM • PARIS • SYDNEY • HAMBURG
STOCKHOLM • ATHENS • TOKYO • MILAN

Published July 1990

ISBN 0-373-70410-0

Copyright © 1990 by Cara West. All rights reserved.
Except for use in any review, the reproduction or utilization
of this work in whole or in part in any form by any electronic,
mechanical or other means, now known or hereafter invented,
including xerography, photocopying and recording,
or in any information storage or retrieval system, is forbidden without
the permission of the publisher, Harlequin Enterprises Limited,
225 Duncan Mill Road, Don Mills, Ontario, Canada M3B 3K9.

All the characters in this book have no existence outside the
imagination of the author and have no relation whatsoever to
anyone bearing the same name or names. They are not even
distantly inspired by any individual known or unknown to the
author, and all incidents are pure invention.

® are Trademarks registered in the United States Patent and
Trademark Office and in other countries.

Printed in U.S.A.

To Barbara and Jim,
who always set a place for me
at their banquet of life...

With fond memories of Ernie,
my very own Zeppo...

And a special thanks to Diana,
who taught me doggy language....

CHAPTER ONE

"WOULD YOU LIKE TO STOP by my place for coffee or a drink?" Sam asked as he pulled out of the Erwin Center parking lot and onto the street, following the line of cars moving slowly before him. Not the most romantic opening, he realized belatedly. Although Leslie didn't seem to mind.

"Why, yes, I'd like that," she murmured, leaning toward him invitingly from the passenger seat.

Sam heard the satisfaction in her dulcet tones. And why not? They'd been dating for weeks. They got along well enough. Wasn't it time he took the expected step and invited the lady into his home and bed?

Lately, he'd begun to notice a certain anxious look that told him Leslie was wondering if she'd made a tactical error in the accustomed mating ritual.

Quite the contrary. Leslie was a model of perfection. A well-tailored, well-manicured, well-informed female of thirty-odd years who could discuss with equal confidence industrial design or the Longhorns' chances of going to the Cotton Bowl. Sam had trouble explaining to himself why he felt an illogical reluctance to make love to this woman.

Other than the obvious fact that he wasn't in love with her.

"I enjoyed the concert immensely." Leslie accompanied her smile of thanks with a light caress of Sam's suit-clad shoulder.

Sam found he had no desire to reciprocate the gesture.

"You were lucky to get tickets so close to the stage," she went on, unaware of his evolving mood.

Luck had nothing to do with it, Sam thought, remembering the price of the tickets. The Super Drum, as the Austin locals called it, had been packed with fans to see the touring rock superstar. For the most part, those fans were dressed-for-success, trimmed-and-tanned couples, with discretionary income and discriminating tastes. They'd all looked, to Sam's way of thinking, like mannequins in a department store window.

Sam decided not to share his observations on their fellow concertgoers. Leslie fit his mental description of them much too well. Nor did he think she'd appreciate the jaundiced review he gave the evening's entertainment.

When the singer had begun a lavish, blatantly sexual rendition of "I'm in the Mood for Love," Sam could almost hear plans being made around him for after-hours seductions.

Unfortunately, Sam was in no mood for romance. He wished Leslie would see humor in the situation.

Not likely.

If Leslie lacked anything it was an eye for the absurd, a kind of laughing perspective that accepted life with all its ironies and appreciated the jokes it played without discretion or discrimination.

Realizing the direction of his thoughts, Sam felt guilty for dissecting his date at a time when he should be captivated by her charms. He glanced Leslie's way and noticed a small smile of triumph on her well-shaped lips.

She has it all planned out.

The night would mark the beginning of a discreet affair, one custom-made for the nineties with a proper amount of commitment and monogamy—you couldn't be too careful in these dangerous times. But with lots of space. And keep it tidy.

Sam suddenly recognized how jaded he felt. He suspected it showed and smiled warily as he caught Leslie's eye. She smiled encouragement.

She's probably speculating on the performance ahead, wondering if it would live up to the advance billing.

Sam would have been stupid if he hadn't realized he was something of a catch. He was a normally libidinous, healthy, attractive, intelligent male, who at thirty-four was a partner in an engineering firm—a *prosperous* engineering firm—that designed ice-cream machines for which dairies all over the world paid a premium price.

To add to his assets, Sam appreciated women. He had a loving, generous mother, three lively sisters, two adoring nieces and various female acquaintances, both personal and professional, whose company he thoroughly enjoyed. Women picked up on that attitude and responded in kind.

Given all this, not even an uninspired coupling would turn Leslie off. With that prediction, wondering how the hell he was going to escape a field test, Sam swung his car into the parking space behind the town house where he lived. He went around to open the door for his date, trying to think of a gentlemanly way to renege on the implicit contract he and Leslie had just negotiated. Somehow his mother's lectures on manners hadn't covered this particular scenario.

Silently, Sam unlatched the gate to the kitchen patio, escorting Leslie to the back door. He unlocked it and gestured for her to enter. After following her across the threshold, he reached for the wall switch and turned on the overhead lights.

When he did, Leslie gasped in alarm.

As well she might.

For before them lay a scene of wild destruction.

In the living room a lamp had been carelessly toppled, its fixture shattered on the carpeted floor. Around their feet was strewn a wide selection of items from Sam's wardrobe—a pair of running shoes, his slippers, a robe, T-shirts, a veritable rainbow of Jockey undershorts, even the jockstrap he'd worn last night for handball. Magazines that once decorated the coffee table now lay wantonly scattered in shreds.

On the table in the dining alcove a vase of flowers had been overturned and dismembered, petals, stems and leaves making a trail across the floor. Water from the vase now dribbled slowly over the table's edge, forming a spreading puddle on the patterned tile.

Even the kitchen countertops looked as if a whirlwind had swept over them. The toaster had toppled to its doom, as had the salt and pepper shakers. A loaf of bread had been thoroughly mangled, as if the perpetrator of this mass destruction had voraciously downed a quick snack in the midst of his assault.

"You've been vandalized! Robbed!" Leslie whispered, horrified. "Be careful!" She grabbed Sam's arm as he stepped forward. "Whoever did it may still be in the house!"

Sam was sure of it.

He braced himself.

From the shadows beyond the stairway came a flash of movement.

Leslie let out a blood-curdling scream.

Sam winced.

As a small, hairy, tan-and-white figure streaked through the living room, trailing items of clothing. It skidded into the kitchen, through the puddle of water, and began to leap madly around them with a joyous bark of welcome.

"Zeppo, down!"

Sam's wirehaired fox terrier ignored the order.

One leap. Zeppo shredded Leslie's lacy black stockings. Two leaps. His wet paws landed breast high on her silk evening ensemble. Three leaps. He managed to lave the end of her nose with his panting tongue.

"Sam! Sam! Get this dog off me!" Leslie screeched, frantically dodging her pursuer. Zeppo, deciding she was the coy type, cornered her against the wall. "Get him off me, Sam! I'm allergic to dog hair! Make him stop licking me! Achoo! Achoo!"

"Zeppo! Down!"

At Sam's voice, Zeppo lost interest in the agitated female and landed with a graceful bound in his master's arms.

"I...I'm terribly sorry, Leslie." Sam cleared his throat, trying to keep his expression serious.

She made a sound somewhere between a growl and a howl.

"Can I get you a tissue? A dishcloth?" Sam rummaged awkwardly through a nearby drawer.

This time, Leslie ignored him as she gazed down, sniffling in despair at the paw prints adorning her dress.

"Actually, why don't I take you home to assess the damage? This place can wait to be cleaned up." He made the offer with lame gallantry, between licks, his arms full of wriggling, affectionate dog.

"I think you'd better." This was said between sneezes and glacial looks. Leslie had already found the doorknob, turned it and backed into the night.

"And I'll deal with you when I get back," Sam threatened the panting face two inches from his nose. Zeppo gazed adoringly into Sam's eyes, unfazed by the ominous tone, as if he sensed the gratitude and stifled laughter that lay behind the threat.

"So DID YOU KNOW?" Sam asked Zeppo thirty minutes later as he and the terrier lounged on the couch surveying the mess.

Sam had managed to see Leslie home without further incident, the lady in question having recovered her customary poise. When he offered to pay for new stockings or the cleaning bill, she'd managed a polite refusal. She'd even invited him in. But Leslie was very understanding about Sam's wanting to get home. Obviously, a shaggy third party didn't fit into her romantic equation. Sam had danced a small jig on the way to his car.

Now he faced the task of reprimanding his rescuer. Still, Sam was willing to give credit where credit was due. "Okay, I admit it, Mutt. I'm eternally grateful. You saved me from making an ass of myself. Given my present state of mind on modern relationships, I should never have offered the invitation to Leslie, no matter how much it was expected. It was unkind, uncouth and unfair to us both."

Zeppo acknowledged the confession by strafing Sam's thigh and planting a wet kiss in the vicinity of his left ear, then nipping his neck playfully.

Sam held the dog to glare at him. "But that doesn't mean you're off the hook. Why the hell do I put up with this?'' He gestured at the havoc around him. ''It's not as if you're here by invitation.''

Far from it. Zeppo was an unreturnable gift. When Sam's great-aunt, Lillith, had died suddenly at the age of eighty-five, she'd willed Sam her most prized possessions—her latest fox terrier and a library of Marx Brothers movies.

It was Zeppo's fate to arrive on the scene just before his mistress departed. It was Sam's luck to be Lillith's favorite nephew.

Now Sam was stuck with his inheritance, having lost a jewel of a housekeeper who'd declared her salary covered only the house and one male inhabitant, the one who was housebroken. Tonight's mess was not Zeppo's first felony. For Sam, coming home from work had become a mild adventure. Each evening presented evidence of new territory Zeppo had claimed for his own.

Sam threatened his legacy often and loudly, but both of them knew the threats were hollow. This time he conceded that ranting was futile, sighed and began to pick up the broken glass from the demolished lamp, which, if he remembered correctly, had set him back two hundred dollars. Zeppo pranced nearby, dangling a sock, trying to coax him into a tugging match.

Sam laughed and shook his head. ''You know what your trouble is, Zeppo? You don't know the meaning of the word shame. Or fear, either.''

Indeed, courage was Zeppo's middle name. Yesterday he'd declared war on the Doberman pinscher in the next town house. They had engaged in a brief but furious skirmish. Sam had intervened, and his fingers had barely escaped the jaws of death.

''You, my fine, hairy friend, are a menace to property. Sanity, too.'' Sam dumped the glass in the trash bin, put his hands on his hips and, with a brooding look, stared at man's best friend.

Zeppo cocked his ears, intrigued by the new tone.

As though reaching a decision, Sam pulled out his billfold and found the business card Nate, his partner, had given him. Nate had assured Sam that a cousin's problems with a petulant poodle had been resolved with amazing success. The dog trainer she used even made house calls.

"Jenny Hunter." Sam read the card aloud for Zeppo's benefit. "Hunter's Kennels, Specialist in Obedience Training and Problem Behavior." He looked to be sure his particular behavior problem was paying attention and spoke sternly. "The fling's over, kid. A lady named Hunter is about to change your ways."

JENNY HUNTER SAT on the Wakefield sofa surreptitiously scratching a new itch as she tried simultaneously to sort out the chaos around her and give her attention to the lady of the house.

". . . afraid Muffin is the most timid of my babies. He won't come out from under the bed. Oh, dear." Mrs. Wakefield caught the significance of Jenny's scratching. "Perhaps we'd better move to the dining table. The living room is infested with fleas."

Jenny could see why. Mutt and Jeff, two dogs of indeterminate heritage, scrambled over the sofa beside her in a game of tag. Sparky, a Scottish terrier, and Lulu, a Yorkshire terrier, tangled between her feet, illustrating their mutual dislike. Peter, a boxer mix of noble proportions, was sitting on his haunches bemusedly following the action. Two poodles whose names Jenny had missed were on the other side of the patio door, loudly protesting their exclusion. Roscoe, an Afghan in his declining years, lay next to the fireplace, pointedly ignoring the fray.

Help! Help! Everyone circle the wagons!

Jenny found herself torn between panic and mirth.

Lot of good circling the wagons will do. Remember, you're the cavalry come to save the day.

Only how on earth was she going to rescue Mrs. Wakefield from her nine darlings? By this time next week she might have added three more.

As though reading Jenny's thoughts, Mrs. Wakefield said apologetically, "You must think I'm crazy having this many dogs. I didn't to begin with, but people started leaving them with me. Pete, Lulu and Muffin were strays. I couldn't just abandon them on the streets to starve."

So she'd established a one-woman animal shelter.

". . . love every one of them," Mrs. Wakefield meandered on fondly. She stroked Pete's head, making him the object of Lulu's and Sparky's ire. "Behave!" she scolded the two dogs and tried to separate them.

"Some breeds," Jenny reminded Mrs. Wakefield gently, "are very jealous. Scotties and Yorkshire terriers think their masters belong to them." She might as well wade in now as later. "I've found that when there's more than one dog in a household, it's better to let them establish their ranks."

"You mean not interfere?" Mrs. Wakefield looked horrified.

"Not unless you have to. There's usually no bloodshed. You'll be surprised how quickly they sort things out."

"Lulu and Sparky can't even be in the same room with Chad and Bitsy."

That explained the two poodles. Jenny filed their names away in her mind.

"...one of the reasons I haven't had the house de-fleaed. Perhaps I should board them with you for a day or two."

"If you'd like," Jenny agreed soothingly, hearing Mrs. Wakefield's underlying hesitation. She tabulated the expense of boarding nine dogs and decided the Wakefield pocketbook could stand the total. Mrs. Wakefield lived in Jester Estates, an exclusive Austin suburb. Clients like her kept Hunter's Kennels in the black. In this particular instance, Jenny was sure she'd earn every penny. Still, she had to admit she liked Mrs. Wakefield. The woman was ineffectual but thoroughly delightful, and Jenny had great sympathy for her misguided efforts. Jenny had decided long ago that people who loved dogs were Best of Breed.

Jenny got out her notebook as they forged a path to the next room. "I'll make a list of the problems you've outlined. The ones you consider most serious we'll tackle first."

"Then you can help me." The lady's face brightened with hope.

Jenny smiled warmly, quashing her doubts. "That's what I'm here for. But you'll need to be involved every step of the way."

"Oh, I understand perfectly." Mrs. Wakefield leaned toward Jenny confidingly. "You come highly recommended. Everyone I talked to said you're wonderful with animals."

Thank heaven Mrs. Wakefield had confidence in her, Jenny thought, more confidence right now than she had in herself. Squaring her shoulders, Jenny began outlining a course of action. Thirty minutes later, they'd set priorities, the next appointment and a possible date

Jenny could pick up the babies to take them to the kennel for a night away from home.

Jenny tried to imagine herself rounding up the nine animals for the trip to the kennel. The idea left her feeling shaky.

Apparently, however, the panic didn't show. Because when Mrs. Wakefield saw Jenny to the door she was all smiles and gratitude.

Jenny let out a gusty sigh as she walked to her truck. She thought over the scene she'd just left and shook her head. Her lips quivered as she tried to keep from laughing. She pressed them together tightly as she drove away.

Oh, Lord, she thought she'd seen everything, and her years as a trainer had provided her with many varied experiences. She remembered the man with two dogs, a Great Pyrenees named Tiny and a Chihuahua called Butch. Then there was the lady who insisted on wearing her hair in the same style as her poodle. Jenny had had trouble deciding who to call to heel. Now came the hapless Mrs. Wakefield, who'd surrounded herself with a perpetual dogfight. Poor Mrs. Wakefield, who was depending on Jenny to solve all her problems. To get dear Muffin from underneath the bed.

At this point, Jenny pulled to the curb. After struggling to repress them, she dissolved into giggles. The road ahead became a blur.

Jenny was laughing so hard tears spilled from her eyes. She wiped them away, struggling for breath.

Suddenly the laughter vanished, and she found herself leaning over the steering wheel sobbing.

Wave after wave of surprise and shock washed over her.

Jenny never cried.

She didn't have time to.

Crying was for those who thought it made a difference. She'd learned long ago tears were a luxury she couldn't afford.

So dammit! Why was she sitting by the side of the road wailing like a banshee?

Because she was tired. Tired to the bone. These past few months had exhausted her. She'd been afraid to turn away customers. Austin's economic slump had lasted two years before it began to ease, and clients like Mrs. Wakefield had been thin upon the ground.

It was only lately the obedience training had started to pick up, and she'd felt justified in making Leia, her assistant, a full-time employee. Now her days were hectic rather than endless. If she was lucky she'd get to bed before twelve tonight. With a six-thirty wake-up to clean out the kennel, that left her with the hope of seven hours of sleep.

Thinking of sleep made Jenny realize how long the day had been—topped off with Mrs. Wakefield. She guessed that was enough to send any trainer into shock.

Jenny rubbed the tears away resolutely. Enough of this nonsense.

She massaged her aching neck, stretched to ease the kinks from her shoulders, turned on the ignition and found her way to the highway toward town. Just as she'd set the truck on automatic pilot heading south toward the kennel, she remembered her last appointment and groaned. It was a six o'clock call on a terrier named Zeppo, whose master, a Mr. Sam Grant, had sounded mildly frantic when they'd talked briefly the day before.

Jenny checked the address in her logbook. She was in luck. It was on this side of Austin. As she approached the street where Grant lived, she noted with distaste the blocks and blocks of expensive new apartments, the town houses and duplexes crowding each other on every side.

A yuppie ghetto. She could never live here. She'd feel stifled, claustrophobic. Thank God, she had the business as an excuse to make her home out of town. Her childhood years of moving from cheap apartment to cheap apartment, from one dingy motel room to another, had left indelible memories that still cropped up in bad dreams in the dead of the night.

Surveying his territory, Jenny formed a mental picture of Mr. Sam Grant. A young executive, no doubt, on the rise in his company. House calls from Jenny didn't come cheap. Probably too absorbed in himself to get married, he'd decided a pet would make a clever addition to his household. Now that he had one, he couldn't cope.

Those were the clients Jenny found the hardest to work with. Her heart went out to the defenseless animals who, through no fault of their own, had become unwanted possessions.

Steeling herself to prepare for whatever situation she might find, Jenny parked and checked in the mirror to see if there were reminders of her crying jag. She brushed her face with powder from the compact she carried, ran a comb through her hair and marched up the sidewalk to Mr. Grant's door. As she rang the bell, there came a duet of barking and deep male voice.

"Zeppo, I think retribution's come calling."

The door swung open and Jenny encountered a pair of blue eyes.

Deep, smoky blue eyes, the color of evening. A lean face that held a hint of amusement. Black hair so dark it shone midnight blue in the golden rays of the late afternoon sun.

Jenny blinked at the vision before her.

The man stared at Jenny.

Their momentary lapse was all that was required.

Down the street strolled the imperious Doberman. Zeppo sighted the enemy. His territory was invaded. He charged with a ferocious growl of rage.

"Ah, hell," Sam muttered wearily and without further hesitation cleared the shrubbery as he gave chase.

Mr. Grant was an athlete, Jenny decided distractedly as she watched the action. He was gaining on Zeppo, which was quite a feat. At this point, however, the race was too close to call. Zeppo had the scent of battle to spur him. Grant, on the other hand, was trying to prevent blood from being spilled.

Just as Zeppo was within reach of powerful bared fangs, Grant took a flying leap—Jenny had to admit it was gracefully executed—and fell on Zeppo, producing howls of frustration.

Taking a moment to catch his breath, Sam scooped up the protesting warrior and offered a profuse apology as he backed away from the elderly neighbor who was straining with all his might to hold his dog.

For the second time in an hour Jenny couldn't help it. She began to laugh and laugh till tears came into her eyes. She was fighting giggles when Sam marched up to her, a wriggling Zeppo secure in his grasp.

"Jenny Hunter, I presume. The dog-training expert. The lady who was supposed to restore peace and order to my life. You're laughing." It was an accusation more than an observation. "Laughing! While I risk life and limb to protect this vandal!"

With an awkward gesture Jenny covered her treacherous lips. Despite her best efforts, more tears of mirth welled up. Frantically she wiped at them, trying to regain her composure.

Sam's mock tirade trailed off. He smiled at Jenny and, still holding the flailing Zeppo, resumed his study of her face.

She was an elf. A wood nymph. A water sprite who made her bed on a lily pad and woke to drink the morning dew from the petals of a flower.

She was laughter and tears and dreams and everything that life was made of.

She was a picture from a storybook he'd treasured as a child. A fairy at the bottom of his garden.

Small, slim in slacks and shirt, she had nut-brown eyes and a delicately pointed face framed with a welter of disheveled curls. Those curls were the color of new-mown hay still touched with sunlight.

She was quite simply the most bewitching woman Sam had ever seen. But at his intense scrutiny the laughter vanished and a wary look appeared. In the blink of an eye, Jenny Hunter seemed poised to flee into the enchanted forest Sam imagined was her home.

He banked the fires stirring inside him and managed with iron control to produce a teasing grin, a grin that in the past had served him well in these matters.

"I'm sorry for staring. You're not what I expected."

"Dog trainers, Mr. Grant, come in all shapes and sizes."

The water sprite had vanished, to be replaced by a cool businesswoman, one who seemed about as approachable as a barbed-wire fence. No, that wasn't a correct analogy, Sam decided. She was too professional to be openly hostile. But the sign was up—Trespassers Beware.

With the opening she'd given him, a variety of retorts came to Sam's mind. He sorted through them and decided on a bland, "Won't you come in?"

"Yes, of course," Jenny said pleasantly, but the faint flush that rose beneath her light tan told Sam she realized the direction her words had led him.

"Once we're inside I can divest myself of the mongrel horde."

Jenny's mouth quirked rebelliously. Sam decided judiciously that her repressed laughter was an enchanting sight.

"You know, Mr. Grant—" Jenny directed the conversation to the reason she was here "—fox terriers are quite territorial. Zeppo was just defending his turf. Weren't you, fella?"

She approached the dog obliquely. Zeppo fell on her proffered hand with damp enthusiasm. Their friendship established, Jenny squatted beside him and began to scratch behind his ears. Zeppo melted into a puddle of adoration.

Grant understood how Zeppo felt. He gazed at Jenny's golden curls and said a little huskily, "Doesn't he realize the canine storm trooper outside could tear him limb from limb?"

"It doesn't matter, does it, Zeppo? You have the heart of a lion." Her voice became a croon.

Sam wondered if she had any idea how sexy that crooning voice was.

He cleared his throat. "Does that mean I now live in a perpetual war zone?"

"No, of course not." Jenny stood, keeping her expression neutral. "Zeppo can be trained to be around other dogs."

"Does that mean he can also be trained not to wreck my house on a daily basis?" He gestured her toward the living room, offered a chair and settled into the sofa across from her.

"That, too." As Jenny sat, she surveyed the room. It was tastefully and expensively furnished, and one wall was devoted to an elaborate high-tech entertainment system that must have cost its owner thousands of dollars. This was certainly not the place for a terrier pup. She looked at Sam oddly. "You know, Mr. Grant, it pays to look into a breed before buying it. Were you aware of the kinds of problems you might encounter when you decided on Zeppo?"

"I didn't decide on Zeppo," Sam said with great dignity. "I inherited him. From an eccentric aunt who did a brilliant imitation of Groucho Marx. Zeppo's Zeppo the Second, really. Aunt Lillith's sixth fox terrier." He waited expectantly.

"And the others were . . . ?"

"Groucho, Zeppo, Harpo, Chico and Groucho II."

Jenny's lips twitched before she could control them.

"Aunt Lillith was quite a woman," Sam remembered fondly. "After her second husband died she decided dogs made better companions. They were a pain to housetrain. However, she claimed it was easier than breaking in a new husband every decade or so."

Jenny lost the battle with laughter.

Sam leaned back, satisfied with his efforts.

After a moment, Jenny collected herself and again attempted to return to the purpose of her visit. "So, Mr. Grant, where shall we start?"

"On a first-name basis. Mine's Sam."

Jenny's face closed. "I don't think . . ."

"Why not? Why should Zeppo get preferential treatment? I was hoping as a reward I'd get scratched behind the ears." As soon as he spoke, Sam knew he'd gone too far.

"Mr. Grant . . ." Jenny started to rise.

"Okay, okay." Sam waved her down placatingly. "I'll be good and not overstep the bounds of the client-trainer relationship." For now.

Jenny doubted his words. In fact she suspected Sam Grant would be harder to manage than his rowdy inheritance. Still, she needed the business, Jenny reminded herself sternly. A polite professionalism would warn Grant off soon enough.

If she could ever reclaim that elusive commodity. Grant was breaking through her defenses with a disarming grin that stirred butterflies in the vicinity of her stomach. He was watching her now with a smile of faint speculation that molded his mobile lips in a distracting way. As though he could sense her inner struggle.

Jenny's backbone stiffened at the unwelcome thought. "I'll hold you to that promise...Sam." She refused to make their names an issue. "You're welcome to call me Jenny. Now, since every minute I'm here costs you money, why don't we get down to business? What behavior of Zeppo's would you like to change? Are you having housebreaking problems? Destructive behavior? Is he disruptive with visitors?"

"All of the above."

"Well, housebreaking could continue to be difficult. Zeppo might be having youthful accidents. But as I mentioned before, male fox terriers guard their territories and mark them. Many owners I know have them neutered after a certain age. It's sometimes the only satisfactory remedy for the problem."

Jenny had been giving her attention to a fawning Zeppo during this entire speech. If she hadn't looked up just then, she'd have made it home free.

She did look up and the expression of comic pain on Sam's face was her undoing.

Jenny flushed bright red and damned the man. This particular bit of advice was a common solution to territorial behavior, one she'd offered her clients for years with professional aplomb. Never before had she, well, considered how a male owner might perceive the procedure.

She blundered on. "I suggest you wait until Zeppo's at least two years old, however. It'll take that long for him to gain secondary sexual characteristics."

Sam raised a brow. Jenny blushed again and decided she just might slap him if he insisted on elaboration.

Sam was, however, a gentleman. He contented himself with saying, "I'm sure Zeppo's relieved to hear neutering isn't an option—just yet at any rate. He comes from championship bloodlines, and Aunt Lillith planned on selling his services. I get the feeling Zeppo was looking forward to that."

"Yes. Well. I also gather you'd like his manners to improve around other animals."

"Very perceptive," Sam murmured.

Jenny smiled brightly. "That's what you pay me to be. I usually handle destructive behavior and housebreaking on an individual basis once a week. To socialize Zeppo you'll need to join one of my group obedience classes. I'm starting a new six-week session this Saturday morning."

Two meetings a week. It was a start, Sam decided.

"How long," he asked, "will the transformation take?" At Jenny's questioning look, Sam clarified, "I mean, how long will it take you to make Zeppo into a model citizen?"

"Actually, Mr. Grant—" Sam's eyebrow quirked at her address "—Sam. You'll be the one making Zeppo into a model citizen. You're his daddy."

This time Sam's well-shaped brow almost made it to his hairline. Jenny flushed. "I mean . . . I'm sorry. I'm afraid that's a stupid habit of mine, to call . . ." *Damn!* He'd flustered her again. If this kept up she'd fall into a chronic state of confusion every time they met.

"You're his master," Jenny resumed carefully. "I'll be training you to discipline him. To reward him for obeying commands and, with the proper techniques, to suppress undesirable behavior. Dogs, like other species, have a definite language. If you learn that language, you can communicate with them. Believe it or not, Zeppo wants to behave."

This time Sam shot Zeppo a highly skeptical glance before he turned to Jenny. "So how long do you estimate it'll take?"

"How old is Zeppo?"

"Eight months."

"And how long have you had him?"

Sam chuckled ruefully. "Three weeks, five days, seven hours and twenty minutes."

This time Jenny stoutly refused to join the laughter. "At this point, Zeppo's developed a set personality, which we'll have to remold. And of course, he's suffering from a lack of companionship. I'm sure loneliness is at the heart of his problems."

"Are you suggesting I get a matched set?"

"No. I'm just saying it could take months to correct his basic behavior and help him adjust to his new circumstances. Longer if you decide you want him more thoroughly trained."

Sam looked at the recalcitrant Zeppo.

Months, she'd estimated, to reform the rascal.

Thank you, Aunt Lillith, with all my heart.

CHAPTER TWO

WHEN JENNY FINALLY made it home that evening, there were three messages on her answering machine. The first was from a Robert Ingram inquiring about classes. The second was from a regular customer canceling a lesson. The third was from Annabelle, her mother. The obligatory weekly phone call they probably both dreaded. There was so much between them and so little to say.

Jenny decided all three messages could wait till after supper. The half-thawed pork chop in the fridge would take too much effort to cook. So she threw together a salad instead, and ate it at the kitchen table under the cooling breeze of a window fan.

It was June. Already the heat was palpable. By July, every day would feel like the inside of a blast oven, and the nights would settle in under a suffocating blanket of darkness. The summer months had to be endured. Jenny's fifty-year-old house sported decrepit cooling units that worked fitfully and gobbled electricity. She couldn't afford to run them except on the most sweltering days.

Besides, Jenny had long ago discovered that retreat from the heat was a psychological blunder. You could catch cabin fever in a Texas August as surely as in a Nebraska February.

Last year, Jenny had bowed to the inevitable and air-conditioned a portion of the kennel. At least her boarders slept in comfort. It was what their mommies and daddies paid for.

Jenny's nose wrinkled in disgust, remembering her earlier faux pas with Grant. Immediately, his image rose vividly to mind.

A troubling image, because Sam Grant was too attractive for Jenny's peace of mind. The hell of it was he knew it. He was at ease with it. His good looks fit him as comfortably as his tastefully decorated home and the casually expensive clothes he wore.

A man not easily dismissed. His lurking sense of the absurd was hazardous to Jenny's usually impenetrable defenses. Irritated with the direction of her thoughts, Jenny mentally pushed aside the disturbing Mr. Grant and glanced around her kitchen with its wooden cabinets and vintage appliances, searching for a distraction.

Calmness settled over her once more. She loved this old rock house. It was small and ramshackle, but basically sound, and it was the first place she'd ever owned. Most important, the place had come with three shaded acres. Only eight miles from downtown Austin, it had been the perfect place to establish Hunter's Kennels. It was a miracle she'd been able to purchase the property as cheaply as she had.

No, not a miracle, Jenny reminded herself. Unless you counted the Caneys' love and kindness a miracle. They'd practically raised her during her troubled teenage years, training her to work with the dogs they boarded, and left her a small legacy along with equipment from their kennel, enough to start this business. After three years of struggle, she was on her way, doing exactly what she wanted.

The ring of the telephone reminded Jenny there were strings attached to her perfect life.

"Hello, Jenny?"

"Hello, Annabelle." At the sound of her mother's voice, Jenny tried to infuse her own voice with warmth.

"Darling, I'm glad to catch you. I worried when you didn't return my call."

"I just got home from a late appointment. I had to meet a new client after business hours."

"A late appointment? Was it with a man?" Annabelle's tone grew worried. "I'm not sure it's safe for you to go to strangers' houses at all hours of the day and night."

Jenny had heard this line before.

Despite her best intentions, she bristled. "They're not strangers, they're customers, Annabelle. Besides, I'm a big girl, remember? I've been taking care of myself for twelve years."

Annabelle was instantly apologetic. "Oh, yes, I know, dear. I didn't mean to hover."

And yet Annabelle couldn't help hovering. It was as though she was trying to make up for the early years, the years when Jenny had been more like the parent.

Hearing her mother's anxiety, Jenny's stomach tightened. She tried to smooth over the breach. "I know you didn't, and I'm sorry you worried. I was going to call you after I finished supper."

"What were you having?"

"A salad...."

"I don't think you're eating enough, Jenny. The last time I saw you, you looked like you'd lost weight." This from a woman who ate like a sparrow and had a fine-boned thinness that reminded Jenny of a fragile bird.

As soon as Annabelle became aware of Jenny's silence, she rushed to fill the void. "Speaking of which, I'd hoped you could come over for lunch this Sunday. Lloyd and I would love to see you. It's been more than a month since you've been out to the house."

Perhaps it was the long, wearing day, or the crying jag, or the unnerving visit with Grant. Or maybe it was just the frazzling heat. But for once, Jenny couldn't allow her mother to hold to the polite fiction.

"Annabelle, Lloyd doesn't enjoy seeing me. We have nothing in common, and it upsets you when we're together and have nothing to say. I don't think coming to the house is a good idea, really. Why don't the two of us just have lunch at a restaurant one day next week?"

"Oh, honey." Annabelle's voice took on a ragged edge. "I wish you'd let bygones be bygones with Lloyd. I know I married him when you were at an awkward age. That when you lived with us, you two didn't get along well. Still, Lloyd really cares for you."

Annabelle's old familiar refrain grated on Jenny. She felt her emotions balling up inside. "Okay, I'll come for lunch, but I can't stay long. Every Sunday I go over the books to find out if Hunter's Kennels is still solvent." Jenny knew she'd made a mistake as soon as she spoke.

"Are you having trouble financially, dear? Lloyd's offered to loan you money."

"I'm doing fine, Annabelle," Jenny broke in hastily. "It was just my feeble attempt at humor. I'll see you this weekend."

Their conversation ended on that abrupt note.

Jenny went outside immediately and took deep breaths of the cooling air, fighting a feeling of claustrophobia. She was met with welcoming barks from the dog runs.

She answered the most familiar one. "Hello, Hilde, sweetheart," she crooned. "I'm sorry Leia cooped you up today. And I'm sorry I took so long getting home. I got to tell you, it's been a hell of a day."

As Jenny spoke, she opened a gate to free Hildegarde, the short-haired pointer she called her own. From the moment Jenny had seen Hildegarde three years ago as a puppy, she'd known this was the dog for her.

Jenny's instincts had proven accurate. Hilde was now her dearest companion, and a creature of great heart, noble proportions, a placid disposition and immeasurable love.

"Have you missed your mama?" Jenny knelt to scratch behind Hilde's velvety soft ears and kiss the chocolate brown muzzle. Hilde sniffed at her legs and hands as though reviewing the day's activities.

After a moment, deciding no other dog had replaced her in Jenny's affections, Hilde leaned against Jenny's leg, nuzzling her hand.

"You want to go for a run, girl?" Hilde immediately pricked up her ears and began to prance about. "We haven't had one in days, have we?" Jenny asked, already feeling better.

That was probably another reason for her earlier attack of nerves. Grooming the animals and maintaining the runs was back-breaking labor, but didn't exactly constitute invigorating exercise.

"Just let me go change into a pair of shorts," Jenny pleaded at Hilde's boisterous impatience.

Within five minutes, the pair took off through the brush, chasing the last rays of twilight. Later, panting yet refreshed, they returned to the house.

As soon as Jenny went inside, she relaxed on the floor in a sprawl and hugged Hilde, whispering, "That's my baby. I don't know what I'd do without you. I missed you today, but tomorrow looks better. I get to take you to the demonstration I'm giving and show everybody what a smart doggie you are.'' Hilde's tail wriggled furiously. She lay across Jenny's lap soaking up the praise.

Dogs were so simple, Jenny thought, as she stroked Hilde's sleek haunches. So straightforward once you learned their language. You loved them, they loved you, without strings or reservations. Without unreasonable demands. Without any complications. They loved you just the way you were.

It was human relationships that were treacherous. They brought pain and confusion—and demands. Always demands. They were filled with undercurrents and complications.

I'll take a dog any day—just like Aunt Lillith.

The name popped into Jenny's head, bringing the image of Grant, a man who could make for complications.

Not that Jenny would let that happen. She had experience keeping men at a distance. She'd been doing it almost as long as she could remember.

Ever since...

Ever since her father had died, long ago, leaving Jenny a small hoard of memories that would have to last a lifetime.

Elusive memories...of a handsome, laughing man who'd swept Jenny up in his arms and carried her piggyback to bed, soothing her to sleep with songs and stories.

Jenny had detested Gordon, her mother's second husband, a man Annabelle met only months after Roy Hunter's death. Even now, thinking of Gordon made Jenny's stomach knot painfully.

The time with Gordon Jenny remembered all too clearly. The constant upheavals, the bleak surroundings, living out of suitcases while he chased after construction jobs. His unpredictable drunken rages, the insults he threw at them over and over.

I don't have put up with your damn brat... Always hiding under the table... You think you're so all-fired special, Miss Beauty Queen... I could walk down the street and pick up a hotter woman in five minutes...

Gordon had abandoned them in a strange town in the Texas Panhandle four years after he and Annabelle were married. He left them for a woman who had come with a little money and without a child.

Annabelle had cried when Gordon left her. But Jenny had hugged her relief like a teddy bear and vowed to look after her mother.

Then had come the period between husbands when Annabelle drifted to Austin, wandering from job to job. She'd been a restaurant hostess, an office receptionist. She'd tried telephone sales. All low-paying work. It was the best she could hope for with no skills and work experience, with no drive to make it on her own.

And there had been men. More than Jenny liked to remember. Some who came and went, others who stayed a while and wandered out of Annabelle's bedroom in the mornings, rumpled and unshaven. They'd treated Jenny with awkward kindness or indifference.

Why, Annabelle? Why do they have to stay? Why can't just the two of us be together?

Lloyd Jarvis had come into their lives when Jenny was thirteen. He was several years older than her mother and owned a prosperous hardware business. Jenny would never forget the first time she met him. She'd been repulsed by his severity. She'd also been certain Annabelle wasn't his type, but she'd never convinced Annabelle of that.

And Lloyd had been drawn in spite of himself to Annabelle's fluttering beauty, unexpectedly proposing marriage. Allowing Annabelle to reclaim respectability.

Once legally bound, he'd seen Jenny as a responsibility he had to accept.

A shudder ran through Jenny when she recalled living in Lloyd's house.

She'd always hated his cold words and disapproving looks, the silence that told her how distasteful he found the burdensome duty of raising a stepchild. Those were the years when she'd escaped to the Caneys at every chance.

Hilde licked Jenny's face consolingly, bringing her back to her surroundings. Jenny wiped her cheek and realized it was wet from more than Hilde's tongue.

She wiped the tears away and stared at the moisture glistening on her fingers.

Crying again? For the second time that day?

Oh, God, what was the matter with her?

Her hands were shaking. Her whole body trembled. For a moment Jenny felt as if she was flying apart. Panic rose in her, drowning reason. Her insides heaved as she fought for air.

No, no! She wouldn't let this happen! She couldn't let it happen!

Anger rushed to Jenny's rescue. And fortified her.

She sat still, breathing deeply, fighting for calm, quiet . . . and control.

She was solely to blame, she told herself sternly. She'd raked over the old, bad memories. She'd let them slip past her guard. She thought she'd outgrown the anxiety attacks that had haunted her childhood.

She had, dammit.

Jumping to her feet, Jenny hurried to the telephone. Taking a further minute to compose herself, she punched in a number.

"Mr. Ingram?"

"Yes?"

"I'm Jenny Hunter. You left a message asking about my obedience classes? I'm starting one Saturday if you'd like to join."

"Well, actually, it's not for me, it's for my son Richard. And Arnie, that's his dog." Bob Ingram laughed. Jenny detected a note of nervousness. "Richard's ten," Ingram explained, "and small for his age. Arnie's a Labrador retriever and still growing. He already outweighs Richard by about five pounds."

"And you're hoping obedience classes will help Richard learn to handle him."

"Yes."

"They will," Jenny assured him. "Size doesn't matter between a dog and master. It's how much authority the master commands."

"You see—" Ingram brushed by her words almost as if he was compelled to continue. "Richard's always been such a shy child. He's withdrawn more since his mother died. He doesn't have many friends at the new place we moved to, and I've... well, my work is taking up a lot of my time. So someone suggested I get Richard a pet for companionship. It's made a difference. He and Arnie are inseparable."

"Then it's even more important that Richard know how to control him." Jenny kept her voice deliberately impersonal. She was a dog trainer, not a child psychiatrist. Robert Ingram's son was certainly welcome in her classes. Ingram had to realize, however, that the focus of her training was Arnie, the dog.

"Where will you be giving the lessons?" Ingram asked abruptly.

Jenny gave him the location.

"How much does it cost?"

Jenny named the price and explained in more detail what she'd be teaching. "The first class is orientation," she ended. "I ask that everyone leave their dogs at home."

As she spoke, Jenny had a sudden inspiration. "However, if you do want to join, why don't you and Richard bring Arnie along?" His response to this request would tell Jenny how serious Ingram was. "I'll use Arnie to demonstrate how we start the training. When I have children they always enjoy watching their dogs perform. Do you think Richard would like that?"

"I think so." Ingram sounded hesitant yet willing to go along with her suggestion. "Richard is very proud of Arnie. I guess he'll enjoy it. Thank you. We'll be there early."

A strange conversation, Jenny thought, as she hung up the phone. Would Richard Ingram end up being a disruptive element? Jenny wasn't used to being around children, and some of the ones in her classes had become real nuisances. Still, she felt she'd gotten the hang of working with them by now.

Deciding not to anticipate trouble, Jenny caught up on her housekeeping chores. Around eleven she made the last rounds of the kennel before securing everything for the night.

In the house, she washed up, slipped into a cotton nightgown, turned on her fan to stir the air and sank into bed, letting fatigue wash over her. Hilde took her accustomed place at one corner of the bed.

Just before Jenny turned off the bedside lamp, she leaned over, stroked Hilde's muzzle and buried her face in the animal's sturdy neck. "It's okay, girl. I'm fine now. The tears are gone for good. Your mommy was being silly. I promise it won't happen again."

She'd locked away the memories.... The old haunting fears... The mistakes of the past... Mistakes she'd never make.

She'd won her independence. She'd fought for it. A stubborn independence she'd never relinquish to a weakness, and vulnerability she'd never let herself feel.

She'd never, ever become like her mother.

"Never," Jenny whispered fiercely. The word became a mantra that lulled her to sleep.

SAM GRANT LEANED BACK in his chair and stared blankly at the computer on the corner of his desk. The screen displayed a brilliantly colored pattern of lines, circuits and cryptic configurations, representing the new machine he was designing for a German firm. When fully realized, it would be capable of manufacturing an elegant frozen torte, complete with layers of cake, ice cream and elaborate icing.

The design was developing slowly, however. Sam's mind wasn't on it. He looked up distractedly when Nate appeared at his door.

"I just got a call from Minneapolis. Their machine's acting up. The bears have no noses, which means the extruder's malfunctioning, and the chocolate syrup is lumpy. Sounds like a defective heating element to me. Could you go service it later this week?"

Later this week? Nate's words penetrated Sam's consciousness. That meant Friday. He'd have to fly back Saturday, and he would miss Zeppo's first class.

"I think Jim could handle this," Sam said casually. Jim was one of their fledgling engineers.

"Do you?" Nate slouched in the chair across from Sam and looked at his partner skeptically. At Sam's nod, he shrugged. "You know best. You're the one who's been training him. What's the matter? You have a date with Leslie you don't want to break?"

"Leslie and I aren't seeing each other any more."

"That was short and sweet." Nate spoke with the frankness of long friendship. "What happened? Did it get too heavy-duty?"

Sam knew where Nate's question had come from. His partner was a hard-core bachelor whose good looks and money made him fair game to the opposite sex. Nate guarded his freedom zealously and had cultivated a light touch in his affairs of the heart.

"Not at all," Sam responded. "Leslie is the soul of reason. The last thing she'd want is a heavy-duty relationship."

"So? You're holding this against her? What a novel reason to end an affair."

"There was no affair, and what makes you think I ended it? Zeppo decided it for us. I don't think Leslie likes my dog."

Nate snorted. "I don't blame her. Zeppo would discourage most females."

"I don't think so," Sam said, remembering a certain female who'd been appreciative of Zeppo's charm.

Something in Sam's tone made Nate's expression narrow. He took a moment, leaned back his chair, propped his well-shod feet on Sam's cluttered work area and steepled his fingers against his mouth thoughtfully. "So, Leslie likes it light and easy. Sounds like my type of woman."

"Be my guest," Sam said absently.

"Thanks, but no thanks." Nate's voice was mildly sardonic. "Our partnership only extends so far."

Sam looked sharply at Nate. "Don't get me wrong. Leslie's a lovely lady."

"But not your type."

"No."

"That's not what you'd have said two years ago."

"Two years ago I was wrapped up in this company. I've been wrapped up in this company since I was twenty-four."

"For which we've both been suitably rewarded."

Sam ignored Nate's wry reminder. "But that's not nearly enough for me now." He stared into space as if he was barely conscious of Nate's presence. "I'm tired of serial relationships. Two lives that meet and touch briefly. Then when it's over, we both walk away bruised, but basically wholehearted. I don't want to walk away again. I don't want to be able to."

"Sam." Nate's voice grew anxious. "Are you having an early onslaught of mid-life crisis? I need to know so I can shelter the stock."

Sam laughed. "You know, old friend, I don't think you have a romantic bone in your body."

"God, I hope not!" Nate stared at his partner suspiciously. "I gather you're telling me you're developing a sentimental streak. It's your mother's Irish influence. I knew it'd come out eventually. Next you'll be telling me you want to fall in love."

"Yes." Sam looked a little surprised at his ready answer. He glanced at Nate sheepishly. Yet as he went on his voice held conviction. "I do. I want to fall madly, passionately in love. I'm bored—with myself, my life, my pretty toys...."

"Does that mean you plan on selling the Mercedes 450 SL? Or the '65 Mustang you keep under lock and key?"

Sam grinned but refused to be sidetracked by Nate's ironic humor. "I mean it, old friend. And I'm especially bored with glossy, earnest, reasonable women. With antiseptic sex. Commitment? I'm sick of that word. It's so damned dry and intellectual. As though in the heat of desire there could be a choice! Space? You do your thing, I'll do mine. I've had that up to here." Sam made a slashing motion. "Give me the basic, primitive human emotions—jealousy, passion, devotion, sexual hunger so overwhelming it sweeps away every obstacle in its path. That's what loving is all about. That's what makes babies."

Nate cleared his throat. "I gather somewhere along in here marriage enters the picture."

Sam smiled at his partner's wary tone. "Yeah, about sixty years of it. Maybe around our fiftieth wedding anniversary, I'll begin to mellow out."

"You know what your trouble is, Sam? You come from a happy home. It creates unrealistic expectations." Nate dropped his bantering tone as he asked curiously, "You really think you can find that kind of love?"

"I don't intend to settle for less."

"But what if this hypothetical woman you fall in love with has different ideas about relationships and love? What if she's not ready to make babies?" As he asked this, Nate watched his friend closely.

Sam shrugged. "I'm old-fashioned. I don't mind doing the pursuing."

"What if she runs?"

"If she's the right one, I'll catch her."

"Catch who?" Megan Grant breezed into the office. She was obviously Sam's sister. She had the same black hair and blue eyes, with a porcelain complexion that couldn't be found in a jar. Sam's features refined by femininity were fairly spectacular.

After surveying the scene, Megan wrinkled her nose at Nate and leaned over her brother to kiss him fondly. "This sounds like a philosophical discussion. I didn't think engineers could even spell the word."

"Better than art majors can read schematic diagrams," Nate came back quickly. "You know the old saying, those who can, build. Those who can't, sit around and talk about aesthetics."

"Oh, another big word." Megan's perfectly shaped eyebrows rose mockingly. "I'll be sure and write a graduate paper next year on the aesthetics of ice-cream machines."

"Children, children," Sam intervened. This sniping between Nate and Megan was familiar and long-standing. Sam decided he had better things to do than be a spectator. "What do you need, Meg?"

"What makes you think I need something?" Megan asked in an aggrieved tone.

Sam's look was telling. "I don't think you came three miles out of your way from work for the pleasure of Nate's and my company."

"Now, brother dear, you know I love your company. I just can't say as much for the company you keep."

The dig at Nate was pointed, even for Megan. Sam wondered why the war had suddenly escalated. Nate must be wondering, too, because after an initial surprised look, his face closed impassively.

"Okay, little sister, act your age. At twenty-three it's time you learned a few social graces."

Maybe Sam's reprimand was sharper than he intended, for the shocked expression that crossed Megan's features certainly disconcerted him. As did the hint of vulnerability that was in sharp contrast to her normally sunny nonchalance. The two men exchanged chagrined looks.

"I'm sorry, big brother." Megan sounded subdued. "You're right, I do have a favor to ask. But since it means helping to get rid of me, I didn't think you'd mind. Could you take a look at my car, please, and see how much I can get for it? I can't leave for England later this summer unless I sell all my worldly goods." Megan was planning a year in Europe to soak up art and culture before she came back to enter graduate school.

"I'd ask Dad," she went on, "but you know he can't tell the difference between an exhaust manifold and a tail pipe." Andrew Grant was a mathematics professor at the University of Texas. Anything more concrete than a prime number left him bemused.

"You want me to take a look at it now?" Sam asked.

"Well, no." This time Megan looked definitely sheepish. "Luckily, I've moved home. Mom let me borrow her car today. Mine won't start."

"Ah, the light dawns," Nate murmured.

Sam was also beginning to get the picture. "So what you really want is for me to take a look at your car, find out what's wrong and fix it?"

"Yes." The admission was unadorned. "I'd hoped you might come over to the house this Saturday."

"I can't Saturday morning. Zeppo and I are going to our first obedience class."

Megan looked intrigued. Her natural buoyancy had returned and, having worked up the courage to make her request, she was ready to corral the conversation in a more interesting direction. "Obedience class? Which one of you is learning to mind?"

"Cheap shot," Nate said, sotto voce.

Megan shrugged. "It's the best I could do on short notice. Honestly, Sam, I'm curious. What does one do in an obedience class?"

"Since I haven't gone to one I'm not sure," Sam said dampeningly. "All I've had till now is a consultation."

"A consultation?" Megan's voice showed the effort it took her to keep a straight face.

"Yes. A consultation. Jenny—" Sam tripped over the name and cursed himself "—Ms Hunter came to my house yesterday. We talked about Zeppo's problems and discussed behavior modification techniques. She explained to me the doggy view of the world. The group obedience lessons are designed to socialize Zeppo to his fellow creatures."

"Sounds more like family therapy than dog training," Megan decided. "Is this Jenny helping you and Zeppo work through your relationship?"

Sam scowled. Megan smiled at him sweetly. "You know what they say, Sammy. There are no maladjusted dogs, just maladjusted masters."

"For someone who wants me to spend precious time and effort on a thankless task, you're playing a risky game."

"I'm not playing games. I'm really curious."

Megan stepped back, made a production of studying her brother. "You know, Sam, there's something about you that's different. An unsettled air. I sense you're going through a major life crisis. Don't ask me how I know." She waved her hand dramatically. "I couldn't tell you. It must be my Irish second sight."

"Second sight, hell," Sam said. "You were eavesdropping."

"Me?" Megan exclaimed at her most innocent. "I don't know what you mean." She went on the offensive. "I'd just like to hear about this Jenny Hunter who makes you stutter. Sam Grant, debonair man-about-town, hasn't stumbled over a woman's name since he was five."

"I can tell you one thing she's not." Nate had been content over the past few minutes to watch the siblings bicker, determined to stay out of Megan's line of fire. Now, however, he caught Sam's eye and challenged him. "She's not glossy, earnest or reasonable."

Sam met his challenge with a crooked smile. "No, she's not."

"Sam," Megan said with sisterly concern. "Something *is* different...."

"I have this awful feeling," Nate interrupted her.

Sam interrupted him in turn. "It's not an awful feeling, Nate. You ought to try it sometime."

CHAPTER THREE

RICHARD INGRAM HAD knobby knees, large brown eyes, a freckled face and a cowlick. Jenny could see at once he was no behavior problem. At least not in the way she'd feared. He clutched Arnie's neck and seemed to shrink against the door of the car as she approached. It was Saturday morning, fifteen minutes before class time, and introductions were in order.

"Hello, you must be Richard."

Richard bent his head and mumbled something, unable to meet her eyes. Bob Ingram cast a despairing look at his son and started to apologize for his timidity.

Jenny interrupted pleasantly. "Mr. Ingram? I'm Jenny Hunter. It's nice to meet you." They shook hands.

Arnie didn't need to be formally introduced. He was a typical Labrador retriever, the good old boy of the canine world, a complete extrovert. As soon as Jenny came within pawing distance, he reared into the air, plopped his feet on her shoulders and licked her face profusely while Richard tugged futilely on his leash.

"That's okay, Richard. We're just making friends. Aren't we, fella?"

Arnie barked raucously.

Jenny rubbed his ears. "We'll teach you later that it's impolite to maul new acquaintances."

A slight smile appeared on Richard's downcast face. Good. He might be shy, but he had a sense of humor.

The smile faded, leaving an anxious look.

Wondering if she was the cause of that look, Jenny turned her attention to Arnie. "What a handsome Lab you are."

Arnie agreed wholeheartedly. He danced around, straining at his leash, and careened into Jenny's legs.

"And you wanna play, too, don't ya?" Proving Jenny's point, Arnie began to tug at her hand as if it were a pull toy. She disengaged herself gently, feeling Richard studying her reactions.

"You know, Richard, Labs are very intelligent. They love obedience training."

For the first time, Richard looked at her directly. "Do they?"

"Oh, yes."

"You mean you won't have to whip him?"

From behind his son, Bob Ingram threw up his hands. So that was what was worrying Richard. Jenny wondered what his father had told him.

"No, I won't be whipping Arnie. Occasionally, I may need to get his attention, and I'll explain later how I do it. But I don't believe in using punishment in training. I've found that dogs learn best with praise.

"And you know something, Richard, almost all the dogs I've worked with enjoy learning the commands. It's a way for them to show off."

Jenny leaned over Arnie and said confidentially, "You're gonna be a real ham, aren't ya, Arnie?"

"Woof! Woof!"

Richard's slight smile appeared again. This time it lingered. And this time his direct look stayed with it. Jenny smiled, feeling satisfaction at her progress. She'd assessed Richard correctly. The way to gain his trust was through his dog.

Bob and Richard Ingram had been the first pupils to arrive at the school parking lot where Jenny held her classes. Now, as it approached nine-thirty, other people began to appear. Some Jenny knew from individual consultations. Other faces she connected with voices she'd heard on the phone. She gave the new clients forms to be filled out, collected payments and glanced at her watch, wanting to start.

This was a small class by Jenny's usual standards. Besides Arnie, there were two shepherds, a boxer, one mastiff and two Dobermans.

Zeppo would love it. David amongst a platoon of Goliaths. Jenny wasn't surprised at the mix. Small dogs could be picked up and banished if they misbehaved. It was harder to play deus ex machina with a Great Dane.

Jenny glanced around. Sam Grant had yet to make his appearance. The thought that he might not show aroused conflicting feelings in her. His absence would make teaching the class easier, but every customer counted.

She'd give him five more minutes before she began.

"Everybody," Jenny said by way of introduction, "this is Arnie." Arnie had already greeted each arrival. "I asked the rest of you to leave your dogs home this morning, but I'll be using Arnie to demonstrate the lessons you'll teach your dogs before next Saturday. And this is Richard, his owner. Arnie is...how old is he, Richard?" she asked without thinking.

Richard Ingram turned beet red and struggled with speech. Jenny cursed her stupidity. Bob Ingram rushed to fill the awkward silence. "Arnie's nine months old."

"A good age to start the training process," Jenny said. She glanced apologetically at Richard. Hadn't she hated to be put on the spot when she was a child?

Jenny, honey, you be hostess while I finish dressing.
This is my daughter, Jenny. Talk to the nice man....

Jenny was so concerned with Richard she didn't realize Sam Grant had arrived until she sensed someone behind her. She turned to find him five feet away watching
her with a expression that was hard to decipher.

She'd forgotten the physical impact of him. For a brief
moment Jenny found herself fighting for breath.

In shorts, T-shirt and running shoes, Sam had obviously dressed for cool and comfort, as she'd advised
them all to do. Even so, he had an indefinable air of ele-
gance Jenny suddenly resented. The heat of the day was
already gathering, and her hair had formed damp, disheveled ringlets around her face.

Didn't the man ever sweat? Sure, he did. And he
probably looked like a male pinup with a faint sheen of
moisture highlighting the play of muscles in his tanned
arms and legs.

Jenny blinked, shocked at the vividness of her mental
imagery. She came to with a start, realizing the others
were standing around her, curious expressions on their
faces.

Jenny smiled brightly. "Well, everyone's here. We can
get started." She cleared her throat. "I am, as you know,
Jenny Hunter, and we're going to be working together the
next few weeks to teach your dog to do what he wants
most—to please you. No matter what their individual
differences, all dogs have that innate desire. It's a char-
acteristic of the species. There's no breed of dog I refuse
to work with. They can all, with proper training, be
taught to obey commands."

As Jenny launched into her speech, she began to relax. "Dogs, as you may know, are pack animals, and
whether you realize it or not, you and your families make

up the pack as far as Fido's concerned. They're very status oriented. Within the pack, there's a pecking order. You know the expressions, top dog and underdog? Well, you'll find they actually hold true."

Several of the class members smiled.

"One of the things your dog will try to do," Jenny went on, "is establish his rank within the family. They're terrible social climbers." A bit of laughter. "So those of you with children need to realize when your dog tries to establish dominance over a younger child. You as the leader of the pack must learn ways to discourage the behavior."

She broached this topic carefully, not wanting to further embarrass Richard by singling him out. "If you bought a dog for a particular child or one of your children feels especially close to your dog, I urge you bring that child with you to these classes. It's very important for children to learn command and dominance in a kind, consistent manner. Those skills will reward both the child and the pet, and, if anything, forge a tighter bond."

With those words she glanced Richard's way and found him giving her serious attention. Arnie had sprawled contentedly on the pavement by his master's feet.

Jenny continued, elaborating on the handout she'd provided, and as time went by the questions began. Orientation was going well, she decided, remembering why she liked smaller classes. They allowed her to really get to know the participants.

Except . . . Bob Ingram was making her nervous. He'd chosen to stand back a little from the group, and he was concentrating more on his son's reactions than on the content of Jenny's words.

Jenny was unsure why Ingram made her uncomfortable until she realized the feeling she got every time she glanced his way.

He was hovering over Richard—with a kind of awkward, fumbling watchfulness. Just like Annabelle hovered. Annabelle, who'd despaired from the start of understanding, much less relating to her introverted loner of a child. Annabelle, who thrived on the company and admiration of others.

Jenny remembered what her reaction to her mother had been as a child. An instinctual withdrawal. A confused anxiety of her own, not knowing exactly what her mother expected. Always wondering if it might be more than she could give.

She knew with sudden insight what Richard was feeling. Why he centered his attention on Arnie. And why she'd felt a kinship with him from the moment she'd seen his solemn face.

She, too, had been a child recovering from tragedy. More comfortable in solitude than with other children. It was only after she'd begun working with dogs that she'd learned to relax and enjoy their masters. As she'd gained confidence in her work, she'd found conversation easier. Maybe self-confidence was a small gift she could give to Richard as they worked together with his pet.

It was something to think about.

When there wasn't a class to teach.

When Sam Grant wasn't nearby to continually distract her. The fact of him. His effect on her senses. An obscure feeling he brought to her that she didn't welcome.

There was laughter at one of her comments, yet only his laughter lingered in her mind. His smile was the one she found her eyes returning to as the class went on.

Although everyone was paying flattering attention as she covered the major points of her presentation, Sam's attention seemed somehow more intense. It wasn't just her words he listened to. He took in her gestures, her simplest movement. He seemed absorbed with the process of studying Jenny Hunter. She'd never been the object of such unwavering regard.

Her developing awareness was new and troubling, also. Her sense of his awareness. As though there were invisible strings linking them together, so that his mind tugged on hers.

When she felt something, he reacted. He raised a brow and she could read his thoughts.

It wasn't just sexual tension between them. Jenny immediately skittered away from that admission.

It was more.

Their eyes met.

Sam knew . . . that he made her nervous.

She looked away. She tried to pull herself together. After a small, breathless moment, Jenny walked over to where Arnie was stretched on the ground.

"Before I end the class, I want to show you the two commands you're to work on for our next meeting, when you'll be bringing your dogs."

As Jenny took the leash from Richard, she allowed her hand to settle on Arnie's thick, golden hair. It was a comforting sensation—the feel of the dog beside her, his trusting eyes looking into hers.

She felt composure return and winked at her pupil. "Arnie, you want to show everybody how smart you are?"

Arnie's tail swept the immediate area, and Jenny reached into her bag for the equipment she needed.

"You notice I'm using a flat chain collar and leather leash. All of you need to get these before next Saturday." Jenny held up the linked collar for everyone's inspection. "Although some people call this a choke collar, it won't hurt Arnie, or your dog, either. The canine neck is very muscular. It's also a very symbolic part of the body in doggydom. Biting the neck is a way to establish rank. So, when you're working your dog and you jerk the leash briskly, tightening the collar, you're merely explaining who's boss."

Jenny demonstrated the correct way to slip on the collar, then attached it to the six-foot leather leash she carried. As she did so, Jenny glanced Richard's way to see how he was responding and saw him tense slightly. "Believe me," she said more for his benefit than for the others, "if you use this collar and leash correctly, it will not hurt the dog. Anyone who's been dragged down the street taking Fido for a walk knows how strong his neck muscles are."

As if to prove her point, Arnie, realizing belatedly he'd been separated from Richard, reared against the leash, straining it severely. For a moment, it looked as if he was going to drag Jenny the twelve or so feet to his master's side.

To Sam's eyes, she couldn't have outweighed the beast by more than twenty pounds.

But it was technique and experience versus fledgling strength. In an economical movement, Jenny snapped the leash, forcing the dog on all fours. Arnie looked up at her, surprised. He reared again, and Jenny repeated her movement. This time, when Arnie eyed her, it was with dawning respect.

"Good boy." Jenny patted him fondly. She looked at the group around her. "I'm going to teach Arnie to heel. This is the first exercise you'll be practicing. So watch me closely."

Jenny knew the next several minutes with Arnie were crucial. Words of wisdom only went so far. There came a time in all her classes when Jenny had to prove to the customer she knew her stuff. She patted Arnie one more time, confidence flowing through her. This was a moment she always enjoyed.

"Heel, Arnie!" She took off at a brisk pace, one hand near the junction of the leash and collar, jerking the leash forward in a rapid movement.

Arnie got the message at once. He surged in front of her, eager to explore new territory. She jerked the leash once more, this time toward her hip, corralling Arnie effectively. Jenny's "Heel, Arnie!" accompanied each tug.

This exercise went on through two wide circles of the parking lot. Periodically, Arnie tested the boundaries of Jenny's patience. Each time, Jenny, with firm consistency, called him to task.

As Jenny suspected, Arnie was a fast learner. By the third circle, he trotted obediently, close by her side, seemingly undiscouraged by his confinement.

Jenny stopped. "Stay," she directed him. Then, before he could launch into new action, she leaned down and hugged him robustly. "Good dog, Arnie! Good dog! What a clever fella you are!"

Sam would have sworn Arnie preened himself. He certainly looked as if he were grinning, his tongue in a pant as he lapped up Jenny's praise. Sam glanced over to where Arnie's young master stood, and found Richard's expression one of rapt awe. Jenny had already made one convert. Sam couldn't help feeling a tinge of proprietary pride.

Then his look took in Robert Ingram, Richard's father. Bob looked pleased and relieved, as if he knew for the first time that his decision to enroll Arnie and Richard in Jenny's class was a sound one. There was something else in Bob's expression, too, as he turned his attention from Richard to Jenny.

Sam knew what that something was, because he was feeling it himself as he watched every movement their teacher made.

Jenny was wearing a pair of bibbed overalls that had been cut off and rolled into shorts. Beneath the bib was a short-sleeved shirt open at the neck. It was a workmanlike outfit, perfect for training, yet it somehow served to emphasize Jenny's faint other-worldly air. It also drew subtle attention to her curves and the neat turn of her slender legs. Legs that looked silken to the touch and were shaded the color of honey.

Sam rubbed a hand against his shirt and noted wryly that his palm was damp.

Oh, yes, he knew with fair approximation the thoughts going through Ingram's head. They could prove a minor complication. Especially since Sam was aware that Jenny was already protective of her youngest pupil.

Sam could appreciate her feelings. He, too, felt concern for the shy, introverted child.

Just as long as Jenny's maternal instincts didn't spill over to include Richard's father.

"The next thing I want you to practice..." Jenny's voice pulled Sam to order, as did a dark look that told Sam she suspected his thoughts.

"The next thing I want you to practice is the 'come' command."

Reaching into her equipment bag, she drew out a twenty-foot leash made of thin nylon rope.

"This is a very important command," Jenny told her listening audience, "and must be taught correctly. It must always produce positive results with Fido, and you must teach it in such a way that he cannot fail."

Feeling like a fool, Jenny felt herself blushing slightly. This was a set speech, one she'd given countless times in her obedience classes. Why for the first time did she recognize its erotic connotations? Hoping everyone would attribute her rosy face to her recent exertion, Jenny hurried on.

"Most untrained owners ask their dog to come for all the wrong reasons, and Fido quickly gets the hint that coming is not a smart thing to do. We say come, but what we really mean is, 'You have to go to the vet, Fido,' or 'I want you outside,' or 'Come here so I can punish you for chewing my carpet.' In those circumstances, can we blame Fido for not minding?"

Jenny paused rhetorically before she answered her own question. "Of course not. So...what we need to do is teach Fido that 'come' is a specific command, and his obeying it will result in a reward, not a punishment. This is how it's done."

Jenny unsnapped the leather leash from Arnie's collar and snapped on the nylon cord, dropping it in a curl next to her feet.

"Richard, would you move over there just a little, please, and distract Arnie? Don't ask him to come. Just call his name."

By now, Richard was so caught up in Jenny's demonstration that he unself-consciously did as she directed.

"Arnie! Arnie!" he clapped his hands.

Arnie took off like a shot, but Jenny was faster. She deftly stepped on the end of the cord, grabbed it and yanked briskly, proceeding to reel Arnie in like a giant marlin, saying all the while, "Come, Arnie! Come!"

Although Arnie resisted her tugging, Jenny was not to be denied. Within seconds he was standing before her, staring into her face with a bewildered look.

"Good boy! Good boy!" Jenny hugged and praised him.

It was clear Arnie hadn't the foggiest idea why he deserved such acclaim. He was more than ready to accept it, however.

Richard caught on more quickly than his canine companion. He beamed at Jenny, and together they repeated the performance. Once, twice, five times. The sixth time was the charm.

As soon as Jenny called out the command and began to tug at Arnie, he reversed directions and bounded toward her, skidding to a halt directly in front of her legs to receive his due.

The entire class watched spellbound as Jenny worked her magic.

It was magic, Sam thought to himself. Not simply technique. Jenny and Arnie seemed to be communicating in ways none of them could see. It only reinforced his suspicion that she was slightly fey.

After Arnie had successfully performed the routine several more times, Jenny profusely praised him once more and unhooked the nylon rope. Her audience broke into spontaneous applause.

She turned to them, flushed.

Radiant, Sam decided.

"This is something you all can do," she assured them. "I've had experience, but you'll get the hang of it. 'Heel' and 'come'—those are the commands I want you to work on over the next week. If possible, for twenty minutes daily. With the correct collar, leash and rope. Then your dogs will be ready to begin group training.''

She dismissed the class with a winning smile.

Sam wasn't ready for school to be let out, however. He was wishing for individual instruction, and not just every Tuesday evening. The other class members didn't seem ready to leave, either. They crowded around Jenny asking questions. Bob Ingram, Richard and Arnie stayed longer than the rest. It was twenty minutes before Sam and Jenny were alone on the parking lot.

By this time it was eleven o'clock. Heat waves shimmered from the pavement, and Jenny distractedly pushed the curls from her sweaty brow as she eyed the determined man before her.

"Yes, Mr. Grant? Do you have a question?"

"How about having an iced tea or a Coke with me? That's a good question. You look as if you could use one.'' He grinned. "A cool drink, that is.'' There was a momentary pause. "And it's Sam, remember?''

"Thank you. Sam.'' Jenny smiled politely. She'd decided cool courtesy would be her stance from now on. "I carry a thermos with me, and you don't need to bother. Besides, I have an individual lesson in—'' she glanced at her watch "—in just a little while.''

"At what time?'' he asked her directly.

"At...'' Oh, why did she have to be so honest! "At one o'clock,'' she admitted lamely.

"Good.'' That grin Sam used so effectively hit her with force. "Plenty of time for lunch, as well. Aren't I lucky?''

"I have a sack lunch,'' Jenny said. "I wouldn't want it to go to waste. Besides, I'm not dressed for going somewhere to eat, and I smell doggy." She realized at once that her excuse was a weak one.

"Do you?" Sam asked innocently. Without warning, he leaned over until they were only inches apart and breathed in deeply. As he let out his breath a fine appreciation appeared on his face. "I don't think so. To me you smell of sunlight, meadows, timid furry creatures and warm earth. Utterly intoxicating."

Jenny took a sharp breath. "Sam..." She held out a hand in an instinctively defensive gesture. "I—I'm not sure..."

As he watched her struggle for words that couldn't come, Sam called himself to bay.

Go slow! Go slow! Go slow! his mind warned him.

Hurry! Hurry! Hurry! his body urged.

He fought for patience, knowing he needed it in abundance.

Sensing that Jenny definitely could not be rushed.

She was wary. She was more than wary. She was on strict guard duty. Which was unusual for an attractive, personable, unattached female of any age.

Was it men in general that so obviously threw her? Sam decided not. She was relaxed with his fellow classmate, the portly architect. Of course, the architect had a wife, and there were three grandkids in town for the summer. Jenny apparently felt safe enough with him.

As she did with the slender, pleasant young restaurateur who'd brought a male companion with him and whose tastes obviously didn't run to Jenny's type.

She'd even been relaxed, if occasionally exasperated, with Bob Ingram. Sam had the feeling she'd put him in the same category as his son.

That thought comforted Sam, but didn't solve his dilemma.

Jenny was definitely leery of one unattached male of a certain age who had designs upon her. Normal, healthy designs, as she must know very well.

After all, it wasn't as if he intended to abduct Jenny and hold her captive in a secluded hideaway while he had his way with her.

Although at this moment, Sam had to admit, the idea had a certain appeal.

He smiled faintly at Jenny, refusing to trivialize the moment. Neither said a word as the seconds ticked by.

Jenny couldn't speak as she stared into midnight blue eyes. She couldn't say stop or go. Or come or no, or yes, or maybe, or I don't know what to do. Or... what's happening between us?

But her face told Sam all she was thinking.

Finally he sighed and spoke quietly as though answering each of her unspoken questions. "All right, Jenny Hunter. You can run for cover. Get into your truck and drive away. Find a nice shady tree to brood under. Take a nice cool drink from the thermos you carry. Eat every bite of the lunch that shouldn't go to waste.

"And think of me. Admit we're attracted to each other. Reconcile yourself to my attentions. Because—" he punctuated the last few words with the lightest of taps on her chin "—I'm not going away."

JENNY, FEELING HOT and harried, guided her truck onto the graveled strip that sided the neighborhood park near her afternoon appointment.

She searched for her thermos, found it on the floor of the cab and grabbed her lunch from the seat beside her. After surveying the scene, she walked to the lone picnic table under the tenuous shade of a willow tree.

The ice cubes she'd plopped in the jug hours before had melted, and the water she poured into its lid was slightly cooler than tepid. The sandwich she'd slapped together at eight this morning had no taste.

As Jenny bit into an apple and stared at the empty swing set nearby, she thought of Sam, just as he'd instructed.

Imagining where she might be right now. In a cozy nook of a cool café, taking sips of lemony iced tea. Nibbling a fresh, crisp salad. Inquiring as to Zeppo's truce with the Doberman next door. Watching Sam's face light up with laughter as she recounted the story of Mrs. Wakefield and her misbegotten brood.

Feasting her eyes on a beautiful male who was giving her his sole attention. Getting to know said male.

Admitting she was very, very attracted to him. Glimpsing an attraction smolder in his eyes. Taking inventory of the slow, lazy smile that seemed to wrap itself around her. Feeling her pulse hammer in response.

Jenny's heart set up a thud in her chest. She felt her body tensing. She placed the apple carefully on the graying wood of the picnic table and struggled for breath.

As she fought the old, bad feelings that never really vanished.

How could she know what Sam expected of her? How could she know if she had it to give?

Jenny hadn't the faintest notion of how to reconcile herself to Sam's attentions.

But neither had she the wildest glimmer of how to send him on his way.

CHAPTER FOUR

DAGWOOD, THE CAT, skirted Hilde's sleeping form, jumped onto the porch railing, stretched herself luxuriantly, licked one paw and leisurely washed behind an ear. She cast an oh-so-casual glance across the fifteen feet of yard to where Jenny and her pupil, Henry, were working. Jenny was alone at the kennel this Monday. Leia, her assistant, had taken the afternoon off.

Henry, a bloodhound still in the novice stage, watched the cat's movements with strained curiosity, whimpered faintly and cast an agonized look his trainer's way.

"Stay, Henry. Stay," Jenny directed sternly.

With a martyred sigh, Henry laid his head on the ground, awaiting release from the onerous command.

After a moment of stillness, Dagwood hopped off the railing into the glare of sunlight and began to make her way daintily toward them through the scraggly grass. Wise to Dagwood's snares, Hilde barely raised her head at the flurry of movement.

But Henry's nose twitched. His whiskers quivered in agitation. Another sigh of torment whispered out between his jowls.

"Stay. Stay, Henry." Jenny refused to comfort him with words of understanding, wary of undoing the afternoon's work.

At last, Dagwood reached her apparent destination—the end of Henry's muzzle. He let out a sharp yelp at the cat's audacity. Dagwood sniffed fastidiously.

Jenny struggled to hold in laughter as she commanded, "Stay!"

Henry settled into the dust with a tragic air.

Tiring of the game, Dagwood circled and rubbed herself against Jenny's bare leg.

It was more a signal of possession than affection, designed to stir envy in any pooch that happened to be close by. Failing to get a rise from Hilde, who was pointedly ignoring her, Dagwood twitched her tail high in the air and set off on her hourly rounds of the outdoor runs, setting up barks and growls of frustration in every cage she passed.

"Heel, Henry!" At last, Jenny said the words that freed Henry from his torture, and he jumped up, demanding praise.

Jenny lavished it on him. "You were a wonderful dog! Yes, you were, Henry. To let mean old Dagwood tease you the way she did."

A soft chuckle made Jenny turn.

"Did you train the cat, or is she naturally sadistic?" Sam asked the question as he approached, his appraisal of Jenny casual but thorough.

Jenny laughed breathlessly, unable to answer. His unexpected appearance, the look encompassing her, had taken her speech away. That and the way he looked in a dress shirt, subdued tie and lightweight gray slacks.

It was irritating, Jenny decided with the corner of her mind still functioning, that standard office attire should fit him so sexily. The bright white of the shirt highlighted his dark good looks. She was especially aggrieved by the contrast between them. He looked cool and collected. She was hot and grimy, dressed in shorts and a T-shirt shrunk from too many washings. The words Hunter's Kennels were a faded scrawl across her breasts.

"W-what are you doing here?" Intruding on her workday. Her peace of mind. Graphically reminding Jenny of how he'd intruded into her thoughts during the two weeks she'd known him.

"Watching your training techniques," Sam answered mildly. "You have unusual methods. Where on earth did you get that cat?"

Oh, Lord, it was hard to be irritated when he smiled that smile. One of his wide repertoire. This one said, "Don't be angry to see me. Laugh with me instead."

She did, still a little breathless, and responded to his question. "Dagwood is unusual, but I had nothing to do with it. She came with the place. Blondie, her sister, took off when the dogs arrived, but Dagwood, for obscure reasons, decided to stay."

Dagwood had completed her parade before the prison inmates. She marched toward Jenny and Sam, intrigued by the new human who'd invaded her domain.

"You must understand," Jenny murmured as she watched the cat's approach, "Dagwood doesn't belong to me. I'm hers, so to speak, along with the house and acreage. She tolerates me because I'm a good source of protein. I supplement her diet of field mice and provide her with diversion when she's feeling bored."

"You must crave a life of danger." Sam addressed this to Dagwood as he knelt and stroked along the arching ridge of her back.

"Don't let her reckless daring fool you. Henry's a wimp, and Dagwood knows it. She has a sixth sense where the dogs are concerned. One time I boarded a bull terrier that ate kittens for breakfast. She took one look at him and ran screeching into the woods.''

Sam stood, stretched a little, and Jenny was reminded of Dagwood's deceptive air of laziness. "Dagwood's a man's name," he said inconsequentially.

"I didn't name her." At once, Jenny's edginess returned in force. "What are you doing here?" she asked abruptly.

Hilde had awakened, and came to inspect Sam steadily, taking a position close to her mistress's side. Again Sam deflected Jenny's question with one of his own.

"And who is this?" He sat on his haunches. "Are you the lady of the house?" He offered his hand to Hilde. She sniffed politely, but maintained a guarded stance.

Jenny let out an involuntary chuckle. "This is Hilde. She's mine. And if she's the lady of the house, what does that make me?"

"An elfin princess, waiting to be awakened from a spell." Sam said this with a whimsical grin.

He was flirting again. Confusing her again.

She took refuge in asking for the third time, "What are you doing here?"

At last, he acknowledged her. "I called and got your recording."

The answer explained nothing. "And?" she prompted.

"I don't like talking to a machine."

"Sam," Jenny said with studied patience, "I have to have an answering machine to take messages when I'm gone or training. It's the only way to run a business."

"What's between us is more than business." The words were provocative, as was the tone he used.

Jenny started to deny it, thought better of it and decided to ignore his challenge.

"What if I hadn't been here? You would have made the drive for nothing."

Sam shrugged almost imperceptibly. "I had an appointment on this side of town. Going a few miles out of the way was worth the risk. Besides it wouldn't have been for nothing. I wanted to see the kennel. And meet Hilde." He scratched behind Hilde's ear. She leaned into his hand with a grunt of satisfaction. He raised his brow to Jenny at Hilde's apparent acceptance and ended, "And I wanted to get a look at where you live."

"Well, now you've seen it." Jenny gestured around her briskly. Taking hold of Henry's leash, she led him to his run. "I don't have time right now for a social visit." She tossed this over her shoulder, not wanting to meet Sam's eyes as she dismissed him.

But she should have known Sam couldn't be so easily dismissed.

"You look like you could use a break and a glass of something cool. Invite me in and I'll join you." He caught up to her with long male strides.

Jenny latched the gate behind Henry and turned to do battle.

"Did you know," Sam asked softly, "that you have a smudge of dirt on the end of your nose?"

Before she could protest, he took the hem of her shirt, twisted it and carefully dabbed the smudge away, allowing the hot sunlight access to Jenny's midriff.

"Not," he went on consolingly, "that I don't find your face utterly enchanting, smudges and all. Hmm, here's another one across your cheek." He tugged at the fabric, making it stretch a little farther, exposing more bare skin to the heat of the sun.

"I—I'll go wash my face." Jenny backed away, yanking at the material Sam held in his grip and stumbling over Hilde.

"Good." He smiled at her sweetly. "While you do that, I'll find something wet for us to sip on the veranda."

"There's iced tea in the refrigerator," Jenny informed him resignedly, realizing she'd lost this skirmish and deciding retreat was the order of the day.

But damn, she hated his coming into her house. Invading her space. Her life. Crowding her. Cornering her. Making unspecified demands. Not that he had, actually. Yet. Made demands, that is. But she was sure the demands were coming.

When Jenny got to the bathroom and looked at herself in the mirror, she groaned. A shower was what she really needed. A quick, cool shower, so she could face Sam with cool composure.

And a change of clothes. Her nipples had hardened with the impact of his arrival and were still plainly visible through her bra and grimy shirt. She wondered if Sam had noticed. She had a feeling not much passed him by.

Twenty minutes later, showered and dressed in a carefully chosen demure shirtwaist, Jenny found Sam, holding a glass of iced tea, obviously surveying the contents of her living room.

Jenny's back stiffened. To Sam her home must look ramshackle. When she'd first moved in, she'd slapped paint on the walls, white to catch the light through the windows, and hung the few prints she'd bought over the years. She'd purchased what furniture she could with the meager budget she'd allowed herself. Every extra penny went into the business. And she'd adamantly refused to accept her mother's offer of help.

"Find what you're looking for?" Jenny asked, without bothering to disguise her displeasure.

Sam turned toward her, not the least embarrassed. "I don't know," he answered simply. "I'm looking for Jenny Hunter. I had a feeling I could find bits and pieces of her in this room."

Jenny was disconcerted by his honesty and had no ready comeback. He took the opportunity to walk to the bookcase.

"For instance, I believe you can tell a lot about people from the books they keep." He smiled disarmingly. "These technical works on breeding and genetics look like heavy reading."

"Any serious breeder," she said evenly, "needs to have the latest information."

"And this row of books by various animal behaviorists. Very impressive. Everyone from Konrad Lorenz to Robert Ardrey."

This time Jenny had more trouble responding. "I have an associate degree," she said finally, "from Austin Community College, but one of these days I hope to get a four-year degree from the University of Texas in the area of animal behavior. I thought it would help if I did some reading on my own."

Sam nodded his understanding, then grinned suddenly. "But it's this shelf that particularly intrigues me." He ran his fingers along the spines of the books in question. "*Watership Down*, the James Herriot stories. What's this? *Winnie the Pooh*? *The House at Pooh Corner*?"

Jenny could see where his grin had come from. She couldn't stop a grin herself. "Silly old Bear," she said softly.

"Who lives by himself under the name of Sanders."

"A Bear of No Brain at All."

"But the very Best Bear in All the World."

They laughed, delighted they shared a favorite author. Still, Jenny was wary of the gleam in Sam's eyes.

She was right to be wary, she decided, as he continued browsing.

"What have we here?" he exclaimed in mock surprise. "*Lassie Come Home*? *The Yearling*? *Black Beauty*? *Old Yeller*? Why, Jenny Hunter! I do believe that under that businesslike facade beats the heart of a closet romantic."

Jenny flushed and stammered. "Those were all my favorite books growing up. I couldn't just throw them away."

"Of course not," Sam agreed with great understanding. While she struggled to regain her composure, he went to the fireplace mantel to study a group of framed photographs.

"Who is this?" Sam took down one of the pictures.

The mood between the two of them changed.

"My father." Jenny's voice was gruff. She cleared her throat.

"This is an old snapshot."

"He died when I was four."

There was a slight pause. "And this couple?" Sam inspected another picture.

"Those are the Caneys. They gave me my first job working at their kennel. Later they left me money and equipment to start my own. They're both dead."

He gave Jenny a penetrating look. "They must have thought a lot of you."

"I thought a lot of them." Again Jenny's voice was gruff. "When I was a teenager, I practically lived at their place. It was the first real home I'd known. They hadn't been able to have children. I think I filled a void in their lives."

Sam took down another snapshot. "And this one? I can tell it's you in the picture. How old were you here? About fifteen?"

Jenny nodded.

"Who's this chap with you?"

She smiled faintly. "Freddy. The first dog I ever had. You could say it was Freddy that got me interested in obedience training. He was run over just months after that picture was taken."

Sam carefully placed the snapshot where he'd found it and turned to her abruptly.

"Is your mother still alive?"

"Yes." Jenny's gaze skidded from his. "Actually, she lives here in Austin with her third husband." Now, what on earth had prompted her to offer him that detail?

"Any brothers or sisters?"

Jenny shook her head and laughed, knowing the sound was thin as it drifted between them. "Annabelle—my mother—isn't the best with children. She decided after me that one was enough."

"You look a lot like your father. You must take after his side of the family."

"Do you think so?" Without realizing it, Jenny's face lit up, as if his words were a surprise she had no right to expect. Suddenly, eagerly, she wanted to take the picture he'd studied and go to a mirror to compare the two faces. She had to restrain the impulse.

"Hasn't anyone ever told you that before?" Sam's voice sounded odd. "The resemblance is striking."

"No. I've never been told. Thank you for seeing it." Jenny turned away and brushed a hand across her eyes. "Don't I get a glass of tea?" she asked and hurried to the kitchen. She found one freshly made, grabbed it and walked onto the porch.

Sam had seen too much. The way he could look into her mind. And she'd known what he'd seen because she could look into his.

Still, his first words as he followed her seemed harmless enough. "I came by to tell you we'd have to reschedule tomorrow's session."

"Oh?" She purposely glanced away from him into the yard. So there was a reason for his visit.

"I'm flying out of town in the morning. I'll be gone a week, so I'll miss Saturday, too."

"Oh…" Jenny could hear the forlorn note in her voice and she cursed it. Hadn't she wanted distance between them? Why did she feel suddenly bereft?

"I'd like you to board Zeppo and keep up his training while I'm gone." He came up behind her. "I wondered if I could bring him over this evening."

"Why, yes, of course. You don't have to drive here, however. I can pick him up at your house."

"No. I want you to come to dinner with me after you get him settled."

"No." Jenny's refusal was instinctive and immediate. She stepped to the railing, realizing only when he turned her around that she was cornered.

"Jenny…" Sam took her hands and began leading her to the rocking chair she kept for summer evenings. He gently pushed her into it, then squatted before her so she was trapped. "Jenny…why?"

"Why? Why what?" Jenny's voice was thin and reedy.

His was little more than a murmur as he watched her closely. "Why won't you go out with me?"

"I've told you I don't date the cust—"

"Not a good enough excuse." He broke through her protest. "I won't let you use it."

"I'm not interested in you. Is that an acceptable reason?" Her chin came up sharply. She spoiled the effect, however, by refusing to meet his eyes.

He chuckled faintly. "Wrong again." Cupping her chin with his fingers, he made her face him. "We both know you're attracted to me. Just as we know I'm attracted to you."

She started to protest.

"I wouldn't argue." He stopped her. "Or I'll be forced to discuss the evidence with you."

A flush rose to Jenny's face as her lashes fluttered shut. At the sound of Sam's harsh breathing she popped them open again.

"That's right. Look at me. See the effect you're having."

As though obeying a command, her gaze reluctantly wandered over his face. She saw the desire in his eyes beneath the intent regard, the tinge of color under his skin. She felt the slight tremor in the hand reaching to cover hers. She could count his pulse, and it matched her own.

"I am," he said deliberately, "an unattached, eligible, age-appropriate male with no communicable diseases. My intentions are honorable."

He paused before continuing. "You are, according to my observations, an unattached, eligible, very attractive female. Why can't we see one another to explore the possibilities between us? Is there something you haven't told me I need to know?"

Jenny mentally went over the list he'd provided, wondering if she could conjure up a husband in Pittsburgh. Or perhaps a terminal illness. She faced him bravely. He studied her intently. After a moment, her look dropped and she shook her head.

"Has someone hurt you? Another man? Do I need to go out and slay a dragon?"

She grimaced, broke through his arms and hurried into the yard.

A man hurt her? Not likely. Her sexual experience, such as it was, had only hurt the other person. And taught Jenny a painful lesson.

"Look, I don't have to answer these questions." Jenny tried to make her tone unequivocal. Instead, she sounded weak and listless. She plowed on. "After all, none of this is your business."

He had a relentless look as he followed her, ignoring her dismissal. "Have you ever been in love, Jenny?"

"No! And I don't plan to be, either."

"That's too bad," Sam said very quietly. "Because I think I'm falling in love with you."

"No!" Jenny's protest rang out, followed by absolute quiet. It was as if the entire immediate world recognized the moment. The dogs in their runs ceased their yammering, the wind lulled and the trees stilled, the birds stopped their afternoon songs.

Hilde, stretched out in the shade, steadily regarded the tableau before her. Dagwood was a sculpted figure on the hood of Sam's car. The universe had hushed in a respectful silence. Only the breathing of the two humans was harsh and loud.

"Sam...listen..." It was hard to get the words out between stiff lips. "I...that would be a big mistake on your part."

"Why?"

"I'm a great dog trainer. But I'd be a lousy lover. No natural aptitude, I guess." She offered her excuses with a smile and a shrug, but Sam could see the labored rise and fall of her breasts.

"Jenny." He moved closer, still giving her space. "I didn't mean to tell you so soon. I realize you're confused by your feelings." His voice was very calming. It reminded her, in her distracted state, of the tones she used to soothe a skittish animal. "But I feel you need to know this isn't a game I'm playing. I'm not flirting with you to pass the time, and I'm not, as they say, making a move on you. At least, not in the way you might think."

He heard a dry wisp of laughter, which was more of a sigh.

"I wouldn't know if you were playing games with me or not. I'm not very good at picking up on maneuvers."

"I'm aware of that. It's amazing how you manage it." Sam tried to coax a smile. "Do you know you've probably left a trail of broken hearts and never even noticed?"

"Don't say that, Sam." Jenny's voice had a catch in it. "I did hurt someone once, although I certainly didn't mean to. A trainer I dated. I don't want to hurt you."

"I'm a big boy, Jenny. I don't need to be protected. And I won't make demands on you that you can't handle. I promise," he added in a gentle tone. "We'll take it slow and easy. Just a dinner to start with. Good food. Conversation. Afterward, I'll bring you straight home and leave. Let's start by being friends with each other."

"Friends?"

"Friends. I think you could use one."

She suddenly realized he spoke the absolute truth.

"Just friends."

"Until you're ready for more."

"What if I'm never ready? What if I don't have more in me?"

Sam's smile was the sweetest he'd ever given her. "Dear Jenny, there is more inside you than you've imagined. More love to give. More passion. Life is inside you, Jenny. Waiting to be lived."

IT WAS THE STRANGEST, most bewildering, most exhilarating encounter Jenny had ever had with a man. Two hours later, as she tried to decide what to wear for their dinner date, she still felt internal tremors.

A closet romantic, Sam had called her. If he only knew. Tucked away in the reaches of Jenny's wardrobe were gossamer rainbows and silken moonbeams. Secretly treasured but never worn.

As a child she'd hated the frilly dresses Annabelle sporadically bought her. Especially when the lacy collars frayed and the hems unraveled. More often than not, she'd looked like a Goodwill version of Shirley Temple. As an adult she'd taken refuge from those memories by simplifying her appearance to the bare essentials.

But, oh, there lurked a gypsy in her soul. And bangles and baubles tucked away in a chest in the bottom drawer of her bureau. Did she dare let that gypsy go out with Sam tonight?

Jenny knew such an action might prove dangerous. But she couldn't make herself put on one of her utilitarian outfits. So she compromised on a navy flared skirt and a peasant blouse belted securely at her slender waist.

As Jenny finished dressing, she felt a fluttering beneath her breastbone and a churning in her stomach. With such a case of nerves, how could she possibly enjoy the meal she and Sam would be sharing?

Surprisingly, she did.

From the moment Sam arrived at six-thirty, he treated her to warm, simple companionship. Having a boisterous Zeppo in tow helped break the ice.

Before Jenny knew it, they were driving toward town arguing amiably about the best place to eat, with Jenny amazed at the easy conversation. Especially in light of their different personalities and life-styles. She'd make a wager the automobile conveying them cost more than she made in a year.

Soon they were ensconced in the booth of a fifties' style diner, the atmosphere cheerful and cozy. And curiously intimate.

Friendly. Like their discussion over the chicken-fried steaks they were served, full of calories and flavor.

Friends. Sam was right. Her life did lack friendships. She and Leia, her assistant, got on well. But that was on an employer-employee basis. The trainers she saw at shows and meets shared news and gossip about the professional world they worked in. But few of them knew anything about Jenny's personal life.

Of course, her customers liked her. Jenny had worked hard to develop a casual but businesslike manner that suited her. She liked her customers as well, which helped.

Yet there really wasn't anyone Jenny knew with whom she felt comfortable enough to discuss the world and their places in it. The way Sam and she were discussing it now. She'd never had the time or luxury to develop such a friendship.

Jenny was curious to learn more about the man who offered it to her.

"So tell me, what do you do? I know you're a partner in an engineering firm."

Sam seemed ready to satisfy her curiosity. "Our company contracts for various custom-made manufacturing devices, but we primarily design and market ice-cream machines.''

"Ice-cream machines?'' Jenny couldn't hide her surprise. "You mean like the ones you crank to make the homemade stuff?''

He chuckled. "A little more than that. How do you think ice-cream sandwiches are made? And all the dairy confections you can buy in the frozen-food department?''

"I don't know. I hadn't really thought about it. You mean machines have to be designed to manufacture each item?''

He nodded.

"Is there much money in that?'' she asked without thinking.

"Enough,'' Sam drawled. "We've sold machines to companies in Germany, France, Italy and England, as well as in most of the fifty states. We work a lot with regional dairies.''

Jenny found herself fascinated by this other world. She drew Sam out, and he began to talk about one of his current projects. As he explained it with animated gestures, she made a startling discovery.

The high-powered convertible he drove, the electronic equipment in his home, those weren't yuppie pretensions. She could tell from listening to Sam that he had an informed knowledge of and appreciation for well-designed, well-crafted objects, and the wherewithal to buy and enjoy them. So how did she fit in with his impeccable tastes?

Jenny realized she'd missed Sam's last few comments when he looked chagrined and apologized. "I'm boring you, aren't I? You should never let an engineer get started on a pet project.''

"Oh, no, you're not boring me at all." Jenny grinned devilishly. "Although I have to admit you lost me when you went on about the stress factor involved."

Sam's expression was rueful. And extremely beguiling.

"Tell me about your family," Jenny requested impulsively. "Are your mother and father..." She stopped, embarrassed by her boldness.

Sam filled in smoothly. "Hale and hearty and happily married. Dad teaches math at the university and doesn't have a practical bone in his body. Luckily, Mother manages the world around him, with time left over for her various hobbies."

"Any brothers and sisters?"

"Three sisters. Two older, Risa and Carol. They're both married with children. And Megan, the baby of the family."

"And you're the only boy."

He glanced at her warily. "I don't like the way you said that."

She grinned and brushed aside his complaint. "Are you and your sisters anything alike?"

"Yes and no. It's the same with any family. Risa's like Mom. Very organized and efficient. Which is just as well, since her husband, Larry, is a Renaissance scholar and totally lost in the everyday world. If it weren't for Risa, Larry wouldn't find his way home from work."

"And Carol?"

"Vague. Rather like my father. But something of a throwback. The feminist revolution passed her by. She's content to stay home and make babies and be kept by her husband, Gary, in the style to which he's accustomed her. Gary's family owns the Mason's Dry Cleaning chain."

"I see."

Sam nodded and smiled. "Carol gets to decorate a new house every time she gets pregnant. Gary says he's indulging her nesting instinct. She's on her third house. And baby, too."

Jenny had to laugh, although his family was beginning to sound rather formidable.

"And Megan?" she asked, not sure what to expect.

"Megan . . ." Sam's whimsical smile, the way he lingered over the name, told Jenny a lot about his feelings for his youngest sister. "I'm not sure how to describe Megan. She's a force of nature. Scattered, impulsive." His expression sobered. "She's pretty much done as she liked up till now."

"Do I detect the hint of disapproving big brother?"

Sam laughed. "That's what she'd tell you."

"And yet I have the feeling you're close."

"Yeah, we are."

"You must have had a wonderful childhood."

"Why do you say that?"

"Oh, we ex-waifs can spot an all-American family a mile away."

"Oh, you can, can you?" Sam knew she was teasing him, but he caught the sudden edge to her humor. "How can you tell I had such a wonderful childhood?"

"Your self-confidence." Jenny crossed her arms and leaned back against the booth. "You're not even conscious you have it. You probably had it before you learned how to crawl."

"And you? Where did you get your self-confidence?"

"Here and there." Jenny's chin went up slightly. "It was one of the traits I set out to incorporate. I didn't have anyone to teach it to me."

"And you see this as a difference between us." Sam's quiet comment was too perceptive.

Jenny took refuge in humor again. "Plus the fact you're spoiled rotten."

"Spoiled!"

"Spoiled." A smile played around her mouth at his indignation. "You think you should get your own way."

Sam was quick to catch her meaning. "You mean about us, don't you?"

Jenny's shrug was eloquent.

He grinned and spoke with a touch of little-boy wheedle. "Just because I'm spoiled doesn't mean I'm wrong."

Jenny's heart thudded. She was helpless to control the reaction. She'd never known someone who could get to her with a smile. "Sam..." She felt a sudden need to establish distance between them. "You must see we have nothing in common. You're happy, secure, you expect the best from yourself and others..."

"Whereas, you go through life leading with your chin."

Damn, he was too perceptive. And determined.

"My turn," he announced.

She didn't understand at first what he meant.

"To ask the questions," he explained, gazing at her steadily. "Jenny." He paused for a second. "How did your father die?"

Jenny realized she'd let herself in for this with the grilling she'd given him. "A training accident," she answered after a moment. "He was in the army, stationed at Fort Hood."

"How long had he been in the army?"

"He joined right after he and Annabelle were married in 1959. The dark ages. Theirs was what used to be called a shotgun wedding. Annabelle was pregnant with me." Now why on earth had she shared the family secrets?

"Do you think your parents resented having you?"

"Oh, no. My father loved me very much. I can remember."

"And your mother?"

"Annabelle's not the resenting type."

"After your dad died, did you and your mother live with family?"

Jenny shook her head. "Annabelle and my father were raised in a little town in Georgia, and that's where both sets of grandparents lived. I hardly knew them. The Hunters died soon after Dad did—Annabelle said of a broken heart. My mother's parents passed away a few years ago. They were very strict and religious. After the scandal, they refused to welcome their daughter in their house. Besides, Annabelle met Gordon a few months later and got married again." All this was said in a clinical tone.

"And Gordon was your mother's second husband?"

"Yes." A kind of dry chuckle escaped Jenny's lips. "You must understand—Annabelle doesn't do well without a man around her. She's the clinging, helpless type. When Gordon left she was devastated."

"But you weren't," Sam guessed accurately.

"No."

Jenny's voice was devoid of color, but Sam sensed the shudder running through her.

"Gordon was an alcoholic and verbally abusive. I spent most of my time staying out of his way. I guess that's when I became a loner."

"Would you characterize yourself that way?"

"You said I needed a friend. Well, those were really the days I could have used one. Freddy. He was the first real friend I had." Jenny's face became expressionless. "Enough about me. Tell me more about your family."

"Why are we changing the subject?" he asked. "What just went through your head?"

"I . . ." Jenny's chin came up. "I don't like to discuss my childhood. When I do, it makes me sad. Then I start to feel sorry for myself. Since I swore off self-pity a long time ago, I try my best not to remember."

"You're leading with your chin again," Sam observed softly.

"Am I?" Jenny blinked and blinked again. "I guess I do sound defensive. I'm trying to get over that," she mumbled. "I'm really working . . ."

"Good." Sam's voice was hearty. "We'll work on it together. And I'll work on being insecure."

It was Jenny's turn to stare at him suspiciously. "Are you making fun of me?"

Sam chuckled. "I'm making fun *with* you. There's a fine distinction. It seems we both have a lot to learn."

He offered her a coaxing smile of friendship that wrapped itself around her and curled into her heart.

She felt its touch all the way home.

CHAPTER FIVE

THERE WERE SILENCES between Sam and Jenny during the homeward journey. Short silences between spurts of conversation. Curiously tense silences.

Being Sam's friend had hidden pitfalls. Because it was hard, very hard to think of him as just a friend.

Jenny could feel his presence on the seat next to her. She found herself watching his hands, remembering them as a compelling accompaniment to his speech.

They were competent hands. Attractive hands. Hands that went about the task of driving with practiced ease. It was the way he'd do everything. With practiced ease.

The way he would touch her. Gently. Knowingly.

Jenny stared out the window and watched the lighted buildings slide by in a blur.

He turned at her mailbox and drove up the graveled road to park beside her house. She opened her door before he could come around and walked toward her porch without a backward look.

But it took only a touch on her shoulder to turn her to him. He was standing inches away.

"You forgot to say good-night and wish me a safe trip tomorrow." Sam's voice was low in the rustling dimness.

"Good night. Have a safe trip." Jenny's pulse thudded in her ears. She tried to move, but found she couldn't. Her mouth was dry, and she had to lick her lips to get them to work. "Sam . . . don't . . ."

"Don't what?"

"Don't . . . kiss me. That wasn't part of the bargain."

"The bargain was, I wouldn't do anything you didn't want. You want me to kiss you."

"How did . . ."

"You told me so in the car just now."

Jenny swallowed hard, remembering several things her silences must have told him.

"Besides," he went on, "this'll be a nice friendly kiss. Nothing you can't handle. Just relax. Watch. It won't hurt a bit."

He cupped her shoulders lightly. She felt his touch in every nerve. Her lashes fluttered shut.

"No. I told you to watch."

She opened her eyes reluctantly to find his face so close she could read every angle. The laugh lines around his mouth and eyes. The whimsical smile he wore.

"I've never kissed a fairy princess before. If I do, will I fall into a spell of enchantment?"

Jenny's eyes widened. Her look told him she didn't understand his meaning.

Sam's whisper of a laugh was warm against her skin. "Too late. I've fallen already."

His lips brushed hers with the merest wisp of contact. They left, then came back to cling for an instant.

Their sighs mingled as Sam drew away.

Hurt? He told her a kiss wouldn't hurt.

But it did. It left her with an ache that burrowed deep inside. And lasted the whole time he was away.

JENNY MISSED SAM. She couldn't ignore it, although she tried. Her sense of being deprived was most unnerving.

Hadn't she spent her entire adult life proving she was self-sufficient? Yet Jenny couldn't seem to fight the need for Sam.

He called late Thursday night to check on Zeppo's progress. That was the ostensible reason for the contact. The real reason was unspoken between them but understood.

Jenny was already drifting to sleep when the phone rang. Her lassitude vanished with the sound of his voice.

So close. So close to her he seemed. She felt as though he touched her.

She was too surprised to marshal her defenses. Too tired to control laughter and a certain husky tone when she heard the same from him. And though the conversation was short and inconsequential, it left Jenny awake and restless. She tossed and turned the rest of the night.

Still, with Sam's absence at the Saturday class, Jenny could concentrate on her other students. On Richard.

The two weeks of instruction had made a difference in his attitude. He was still shy and reserved, but his anxiety had vanished, and he watched and listened with intense concentration. He was a fast learner, just like Arnie. Jenny could tell they practiced faithfully every day. It was only fair she praise their efforts. After all, they were turning out to be her prize pupils.

Just as Arnie had basked in her praise the first day, Richard, in his own guarded fashion, was blossoming under her tutelage.

He was drawn to her. Jenny felt the tug below her consciousness. Just as she was drawn to him.

Strange. Most of the time she coped with children rather than enjoyed them. Children were alien to her. Perhaps because she couldn't remember being a child herself.

But Richard was ten going on fifty, with an adult control that put some people off. Jenny recognized the necessity of that control, the reasons for it, the vulnerability that underlay it. She could no more have ignored the instincts drawing her to coax a smile from that solemn little face than she could have ignored a dog that was lost and frightened.

All she really wanted from Richard was a grin. A childish giggle or two. A burgeoning self-confidence she could sense as he called out commands to Arnie with a new authority. She had no wish to breach the reserve so necessary to him.

She remembered too vividly those well-meaning adults who had tried to pierce her reserve, who considered it a challenge to their charm. As though her shyness were an insult.

A rejection.

She found herself wanting to take Bob Ingram and shake him soundly. Didn't he realize his anxiety at Richard's withdrawal only compounded the problem? Bob was affected by his wife's death; why couldn't he see the ways it had affected Richard? Was it guilt that blinded him to his son's needs? Didn't he realize he was withdrawn himself?

"Miss Hunter?"

"Yes, Richard?" Once again, Richard and his father had stayed behind after the others were gone.

"I wondered..."

"Yes?"

"You know, you said you train people's dogs for them, sometimes."

Jenny felt the cold wind of discouragement blow over her. Had the growing confidence she'd sensed in him been an illusion?

"I do train for people on occasion, Richard. But you're doing so well, I—"

"Oh, no!" It was a measure of his distress at the misunderstanding that Richard rushed to interrupt her. "I don't mean train Arnie for me. I just wanted to watch and, well, see you giving the commands. I figured I could learn a lot watching. If that—if you don't mind, that is."

Jenny found herself smiling foolishly. "I don't mind. As a matter of fact—" she caught Bob Ingram's eye "—I'm working with Zeppo this afternoon. I don't know what your dad has planned..."

"I have to catch up on some work at the office, Richard," Ingram said, rather abruptly—and reluctantly, Jenny had to admit.

A bleak mask replaced Richard's look of cautious anticipation. Once more Jenny's hands itched to grab hold of Ingram's shoulders and deliver a good shake.

"Why don't you drop Richard by the kennel while you go to the office?" As soon as Jenny spoke she realized she'd curbed her instincts with Ingram only to give in to another impulse. Impossible to take back the invitation. "He can watch me work with several of the dogs."

Ingram seemed hesitant. "Are you sure you don't mind?" His tone implied she would.

"I'm sure. Leia, my assistant, doesn't come on Saturday." Jenny spoke directly to Richard. "I could use some help in return for my expert demonstration. Is it a deal?"

Richard looked up at his father with the polite mask still in place. "Is it a deal, Dad?"

Ingram shrugged and seemed relieved. "Sure, why not. But you have to promise to be good and not get in Jenny's way."

It was such an incongruous set of instructions, considering Richard's perfect manners, that Jenny began to wonder if Bob Ingram knew his son at all.

But it wasn't that. Ingram was simply floundering as a parent, conjuring up words from a memory bank. Jenny wondered how many other conversations between father and son were so curiously inept.

"I'll be good and not get in Miss Hunter's way," Richard promised with no color in his voice.

Jenny remained wisely silent during the exchange.

RICHARD WAS A MAN OF HIS WORD. And few others. He might have been a ghost at the beginning of his visit. Except a ghost wouldn't have followed her few instructions to the letter. A ghost wouldn't have laid a timid hand on Dagwood's sleek fur when she decided to court him.

A trace of a smile appeared on Richard's face when Dagwood nipped daintily at his fingers. He and Hilde were introduced with formal politeness, but it was only when Zeppo was let loose from his run that Richard began to loosen up.

For, contrary to Zeppo's attitude toward Dobermans, the terrier never met a boy he didn't like. All boys belonged to him by fiat, and he assumed from each a felicitous response.

As soon as he saw Richard, Zeppo bounded over, madly circled him, tumbled them both to the ground and began to lick Richard's face, sending the child into helpless gales of laughter.

Jenny squatted beside them and threw an arm around Hilde, who had come over to investigate the proceedings. Childish squeals never sounded so good.

"Wha—what kind of dog is he?" Richard asked breathlessly as he halfheartedly fended Zeppo off.

"A fox terrier. They're exuberant, like Labs. They seldom meet a stranger." By this time, Zeppo was avidly sniffing Richard. "He smells Arnie, and he probably remembers you from the class."

"Yeah, I think he does. Hi there, Zeppo. You wish Arnie was here to play with?"

Jenny shook her head wryly. "I don't think they'd play well together."

"Why not?"

"They're both males, for one thing. Male dogs very often don't get along. They feel the need to defend their territory, which in this case is you. Arnie knows you belong to him, and Zeppo would like to claim you. You've heard of dogs fighting over a bone. Well, consider yourself a nice, juicy sirloin steak."

Richard grinned appreciatively at the analogy. "Are all the breeds like that? I mean, do they all have different..." Richard struggled to formulate his question.

"All breeds were developed for different reasons, Richard, some to hunt, some to herd, some to guard, some to be companions. Even though many dogs aren't used today for their original purposes, each kind of dog has characteristics that are unique to that breed. And of course, every dog has his or her own personality. That's why it's so interesting working with them." Jenny was afraid she'd begun lecturing on a favorite subject, but Richard's face told her he was fascinated.

"Yeah. Dogs are neat. I never had one till I got Arnie. Mom was allergic to animals. What's a Labrador supposed to do?"

Jenny was surprised to hear Richard mention his mother in passing. She wondered if he expected a question about her, then decided to stick with his query. "Arnie's a retriever, like his name implies. He's a Cana-

dian dog bred to go hunting with his master in the cold
and damp to retrieve the kill." Jenny smiled to soften her
words. "That was back in the days when we couldn't get
our supper from the supermarket. Labs are very hardy
and loyal. They're also very affectionate."

"Like Zeppo." Richard giggled. Zeppo was nibbling
on his ear. It was obvious Zeppo had charmed another
subject, but Richard wasn't ready to switch his alle-
giance. His face sobered as he looked Jenny's way.
"Zeppo's fun, you know, but Arnie's special." It was
almost as if he felt disloyal, playing with another dog.
"Arnie likes me better than anybody."

"I'm sure he does."

"He follows me around," Richard informed her earnestly, "and sleeps on the foot of my bed. Sometimes I
think he knows what I'm thinking, and when I'm feeling
bad. Dad doesn't believe me, but it's true."

"You know, Richard," Jenny said carefully, "there's
something very special between a dog and his master, a
magical bond other people can't see."

Richard nodded sagely.

"Unless you have a dog of your own," she went on,
"that you're very close to, or you work with dogs like I
do, it's hard to understand how close the bond really is.
I know your dad is pleased with how well you and Arnie
get along."

"Sure." Richard shrugged. "Now he doesn't feel so
bad leaving me alone when he has to work or something.
He says I have Arnie to keep me company."

Jenny went cold for a moment in the afternoon heat.
How many nights had she waited for her mother to come
home from a date or an evening shift at the restaurant?
With only Freddy to keep the dark at bay. She tried to
keep her voice light.

"Isn't it great, then, you and Arnie have each other for pals? Sounds like you can even share your private thoughts with him. That's what pals are for."

"How did you know Arnie and I talk to each other?" Richard's face was filled with amazement.

Jenny smiled. "Because when I was your age I had a pal, too. His name was Freddy. He wasn't as handsome or dashing as Arnie, but he was my very best friend, and I could tell him anything."

"I talk to Arnie a lot." Richard's voice fell to a whisper. "I tell him about my mom. Everything I remember about her..." He turned away from Jenny, his lashes blinking rapidly.

Jenny sat beside Richard in an aching silence, at a loss as to how to react to his sudden struggle with tears.

Zeppo, with his usual savoir faire, came to their rescue.

"Woof! Woof!" he barked raucously, stretching his paws and assuming a crouch. *What's going on here? You can't ignore me! I want to play!*

He pounced on Richard and fell with him into the grass. Richard's tears turned to laughter as the awkward moment passed.

Jenny took her cue from Zeppo, deciding his lesson would rescue the day. She found the leash where she'd dropped it, hooked it to Zeppo's collar, then stood and brushed off her shorts.

"Okay, Zeppo, enough of this. It's time to work on your manners. Heel, Zeppo. Heel."

Zeppo tried his best to dismiss the new subject of discussion. But Jenny could not be ignored. With a brisk jerk of the leash, she commanded his attention. Reluctantly, he agreed to the task at hand.

The maneuver gave Richard time to regain his composure. When she glanced at him wryly and said, "As you can see, terriers like to be the main attraction," Richard could smile and nod his understanding. "They're fiercely independent, too. The breed was developed to hunt on their own. Sometimes they're stubborn and hard to train."

"Not like Arnie." Pride laced Richard's voice.

"Not like Arnie," Jenny agreed solemnly.

After that, the afternoon sped by. The initial awkwardness between them had vanished. And Jenny's handling of Richard's moment of vulnerability had somehow earned his trust.

Jenny was amazed she could entertain a boy of ten for three hours without groping for words or activities. But she did what she always did, and Richard tagged along, careful to stay out of her way, asking the occasional question, showing his interest and intelligence. Often, there was silence between them. Now it was an easy silence. They felt comfortable with each other. They had something to share.

By the end of the afternoon, it was impossible for Jenny not to recognize that underneath Richard's polite dignity was the need for a woman's attentions. It stunned Jenny to realize that she yearned to reach out to this child and envelop him in her arms.

She couldn't do that, of course. It would have embarrassed both of them. Still, when Ingram came to pick up Richard, Jenny sang Richard's praises as a helper and invited him back.

Had she been too effusive? Had Richard seen through her? Jenny glanced his way and found an eager smile plastered across his face.

"Next Saturday, Dad?" he asked with rare temerity. "Could I come next Saturday after the lesson?"

"Sure." Bob Ingram was just as eager. "If you're sure Richard's not a bother, Jenny."

"I wouldn't have asked him if he was."

AFTER BOB AND RICHARD LEFT, Jenny realized her life was suddenly cluttered with males. Males who disrupted the cadence of her existence.

Sam, who stirred restless urges in her. Richard, who tugged powerfully and insistently at her heart. Bob Ingram, with his needs and sorrows.

Bob called her the day after Richard's visit.

"Richard talks about the kennel and you nonstop."

"Does he? Well, I told you what a help he was."

"I can't tell you how much I appreciate the interest you've taken in him. I realize Richard's not an easy child to know."

Jenny felt herself bristling. She wondered if Richard was listening to the conversation. "I like Richard, Mr. Ingram. He's very bright and good with the animals. I find him easy to be around."

Ingram didn't seem to notice Jenny's stiff tone. "Listen, call me Bob." He cleared his throat. "You two sure must have found something to talk about. I haven't heard him chatter like this in years."

To Jenny's ears he sounded wistful. "It's because we share a common interest," she placated him. "I think having Arnie has opened up a whole new world to Richard."

Bob laughed briefly. "Yeah. Next thing you know he'll decide he wants to be an animal trainer."

"There are worse things he could want to be," Jenny said, trying to empty her voice of irony.

"Oh, certainly, certainly." Bob recognized his misstep and hastened to his purpose in calling. "What I'm trying to say is... I'm so happy about him wanting to get to know you. It's quite a breakthrough. He hasn't been around women much lately. He and his grandmother—Doris's mother—aren't very close. She was badly broken up by the accident, and frankly, her nerves aren't the best. My parents live out of state and we hardly see them. So I haven't had any family to turn to for help. I'm grateful for yours."

He paused for a moment. "Sometimes I feel like I'm doing everything wrong. Ever since Doris died...it's like Richard and I live in the same house, but we have nothing to say to each other. You'd think we'd be close...but we're not."

Jenny felt uncomfortable with the conversation. Bob Ingram's neediness made her want to retreat. But she couldn't stop the compassion and sympathy welling up in her.

"How long has it been since your wife died?" she asked.

"Two years. Two hellish years." Jenny's question opened the floodgates. "It was a car accident. Totally senseless. If I'd been with her the wreck never would have happened. It took me a year to realize she'd gone. She was a lovely person. So good with Richard. When we had him, she gave up her career to be a full-time mom. That was important to Doris. To make a home for us." His voice faltered. "I've been lost without her. And work these past two years has eaten me alive. Although... maybe I've been lucky to have it."

"Perhaps you have," Jenny commented noncommittally, thinking of Richard and his unmet needs.

Bob seemed to sense her withdrawal. "Well, anyway...I didn't mean to talk your ear off." He paused. "I just wanted to thank you."

"You're welcome. As I said before, Richard's a neat kid."

"So I'll see you next week."

"Next week," she confirmed pleasantly.

After they traded goodbyes, Jenny sat looking at the phone. She had a premonition she was getting in over her head with Bob and Richard. The conversation strengthened her forboding.

She grimaced. Hell, that wasn't the only situation she should be wary of.

Sam's return loomed in her mind.

WHEN SAM FLEW INTO TOWN and came to pick up Zeppo, Jenny found herself sharing another dinner, this one king-size cheeseburgers, which they took to Zilker Park to eat.

Evening settled as they argued over the last French fry and sipped giant root beers. Yells and laughter drifted from the swimmers in Barton Springs. Pecan trees offered shade and the hint of coolness as they walked off the calories.

"If you feed me too often, I'll be a blimp."

He took the opportunity to survey the finer points of her figure, only partially hidden by the hiking shorts and blouse she wore. "You realize," he said, "that statement's ridiculous."

"I beg your pardon," she said indignantly to hide her confusion.

"Okay. Okay." Sam threw up his hands, his smile conciliatory though suspect. "I will do my gentlemanly duty. Every pound is divine. Several more would only add to the view."

"Are you saying I'm too skinny?"

"Far from it," he protested, an odd gleam in his eyes. "Your figure's enchanting."

Sam's extravagance always rattled Jenny. She flushed. "I wasn't trying to wheedle compliments." Or was she?

Sam smiled at her. "Whether you were or not, it's only the truth."

Jenny's flush deepened, and she wondered if it showed.

She, Jenny Hunter, was flirting. And enjoying it. Another first in this new life she led.

Still, she was relieved when Sam changed the subject, asking her how her week had been. She found herself discussing Richard and his father.

"I'm not usually good with kids," she explained carefully. "I feel inadequate around them. Richard's different somehow."

"Why is that, do you suppose?"

"Well, I'm no Freud, but I suspect it's because he reminds me of me at the same age. Did you know he lost his mother in an auto accident?"

Sam shook his head slowly, his expression somber. "So that's why he's a miniature adult. Do you think having Arnie is helping?"

"Of course. Didn't you know pets have the power to cure all ills? Getting Arnie for Richard was one of the few smart things Bob's done."

"You sound as if you don't like Ingram."

"I don't mean to. I'm certainly not an expert, to give him advice. And I don't mean to sound callous. I know he's still getting over his wife's death. He evidently loved her very much. I just get impatient with the man. He's making demands on his son without understanding the consequences. Half the time he hovers, which makes Richard uncomfortable, the rest of the time he's buried in his work. How can Richard cope with such mixed messages?''

Sam stopped, faced Jenny squarely and pointed out, ''You could probably answer your own question better than anyone. You may not be an expert, but you could use your own experience to help Ingram understand his son and the relationship between them. And what Mrs. Ingram's death has meant to them both.''

Jenny immediately shied away from the notion. ''I wouldn't know where to start. I'm a dog trainer, period. I'm no good at rescuing people. If I tried, I'd probably drown myself.''

Jenny realized belatedly the remark had been revealing. She was surprised when Sam didn't follow up on it.

Instead, he asked, ''Does Bob Ingram remind you of your mother?''

Sam's question was unexpected and left her at a loss. ''No. I mean, not obviously.'' Yet, when she thought about it, she had linked the two of them in her mind. ''In a way I guess he does. I have a hard time explaining Annabelle to people. You'd have to meet her to understand.''

''Why do you call her Annabelle?''

''I'm not sure. I called her Mother when I was very young. Then, after Gordon left, it didn't seem like we were mother and daughter. I took care of her as much as she took care of me. I started calling her by her name, and Annabelle never objected.'' Jenny shrugged dismissively, wanting to drop the subject. ''It's hard for me to think of her any other way.''

''Tell me more about your mother,'' he pressed her.

Jenny's eyes flew to his. "What do you want to know?" she asked with a hint of belligerence.

"Whatever you tell me," he responded quietly.

Jenny took a deep breath, not wanting to do this, but knowing Sam well enough to realize he wouldn't let the topic lie. "Annabelle's almost fifty, and she's still quite beautiful."

"Like her daughter?"

"No. You were right the other night. I take after my father's family. Mother's tall and willowy with classic features. We don't look a bit alike."

Jenny paused for a moment and stared into space. "It's funny. Her mirror shows her how lovely she is, yet she only sees her beauty when it's reflected in a man's eyes. Annabelle's not a very self-reliant person. I mean, she's not whole unto herself."

"Like her daughter."

Jenny breathed in sharply. Sam was too perceptive. "I try," she said evenly.

His lips curved faintly in a smile that said more than words. "You said your mother was lost after your father died."

"Totally. And she had this kid she didn't know what to do with."

"This is how your mother reminds you of Ingram."

"Yes. Please understand, I don't blame her any more than I do Bob." Or did she? "But Annabelle's helplessness gets her into trouble. She needs constant male attention. She married Gordon because of that. It's one of the reasons she married Lloyd."

"Tell me about Gordon and Lloyd."

"I don't like to talk about them."

"I know. That's why I want you to."

Jenny folded her arms and looked at him challengingly. "Just what is going on here? Should I draw up a couch, Doctor, and bare my soul?"

"Among other things."

She'd walked into that one. She flushed and had to look away.

"Hey." He caught her chin and made her face him. His smile was whimsical. "I'm sorry. I keep losing my place. We'll get to that subject another time. We're friends. That's what's going on here. Friends share the bad as well as the good. Have you ever talked to anyone about your mother's husbands?"

"No."

"Believe me, now's a good time to start. I'm an experienced listener."

Somehow, Jenny believed him. "Okay," she said brusquely. "We'll start with Gordon. He was cruel to Annabelle. He could be charming, but he was violent. There was a stream of other women. He detested me."

Sam started to speak, decided not to. His silence somehow helped her to go on.

"Do you know—" Sam felt her shudder faintly as she spoke "—when Gordon told my mother he was leaving, she begged him to stay. Begged him." Even now, Jenny could remember lying in her bed in the dark listening to Annabelle in the next room crying and pleading. Even now she could remember her feelings of shame and revulsion at what her mother had come to. "Gordon was a drunk, he was brutal and he was openly unfaithful. Yet Annabelle was so frightened of being alone, she begged him to stay."

There was a moment of silence after Jenny stopped speaking while each one of them digested what she'd said.

Then Sam asked with a faint rasp in his voice. "What happened after Gordon?"

Jenny gathered herself and shrugged. "We came to Austin. Annabelle tried to support us. There were more men."

"Like Gordon?"

"No. None as bad as Gordon. Just . . . men. Then she met Lloyd. He seemed the solution to all her problems. So she married him. They've been married over fifteen years."

"It sounds like this marriage was successful."

Jenny was silent. She felt chilled and a little battered. "I think my hour's up, Doctor. How much do I owe you?"

Sam could see she'd had enough. He rubbed his hands up and down her arms as if warming her from the cold that crept through her, then leaned to brush her forehead with a kiss.

"Is that your payment?" Jenny asked, a weak smile appearing.

"A first installment." His own smile came and went. He studied her features as he said unexpectedly, "I hope some day you'll let me meet your mother and Lloyd."

Jenny couldn't think of anything she wanted less.

IT WAS TEN O'CLOCK when they made it to Jenny's house, and the last hour and a half had been pleasant and undemanding. They'd walked down the hill to indulge in an ice-cream cone at the concession stand by the pool. And leaned over the fence to watch the swimmers cavorting. After a short tour of the park, they'd driven north to Mt. Bonnell to catch the last rays of sunset over the western hills. Then Sam had insisted on a cup of coffee at what was now their favorite haunt, the diner.

Sam sensed Jenny could handle only so much probing. When she asked him about his trip, he'd taken his cue from her and explained with some humor the problems of custom designing an ice-cream machine.

"So the vice-president in charge of product development is asking me if I can mass produce an ice-cream bar that looks like Big Foot. Based of course on a composite description from his various sightings."

Jenny broke into laughter. "And what do they plan on calling it? The Yeti Bar?"

Sam's heart tripped as he watched her face light up. At least he could make her laugh. When that happened he was always reminded of the first time he'd met her. How she'd been helpless with laughter at Zeppo's antics. Though he hadn't known it at the time, he'd caught a rare sighting of the magical creature who dwelt inside Jenny. A creature she seldom let anybody see.

Jenny, for her part, was restless by the time the evening ended. It was easy being around Sam. So very easy.

Yet so very difficult. To keep her pulse steady. To meet his look and hear his voice and keep a cool head. She kept remembering the way they'd ended the other evening. She kept remembering, wondering how his lips would feel against hers.

When they touched casually. When he guided her briefly by the arm as they left Mt. Bonnell. When his laughter caressed her in the gathering gloom. A shared moment over coffee when their fingers had entangled.

She fell into silence as he parked his car by her house and turned off the key. They got out and he walked her to the door. The barking of dogs announced their arrival and disguised the silence. Still, they both felt it.

Jenny felt his hand brush her shoulders and linger to drift over the small of her back. She turned. His other hand smoothed her curls and settled in a light caress around her neck.

She trembled and knew he felt her trembling.

"Jenny," he murmured, "I promised I'd let you set the pace, but I think you want this as much as I do."

She could hear in his voice both longing and a question. An inchoate yearning washed over her. She swayed. He took her silence as an answer.

Slowly his face drew nearer until his lips met hers.

She hadn't known what kind of a kiss it would be. She hadn't known how the past week, the first kiss she remembered so well, had left her hungry for him.

She hadn't understood the intensity of that hunger building inside. Until their lips met, sending a wave of desire rushing over her.

She moaned faintly and was shocked by her response.

She felt the shock rippling through Sam's body. He moved nearer, and his mouth settled more firmly over hers and began a tantalizingly gentle conquest. Her lips opened naturally, eagerly. He groaned, and the kiss became a tangle of lips and tongues and the sweet taste of arousal.

Her hands...how had they come to be smoothing over the muscles in his arms? How had they found the breadth of his shoulders?

His skin scorched her fingers.

His body against hers was hard and soft and heated and encompassing.

She realized she'd pressed herself against his chest and was clinging helplessly.

No demands. Not yet. But there was the promise of an explosive passion that left her feeling dizzy with anticipation.

When Sam ended the kiss, they were both breathing heavily.

He took her face in his hands to stare at her, and Jenny felt their slight tremor. She could tangibly sense him gathering control. He backed away until only his hands touched her.

"Sam . . ." Jenny wasn't sure what she wanted to say, what there was to say.

"Shh." He closed her lips with his in a butterfly touch. "Don't say anything. Just think about it. Good night."

Jenny went in, closed the door and leaned against the wall as she listened to Sam drive away.

And knew she'd never experienced such a jumble of emotions.

There was a wild exhilaration at the desire they stirred in one another. So this is what the poets write about and why ballads are sung. It was an incredibly intoxicating feeling.

But the loss of control was terrifying. She'd had no will to pull away. It was Sam who'd stopped. He'd understood the danger of the passion that shook them. He'd known she wasn't ready.

Her body had betrayed her.

But Sam hadn't.

Gratitude, anticipation and a giddy anxiety shared Jenny's bed with her that night.

CHAPTER SIX

THE TELEVISION in the Grants' family room was tuned to the all-star game, and Andrew Grant, Sam's father, was following the action, providing Sam with statistics on every batter who came to the plate. Andrew was a long-time fan, make that a fanatic, of the Longhorn baseball team and the Houston Astros. One balanced out the other, he explained to anyone who'd listen, since Texas was a perennial collegiate power and Houston was an annual also-ran. Andrew had gone to the college World Series six out of the last seven years to see the university team play. Hope sprang eternal in his breast that one day he'd see the Astros in the World Series.

Sam's brother-in-law Larry, Risa's husband, was in the kitchen with Megan. They'd drawn K.P. duty and were clearing the dinner dishes from the table, loading them in the dishwasher, and deciding the fate of the few leftovers. Sam could faintly hear them discussing Megan's upcoming trip. Larry had spent two years in Florence as a graduate student, and he was compiling a list of sights she must see when she went to Italy.

Sam's other brother-in-law Gary, Carol's husband, was on the backyard patio with Molly Grant, admiring the brilliant colors of his mother-in-law's bougainvillea and lamenting the lack of rain on his own newly sod lawn. Risa was herding Sam's assorted nieces and nephews while Carol lay in the guest room napping. She was in her seventh month of pregnancy and feeling the strain.

It was Sunday. The traditional once-a-month Sunday, when the Grant family gathered to share current domestic events and renew the ties that bind. This after-church dinner was a long-standing ritual in the Grant household, and though Molly was wise enough not to monitor her children's religious habits, the tradition had continued in modified form. It was a custom Sam enjoyed and took for granted.

Now he was trying to see it through Jenny's eyes. He'd briefly considered bringing her today, but he'd known their relationship was still too tentative to see Jenny through an afternoon of amiable scrutiny.

She could hold her own with his family. He recognized that. Her quick intelligence and composure would have saved her from panic. But today would have presented a new challenge, because she wouldn't be there as a businesswoman but as his guest. A role that didn't come easily to Jenny. Still, thinking about her led him to view the activities in a new light.

The Grants were a typical family, with the usual history and traditions. Yet they were most atypical in their good fortune and closeness.

Oh, they'd had their troubles. Andrew developed angina in his fifties, and Molly monitored a strict diet and exercise regime. Risa and Larry's older daughter had suffered from asthma as a baby. They'd almost lost her once. Luckily, she'd outgrown the condition. With the spoiling she'd gotten and her rebellion at being overprotected, however, Sam didn't envy Risa and Larry her teenage years. Carol and Gary had had to make adjustments at the beginning of their marriage. They'd been childhood sweethearts and hadn't anticipated the turbulence of the post-honeymoon period. But they'd worked to deal with their problems before the first child came along.

How very fortunate they all were. And perhaps a little complacent. How different it might have been if tragedy had struck their lives.

Spoiled, Jenny had called Sam, and she was right. Security and a sense of self had been handed to him on a silver platter.

He knew he got his mechanical bent from his mother. She was the household handyman. Her father had developed a prosperous plumbing business in the neighborhood where she'd been born.

His dad? Sam studied his father for a moment. Andrew was totally absorbed in the game. He had that talent for complete concentration. If Sam had been blessed with the gift of creative vision, he had his father to thank for it. Andrew Grant was widely acclaimed as a mathematician. Two of his books on theoretical equations had become standard college texts.

Sam had Grandpa Grant to thank for the fact that he was more than an illiterate engineer. Andrew's father, a poet and dreamer, had opened new worlds for Sam in literature and the arts.

No such gifts had been handed Jenny. There'd been no family to provide her roots. No father to adore and admire her. Instead, she'd been left with a childish, dependent mother. She'd had to learn to take care of herself.

No wonder she empathized with Richard. They'd both learned the hard way that life awards no sinecure of happiness. She hid her wariness behind a professional facade and a mask of good humor, which fooled the casual observer. Only Sam saw the haunted child that hid inside.

Jenny wanted him. He knew it. Just as he felt sure she'd never wanted another man before him. And her hesitant, awakening desire flamed a unique and unprecedented urgency in him.

Only an iron control kept him at the level of lovemaking his intuition prescribed. He'd gained her trust with his control. But would she let him love her? Would she allow herself to need him? Could she lower her guard and let him into her heart?

Sam didn't have answers to those questions, and he was frightened. For the first time in his life, he yearned for something perhaps beyond his reach.

His comfortable world had crumbled at the sight of a woman's face and the sound of her voice. His spirit was challenged by her mental toughness, and her soft, womanly body made his body ache.

Sam had gotten what he wanted with a vengeance. Nate would be amused. Because now that Sam had been seized by a grand passion, he couldn't walk away.

Would he want to?

No.

Never.

Still . . . when Sam heard his name and was recalled to his surroundings, he realized he'd broken into a cold sweat in the air-conditioned room.

"Sam?" Wiping her hands on a dishcloth, Megan stood at the door of the kitchen. "Can I tear you away from the game to perform automotive surgery?"

"Yeah." Sam had worn jeans and brought his tool-box, knowing Megan meant to hold him to the promise she'd extracted. "But I never operate alone."

Megan sighed resignedly. "Okay. As long as you realize you're getting a woefully ignorant assistant. Let me change. I'll be right there."

Ten minutes later she joined him on the driveway where he'd opened the hood of her car and disappeared beneath the front end.

She leaned over and peered into the crowded gloom. "Hello. See anything interesting?"

Sam scooted out on his back, wiping hands that were smeared with oil. "When was the last time you had this car serviced?"

"Oh, I don't know," Megan answered vaguely. "Three or four months..."

"A year," Sam estimated dryly.

Megan tried to work up indignation. "Am I going to get brotherly lecture number forty-two on automotive care and maintenance?"

"It comes with the privilege of repairing the neglect. Hand me the torque wrench."

"The torque wrench?" Megan went to the tool chest and stared into its innards as though she was facing the contents of Pandora's box.

Sam grunted, sat up and leaned against the car. "Never mind. I'll get it in a minute. As a helper, little sister, you leave something to be desired."

Megan grinned. "I told you that already." She made herself comfortable on the concrete beside him. "You love me anyway. You can't help yourself."

Sam's expression was surprisingly thoughtful. "I wouldn't want to help it."

Megan studied his face as she added lightly, "And I love you, which is why I sit through your lectures." When he didn't respond, she touched his arm. "Sam? What's wrong? I can feel there's something. Would it help for us to talk?"

Sam let out a small sound of frustration. "I don't know. Perhaps. I certainly can't go to Nate for advice. He'd just lecture me on the dangers of involvement."

Megan harrumphed. "Nate's phobic about involvement. He's the last person you should go to."

Sam looked at her oddly. "You're too hard on him, Megan. Nate didn't come from what you'd call a loving family." His voice changed timbre. "Have you ever wondered what we'd have been like if Dad had died? Or Mom? Or if they'd divorced when we were kids? Do you realize how lucky this family's been?" He turned to face her. "Do you realize none of us has ever wanted something we couldn't have?"

A moment passed before Megan responded. "That's not true, Sam. Nobody ever gets everything he or she wants. We're no exception."

"And what have you wanted that Mom and Dad couldn't give you? They provided you with brains, beauty, love, the creature comforts. Come on, Megan."

Her smile was ironic. "I hope I'm bright enough to know how lucky I am, if that's what you're saying. But I'm not a little girl any longer, remember? It isn't within Dad and Mom's power to grant me everything I want."

Sam took her rebuke in the spirit she intended. "I'm sorry. End of brotherly lecture." He started to rise.

"Wait." She held his arm for a moment. "Is Jenny Hunter the problem? I know you've been seeing her. Has your legendary charm failed you for once?"

At the look on his face, she muttered a swear word. "I'm sorry. There I go with the brat routine. I'm fumbling for words because this is a new role for me. I gather this thing between the two of you is serious."

"On my part it is."

"But she's not ready for a serious relationship."

He sighed. "Jenny doesn't know what a serious relationship is. She doesn't want to know. She hasn't had much luck with people." He gave her a brief summary of Jenny's life.

After he finished, he ran his fingers along his jeans in a harried gesture. "I don't know what I'm getting into, Megan. Whether we can make it together. But it's too late now to back away."

"Oh, Sam." Megan's protectiveness surfaced. "This isn't what I want for you. A girl who doesn't know how to love."

"Jenny knows how to love," he countered forcefully. "She pours love into her animals. She's just afraid to take a risk."

"Aren't we all? That's one of the joys of growing up. Everyone has to risk sooner or later, in order to get the gains."

"You and I know how much there is to gain. Jenny doesn't. I want to teach her, if she'll let me."

"Sam, you can't undo Jenny's life, you know. Maybe the scars run too deep."

"Jenny believes they do. She doesn't think she's capable of loving me. She doesn't understand how strong she is, or the depth of her courage. The picture she has of herself is constricted and distorted. She doesn't appreciate what she has to give."

"Maybe you can help her know herself as you do."

Sam shook his head. "Maybe. Maybe not. Jenny told me once that her mother could only see herself through another's eyes. Jenny's fought against the same kind of dependence. Fought against being like her mother. And she's one of the most fiercely independent persons I've ever met. I swear, though, she's hurting. She may not admit it, but she needs me."

"Sam." Megan squeezed his hand, held it. "I hope you're right. For both of you."

Sam's fingers curled around Megan's. He had no reassurances to give her.

All he could do was answer, "For both of us, I hope so, too."

ANNABELLE AND SAM met each other for the first time on an evening in July. Jenny couldn't have imagined more awkward circumstances or a scene more guaranteed to fuel Annabelle's fancies.

It all started when Leia came down with a case of the summer flu.

Then after several postponements Mrs. Wakefield consented to board her babies. "My son visited me, and I'm afraid he was a little upset about the fleas. He won't come back until I've fumigated the house."

Jenny knew she couldn't handle the transportation of the Wakefield dogs single-handed. Reluctantly, resignedly, she accepted Sam's offer of help.

They'd fallen into a curious routine. He phoned or came by the kennel almost every day. After finding that she usually ate a haphazard supper, he'd taken to feeding her, over all objections.

Sam being insistent was hard to resist.

Jenny didn't resist his kisses. When they came. And each time they came Jenny was once again shaken by desire. Yet Sam seemed to be holding back. He was on guard as she began to relax in his presence. As she became comfortable with the fact of their mutual attraction.

Although Jenny hated to admit it, she was becoming disgruntled, not to say frustrated, by his gentlemanly restraint.

The evening of the infamous meeting, as they discussed the logistics of unloading the nine Wakefield animals, Jenny found it hard to concentrate on anything other than the way Sam's face arranged itself into a wry grin. The quirk of his brow. The faint lines of laughter around his eyes and mouth. The flash of straight white teeth.

"So who do we put together and who do we separate?"

"W-what?"

"Earth to Jenny. I said, who can we put together and who needs to be at opposite ends of the runs?"

"Chad and Bitsy can bunk together. They're fond of each other. But we need to separate Lulu and Sparky. They're archenemies and could keep the other boarders in an uproar." Jenny saw a harried look replace Sam's grin. "I told you arranging accommodations for this crew was worse than figuring the seating at a presidential dinner."

"I had no idea running kennels required diplomatic skills." He squared his shoulders and let down the back of Jenny's pickup, where eight of the darlings were yelping from their cages. Muffin was in the front seat, cowering. Jenny hadn't decided yet what to do with her.

She wasn't ready to decide. Instead, she found herself concentrating on Sam's movements. She knew he was an athlete. That he skied every winter and was a member of an amateur soccer team. He had the unconscious grace and bearing of an athlete. She loved the way he held his head.

His hair was blue-black as it caught the light. She'd noticed his hair the first time they'd met. It was disheveled now, and windblown. She loved the way it waved around his ears. Nice ears. Too sinfully nice for a man to claim them. Did he have any idea how his profile affected her?

"Jenny?" Sam cocked his head and studied her intently. Just as she'd been studying him.

He knew the direction of her thoughts. He always knew.

"Like what you see?" he asked softly. "It's yours free of charge. I even come equipped with experience at refereeing dogfights."

"Yes." Jenny grinned, fighting confusion. "But can you lure Muffin out from under the seat?"

He moved closer, ignoring, as she did, the canine clamor. "I've been told I'm very persuasive with the ladies." He ran a light finger along the delicate curve of her jawline. "At least one lady I know is tempted by my charm."

"You're so vain, Sam Grant." The husky tone of her voice belied the words she spoke. That and the smile she wore that was as old as Eve's.

"You're so beautiful, Jenny Hunter." His own tone was husky and utterly sincere.

She drew a sharp breath at the unexpected compliment and was prevented from exhaling by the pressure of his lips.

It was a kiss that began teasingly, intensified with a murmur and gained momentum.

Until it was abruptly interrupted.

"Jenny, darling! Yoohoo!"

Jenny broke away, appalled.

Not thirty feet from them, Annabelle stood waving and peering.

The uproar of the dogs had obscured the sound of her arrival. Although Jenny had to admit both she and Sam would have been oblivious to a minor earthquake.

She had a premonition some similar upheaval was about to ensue.

"Dear, don't be angry with me for dropping in unannounced." Annabelle hurried up to them. "I just took the chance you were home, because we haven't seen you in almost a month, and I was worried."

SAM WOULD HAVE KNOWN Annabelle's identity even without Jenny's reaction. Lovely in a faded sort of way, as frail as Jenny was sturdy, she wore a flowing chiffon dress that would have been perfect worn with white gloves, a picture hat and strappy sandals to a 1950s Georgia garden party. It made Annabelle look like Blanche DuBois.

Sam wondered if this was her usual costume. Her makeup was certainly artfully applied, yet it emphasized her age rather than obscuring it.

She smiled at Sam, and he recognized the look. It was a smile men learned about as they grew wise to the ways of the world. A smile asking for male admiration and approval.

However, Jenny beside him was as tense as a bow string. And until he better understood the mother-daughter relationship, he chose to grin noncommittally.

Annabelle's hurt look was transparent.

"You know I like you to call first, Annabelle." Jenny barely got the words out between stiff lips. "Sam and I are working."

"Sam?" Annabelle looked at her daughter questioningly.

"Annabelle, this is Sam Grant." Jenny made the introductions brusquely. "Sam, my mother, Annabelle Jarvis."

The two exchanged formal greetings.

"Isn't Leia working for you any more?" Annabelle asked, though it was plain she didn't think Sam was a newly hired assistant. She'd witnessed their kiss. That fact was plain as well.

"Leia has the flu. Sam offered his help in her absence."

"How friendly of you." Annabelle gave Sam a questioning smile. Once again Sam deflected it carefully. She plowed on. "I worry about Jenny, you know. Living alone like this. Meeting strange people. When I don't hear from her…well, I'm afraid my imagination is a vivid one."

"Overactive's more like it." This time Jenny had to struggle not to grit her teeth. "We've gone over this before, Annabelle. I have Hilde for protection, and no one could sneak up on this house with all the dogs around."

"I know, dear. It's silly of me. But you are my only child. I can't help worrying." After visibly hesitating, Annabelle reached out to Jenny with a hand that was amply bejeweled.

The contrast between Annabelle's creamy complexion and the golden skin of Jenny's forearm was striking.

Jenny unconsciously stiffened at the touch.

Annabelle caught the reaction and she withdrew her fingers with an awkward flutter.

Sam caught it, too, and found himself unexpectedly feeling sorry for this frivolous woman. She hadn't the foggiest notion of how to deal with her prickly daughter. Sam had a feeling the scene he was witnessing had been played countless times before.

He heard himself say, "Don't worry, Mrs. Jarvis."

"Call me Annabelle." Jenny's mother offered him a wistful smile.

"Annabelle. I'm around these days to keep an eye on Jenny."

Jenny's head jerked around and she glared at him hotly.

His return smile was bland. *In for a penny, in for a pound.*

"Oh, I'm so glad!" Annabelle was more than that. She was openly ecstatic. "Jenny's so used to being by herself. I've been afraid she'd turn into a hermit. I was beginning to think . . . well, she is absorbed with her work and, well, she has no idea how attractive she is." The last should have been a non sequitur. Except the two people listening easily followed the direction of her thoughts.

"I'm very appreciative of Jenny's attractions," Sam said smoothly, ignoring Jenny's continued glare.

"You know—" Annabelle's look was coy "—I said to myself as soon as I saw you, Sam, that you were a discriminating man." She couldn't help playing up to him. It was an automatic response.

Jenny had had enough. "We're working, Annabelle. I don't have time to visit."

"I understand, dear." Annabelle was instantly apologetic. "I realize I've intruded. I was just hoping you could come to the house again Sunday. And you, too, Sam. Lloyd, my husband, would love to meet you. We don't get to see enough of Jenny's friends."

"I'd love to come . . ."

"I don't think . . ." Jenny and Sam spoke in unison.

Sam's voice overrode hers. "When would you like us to be there?" He threw his arm around Jenny's shoulders when she would have vociferously protested. Her look told him plainly what she'd say when they were alone.

"About one-thirty?"

"Fine."

"Now I'll let you two get back to whatever you were doing." She gave them an arch look, waved breezily and was gone.

Jenny was seething.

"How dare you do that to me!"

"Do what?"

"We'll *have* to go now," she said, ignoring him, "or I'll never hear the end of it."

"I have every intention of going and enjoying myself."

"You know what it'll be like."

"Probably the same as when we visit my family."

Again she ignored him. "Annabelle's so anxious for someone to take pity on her spinster daughter."

Sam was aware he was treading on dangerous ground. "I'm not sure pity is the word I'd use."

"Can't you tell? She doesn't understand what a man would see in me. Bless her heart, though, she keeps trying to find one for me. She can't do without men, so she thinks I can't, either. She doesn't realize I'm alone by choice."

"I can tell she doesn't understand you very well. You and she are just as different as you told me."

"Yes, sirree, we're certainly different! She's the beauty of the family. I'm the . . ."

"Jenny." Sam interrupted her tirade, tilted her face with a finger so she had to look at him, and asked gently, "You're not jealous of your mother, are you?"

"Me jealous? Of course not!" But as she made the vehement denial, Jenny avoided his eyes.

"Because there's no need to be. She is lovely. But she hasn't the class her daughter has."

"Class?" Jenny's look flew to his.

"You're just about the classiest lady I know. And much more to my taste than Annabelle. However, she is, as they say, a gentleman's lady, and being a gentleman I'll give her the admiration she expects. Do you understand me?"

"Perhaps." It was a reluctant admission. "But I'm still not happy about Sunday. I didn't want Annabelle to know about us."

"Why not?"

"Isn't it obvious?"

"Not entirely."

"She'll jump to conclusions. I don't want you to feel backed into a corner."

"You mean, you don't want to be backed into a corner."

Jenny waved dismissively. "If that's the way you want to look at it."

"What's between us is private. You can trust that I'll keep it that way."

"Like you did earlier? 'I'm around these days to keep an eye on Jenny.' Those were your exact words."

Sam sighed. "She'd already drawn her own conclusions. I decided to clear the air."

"Clear the air? You've put me in an impossible situation."

Sam decided subtlety was of little use. "Nonsense," he announced roundly. "It's a perfectly possible situation. Probable even." He grabbed hold of her before she could protest and swung her around and around in his arms.

It was impossible for Jenny to maintain her dignity, much less her indignation, in the face of his surprise maneuver. Before she could help it she'd joined him in laughter. When she thought about their conversation, parts of it really had been absurd.

He stopped when he knew he'd defused her anger, then gazed at her with an openly provocative smile. "This Sunday I meet your folks. Then you meet mine. It's time to take this act of ours on the road."

CHAPTER SEVEN

"I FEEL DECADENT." Jenny popped a nutty sliver of chicken and almonds into her mouth and licked her fingers. She and Sam were in her kitchen lingering over an assortment of Chinese takeout cartons.

Mrs. Wakefield's brood had been tucked in for the night, supper had been ordered and delivered per Sam's instructions, and Jenny couldn't remember when she'd had so much of an evening to call her own. Finishing the chores had come as a welcome diversion after the scene with Annabelle. That unfortunate half hour was being ignored if not forgotten.

Jenny watched Sam explore the sweet and sour shrimp with the chopsticks he'd requested. She had to admit he handled the utensils with flair.

"You're a show-off, you know that?" She'd struggled for five minutes with the stupid things before giving up in disgust.

"On the contrary," he chided with a hint of moral superiority. "I'm just open to new challenges. You shouldn't have given up so easily. It's all in the wrist."

He lost the shrimp he'd captured as he demonstrated technique.

"All in the wrist," she murmured.

He sent her a sour look and retrieved the shrimp. Jenny didn't think she could eat another bite.

She confessed as much, then reconsidered. "Well, perhaps a snow pea. How much damage can a snow pea do me?"

"What kind of damage were you referring to? Shall I go into my gentleman routine?" Sam leaned back in his chair and smiled at her lazily.

"Now Sam—" Jenny's tone was faintly ironic "—you're always a gentleman."

He cocked a brow. "Methinks the lady sounds a trifle piqued. Who would she prefer, the gentleman or the show-off?"

How far did she dare take the challenge? With unaccustomed boldness Jenny lifted a shoulder in a dainty shrug. "Gallantry has its uses, of course. But it can be awfully dull on occasion."

Something flared in Sam's eyes.

Jenny scurried to her corner and waved her hand over the numerous cartons. "Are you always this hungry?" she asked, trying to distract him. She failed.

The look that had flared in Sam's eyes settled into a slumbrous flame. "Yeah," he grumbled softly. "And getting hungrier."

He captured her waving hand and began to nibble on her fingers, licking off the remains of the chicken and snow peas. His unexpected touch jolted her nerve endings.

Jenny pulled at her hand halfheartedly. "Sam," she said with a catch in her voice, "you're being a show-off again."

He ignored her feeble attempts to escape and made his way to her wrist, beginning to explore with his mouth the smooth skin of her lower arm.

"It seemed to me," he murmured between delicate bites, "that's what you wanted." As his words brushed over her sensitive flesh, Jenny shivered with exquisite pleasure.

She'd had no idea how responsive she was in that particular area of her body. He was beginning to set off a reaction in other places as well.

"Now I really feel decadent," she whispered, not at all sure where this was leading them.

"Fun feeling, isn't it?" He breathed against her skin.

"Mmm," was all she could manage.

It was answer enough for Sam.

In one motion he stood and pulled her against him urgently. His lips covered hers. It was a kiss that dispensed with preliminaries. Intense, seeking. Jenny began to tremble.

Sam's hands felt the trembling and moved restlessly up and down her back in sweeping caresses that left her leaning against him, unable to stand alone. As his kiss deepened, one hand molded her waist, then moved slowly until it cupped a breast. His thumb began to tease her nipple slowly.

Jenny's breath caught at the intense response that flashed through her. She moaned. Sam captured her sigh with his mouth, and his tongue delved more deeply.

Challenges were forgotten.

Their laughter turned to passion.

The heated attraction between them ignited into physical need.

This was a Sam Jenny had only glimpsed before.

A new Sam. The lover. And if what was happening between them was a sample of his lovemaking, Jenny thought she might die if he ever stopped. She certainly didn't seem capable of halting him. Her will had fled along with her mind.

He was the one who broke away when the phone began its insistent clamor. They stared at each other blankly, their breaths coming out in spasms as if they'd just run a mile. Like an exhausted runner, Jenny couldn't seem to walk over and answer the call.

Ring.

Ring.

Ring.

Click. "You have reached Hunter's Kennels." Jenny's voice echoed hollowly around the motionless couple. "I am unable to come to the phone right now, but if you will leave your name, number and a message after the tone, I will get back to you as soon as possible."

"Jenny?" A child's voice sobbed faintly. "This is Richard. I—I guess you can't hear me. I . . . just . . ."

Feeling like she was waking from a dream, Jenny dived for the phone. "Richard, I'm here. What's wrong?"

"Is that you, Jenny? I didn't think . . ."

"It's me. Richard, is your father with you?"

"No, I'm alone except for Arnie. Dad h-had some work he had to do. When I called his office he didn't answer. Arnie keeps barking at something. Outside the window. I can't tell what it is." Richard's voice broke and he began to cry in earnest. "Jenny, I'm s-scared. What if someone's out there?"

"We'll be right over. Sam is with me." She flipped through the client file beside the phone, pulled the card with the Ingrams' address. Repeated it for Richard to verify. She was thankful she had an idea of the side of town he lived in. "It shouldn't take us more than fifteen or twenty minutes," she calculated quickly. "I'm sure it's nothing, Richard. But just in case, wait until you hear us call through the door. Don't open it for anyone else, unless it's your dad. Okay?"

"Okay. W-will you hurry?"

"We're leaving this minute."

It was a literal statement, because as Jenny hung up the phone, she grabbed her purse and beckoned Sam out the door.

Her voice was strained as she recounted the conversation.

Sam put the car in gear and backed out the drive. "There's a map in the glove compartment," he instructed, as he headed in the general direction she indicated.

She fumbled with the map while he sped through the darkness. She found the street and located it on the grid. Once again, her voice was tight as she gave directions. He glanced at her face. It was tense and pale. He reached over and squeezed her hand.

"I'm sure he's okay, sweetheart. Arnie's a pup. You know he'll bark at anything that moves. If someone is trying to break in, one look at Arnie would scare them away."

"You don't understand."

"What don't I understand?" he asked, thinking it might be good to keep her talking.

"What Richard's going through." She turned her head to stare out the window, her chest so constricted she could barely breathe.

"Tell me."

"He's alone," she burst out. "He's scared. He feels abandoned. How could his father do this to him?"

"I don't think Bob understands what Richard's going through, either."

"Then he's blind!"

"Or consumed with grief. It comes to the same thing. I've wondered what it would be like to be in Bob's shoes.

To have lost a young wife I loved very much." Sam's tone was stark in the darkness between them. "To be left with a child who must be a constant reminder of her."

"But wouldn't that make you love the child even more?" Jenny's words had a desperate edge to them.

"Yes. But grief takes people different ways. With Bob, his grief's imprisoned him."

"You mean he's incapable of loving Richard?" Sam's answer seemed inordinately important to Jenny.

"No, I don't mean that," he responded carefully, sensing the origin of her question. "I believe loving Richard might eventually be what saves Bob."

Other than Jenny's instructions, no more words were spoken in the time it took them to find the Ingram house.

As they approached the front door, Arnie barked raucously.

"Richard! It's Jenny and Sam!" Jenny shouted over the din as she knocked briskly.

Arnie's barking changed its tenor, and Richard threw open the door. He was too frightened to be inhibited. As soon as Jenny entered, he launched himself at her. Without hesitation, she enfolded him in her arms.

"It's okay," she murmured into his hair. "We're here. And Sam's going to look around to see what Arnie's fussing about."

Richard said something, but it was unintelligible through the tears and Jenny's shirt.

Apparently Jenny understood him. "I know," she said soothingly, "sometimes you wonder if they're more trouble than they're worth."

From her arms came a muffled protest.

"Of course, he is. I know you love him. He just has to learn not to bark at everything he hears."

As if to prove her point, Sam returned at that moment with the object of Arnie's ire. It was mewing piteously in the palm of his hand.

"A kitten." He held it up for all to see. Arnie began an immediate investigation while the kitten cringed and hissed balefully. "Hey, watch it, Arnie, I'm the one getting scratched." Sam's look encompassed the small assemblage. "I think we have ourselves a homeless transient."

As soon as Sam entered the room, Richard pulled away from Jenny awkwardly, making an effort to gather his tattered dignity about him. Now, his eyes wide at Sam's discovery, he went over and took the protesting kitten, cuddling it to his bony chest. Immediately, the cat made itself comfortable.

"Poor kitty," Richard whispered, his voice still a little wobbly. "Were you alone and hungry in the dark with no one to take care of you?" He turned to Arnie, who'd lodged his head firmly in the bend of Richard's arm and was nuzzling the cat, much to its disgruntlement. "Is this what you were trying to tell me? The kitty wanted in?"

A thought occurred to Richard. He stared at the two adults, his face bright red through the tear stains. "I— I'm sorry I made all this fuss. I should've gone and investigated. I should've known Arnie was trying to tell me something. If I hadn't been such a nerd..."

"Hey, wait a minute." It was Sam's turn to provide Richard solace. "You think I wasn't being cautious when I made the turn around your house where those tall bushes take over the yard? I can tell you I was relieved when I found out this—" he reached to scratch the kitten "—was our culprit. I'm sure your dad would tell you never to go out at night to investigate suspicious noises.

You did the right thing calling Jenny when you couldn't get hold of your dad.''

The reassurance was smoothly given, and coming from a man like Sam it carried the needed weight. Jenny sent Sam a grateful look he acknowledged briefly. But it was Richard he watched keenly, and this time Jenny was left out of the unspoken communication that was exchanged between the two males.

"If you think so, sir." Richard's impeccable manners were back in place. Then the earlier frightened child reappeared briefly. "You sure you don't think my dad'll be mad when he hears I called you?"

"Very sure." Sam meant to have a say in that.

"I don't guess he'd have to know," Richard said haltingly. "Not that I wouldn't tell him. But if you all are in a hurry and need to go…" His eyes slid away from theirs. He was trying hard to hide his concern at their leaving.

"We're in no hurry," Jenny said firmly. "However, rescuing kittens can work up a thirst."

She'd reminded Richard of his hosting duties. Still clutching the kitten, he brushed the last of the tears away with his free hand and asked, "Would you like coffee?" He stopped for a moment, obviously pondering the matter. "I'm pretty sure I know how to make it. Or there's beer and orange juice in the fridge."

"I'll take orange juice." Jenny threw her arm around his shoulders casually. Richard leaned against her oh-so-slightly, his face revealing in its vast relief.

"I'll have a beer," Sam said, following them into the kitchen. Arnie, not to be left out, made up the tail of the procession.

That's where Bob Ingram found the five of them when he arrived. His initial look was one of blank astonishment. "Well, hello. Is this a party? Am I invited?" He turned to his son, obviously wanting an explanation. "Richard, I didn't know you'd asked Jenny..."

Sam decided now was the time to take over the explanations. He began with, "Consider us visiting firemen on a rescue mission."

At this point, Richard proved he had his own brand of courage. "Dad, I called Jenny. I got scared here in the house. I tried not to. But Arnie kept barking and barking at something in the backyard. When you didn't answer your phone, I found Jenny's number. It's all my fault."

"It's nobody's fault," Jenny intervened.

"No...of course it's nobody's fault," Bob agreed hastily. He wasn't angry, just acutely embarrassed. "Unless it's mine. I'm sorry you couldn't reach me. I stepped into Phil's office for a moment to check a report. That must have been when you called. I thought with Arnie here...." He shrugged helplessly. Bob's reddened face looked remarkably like his son's.

"Arnie was trying to tell Richard something with all his barking." Sam came in strategically. "Richard, show your dad what Arnie found."

Richard went to his father, the kitten in hand. His face still had a wary cast to it.

"Well, hey. What have we here?" Bob asked with forced joviality.

"He was lost and frightened." Richard held the cat up for Bob's inspection.

"Well, he looks pretty happy now."

"I just finished feeding him some milk."

"But remember, tomorrow you need to get him kitten chow," Jenny reminded him. "Cow milk isn't good for cats."

"Tomorrow?" Bob asked, floundering.

"I have to find out if he belongs to anyone in the neighborhood," Richard explained carefully.

"And if he doesn't?" Bob asked, comprehension dawning.

After an awkward moment, Jenny said, "You can always bring him out to my place, Richard, if you can't find him a home."

Richard's eyes were fixed on his father.

Bob grimaced in what should have been a smile. "That...probably won't be necessary, Jenny. How do he and Arnie get along?"

Richard's face cleared. "Arnie likes him a lot, Dad."

"Albert's not quite so enthusiastic," Sam interjected dryly.

The adults smiled.

"Albert?" Bob asked with mock dread.

Richard had not joined in the small joke. Now his back stiffened. "It's what I decided to call him. Until we find out if he has another name."

"I see. Well, Albert looks like he's had a busy night. And you do, too. It's past your bedtime."

Richard's hands tightened around his new pet. He looked at his dad anxiously. "Can I take him with me to bed?"

"Sure. Why not? But Richard, I think we've reached our quota of pets. If that bed of yours gets any more crowded, we'll have to exchange it."

Richard's brilliant smile took them all in. He hooked his free hand around Arnie's collar and, not wanting to give his father a chance to renege on the bargain, urged him from the room.

Bob grinned weakly at Richard's transparent tactics. After Richard had gone, however, the smile vanished. He sank into a chair and rubbed his hands over his face, his

agitation obvious. "I'm sorry about what happened tonight, Sam, Jenny. Sorry you had to come over. I know
I shouldn't leave Richard, but I thought with Arnie..."
He shook his head wearily. "I could see he'd been
crying."

"He was all right as soon as we arrived," Sam assured
Bob quietly.

Bob sighed raggedly, the cracks in his control beginning to show. "It's Richard who deserves the apology
from me. Hell of a father I am. Doris would hate me if
she knew. It's been so hard to go on without her." His
voice broke with the emotions he was fighting.

Any lecture Jenny had prepared for Bob vanished from
her thoughts. As she stared at his stooped shoulders, the
lines of despair to be read in his bowed head, an unbid-
den image rose in her mind, almost forgotten but suddenly vivid.

Of Annabelle...crying...and crying...and crying.
And Jenny, four years old, huddled beside her, wanting
to comfort yet not knowing how.

Her mother had been little more than a child when
Jenny's father died. Much younger than Bob Ingram. No
wonder she'd been utterly lost without the husband she
loved and leaned on.

Just as Bob was.

Jenny must have sucked in her breath at the sudden
ache, or maybe she made a random gesture, because she
looked up to find Sam watching her intently.

She sat beside Bob and reached out her hand. "I know
how hard these past two years have been for you."

Bob's fingers gripped hers as though he'd discovered
a lifeline. "Thank you for caring enough to come when
Richard called. You must wonder..." He stopped, tried
again to say what he wanted. "I do love Richard, you

know, very much. He reminds me so much of her..."
Bob's voice faltered again, his control wavering.

"Richard needs you very much. Arnie's not enough,"
Jenny said gently.

"I know." He lifted his head to look at her. "Don't
you think I know that? I'm trying. But sometimes I feel
so empty. Like there's nothing left for me to give." It was
a stark admission. No one had a response to it.

"Dad? Jenny?" Richard stopped at the door as though
he knew he'd interrupted something "I'm ready for
bed."

Bob pulled himself together and held out his hand.
Richard went over to him. They embraced awkwardly.
Bob held him for a moment convulsively, then relaxed his
hold.

"Good night, son."

"Good night," Richard mumbled.

He looked Jenny's way, his expression torn between
doubt and hope. His Adam's apple wobbled in his throat
as though he were trying to speak. Intuitively Jenny knew
what he wanted, what he needed very badly.

She opened her arms and invited him in.

"Thanks again for coming," he whispered against her
shoulder, his fingers clutching her.

"Any time." She dropped a light kiss on his forehead,
fighting a tide of emotions. "That's what friends are
for." The two men in the room watched the poignant
scene with a variety of feelings.

Richard eased reluctantly from Jenny's arms. "Good
night..." He hesitated, staring questioningly at his other
rescuer.

"Sam. Call me Sam. Good night, Richard." Sam
dropped a warm hand over Richard's shoulder and
squeezed it. "Take care of Albert for me."

"I will."

Moments later, after strained goodbyes, a sober couple left the Ingrams' house.

"Do you think we should have stayed longer?" Jenny asked as Sam pulled away from the curb.

"They'll be okay for now. Bob has enough to think about. I'm not sure—" he glanced Jenny's way "—he could have handled any more guilt tonight."

"I wasn't going to make him feel..." Jenny began instinctively. "That is, I was, but when I realized..." She broke off and admitted, "You're right, I had prepared a lecture. I was furious with him. But it was clear, what you'd said earlier. How depressed he's been."

"Jenny..." Sam paused for a moment, as though trying to decide how to frame what he was about to say. "Remember you told me a few weeks ago you might be getting in over your head with the Ingrams? I think you were right about that."

When she started to protest, he held out his hand. "I don't mean going there tonight. We had to, that's clear. It's Bob I'm concerned with."

"I am, too. There's so much I want to tell him, but I'm not sure he's strong enough to hear."

"He's a very needy man." Sam glanced at her as though he wanted to gauge her reaction.

"Yes." Jenny bowed her head. "I've seen that all along. Tonight I understand him better."

"He may turn to you for help."

"Help? How? Half the time I want to shake him silly."

"I know. You're very ambivalent toward Bob. I understand why. Bob's so needy he doesn't pick up on your ambivalence. He just sees what you're doing for Richard. Don't be surprised if he begins to fantasize what you can do for them both."

"Are you saying—" Sam had startled her initially with his suggestion. Now she was becoming indignant. "You're not implying that Bob would look at me, well, romantically?"

"I think," Sam said coolly, "he might begin to imagine you as Richard's substitute mother. Draw your own conclusions from that."

"You're not jealous of Bob, are you?" She asked with mock incredulity, trying to take the offensive.

"No." Sam's denial was calm. "I know you too well." He paused. "But Bob doesn't. Jenny, listen to me. Don't ignore what I'm saying. Face the fact you may have a problem on your hands."

"Well, I certainly can't turn my back on Richard. You saw him tonight. Bob says I'm the first woman Richard's related to since—since his mother died."

"I'm not asking you to turn your back on Richard. I just want you to understand how much you identify with him and how much you already care. Get it straight in your mind why you've become friends, and what role you can play in the situation."

"How will that help with Bob?"

"It'll keep you from sending him mixed messages. It'll help you be clear with him when or if he comes to you with whatever scenario he's dreamed up." Again, Sam paused and took a deep breath. "Of course, it would be good if you could separate Bob from Annabelle in your mind. How old was your mother when your father died?"

The sudden direction of Sam's question left Jenny momentarily speechless.

"How could you tell—" her voice was rough when she finally spoke "—what I was thinking?"

She could see a hint of Sam's wry smile by the flickering lights of the oncoming cars.

"Haven't you found out by now," he asked after a moment, "I can read your face?"

"It's not fair, you know—" she sounded faintly bitter "—when I can't read yours."

"You can. You just don't want to."

They were at her house before she spoke again.

"Annabelle was very young." Her voice was so soft it was hard for Sam to hear her. "Eight years younger than I am. And she had nobody. She adored my father, you know. He was the great love of her life. I have a picture of the three of us. Dad was holding me in one arm, the other was around Annabelle. They were laughing together. You can see how she felt in her eyes."

"Why don't you have that picture on your mantel?"

"I can't look at it. The memories are too painful."

"Like the memory you had tonight."

"Yes." Her breath fluttered out.

He put his hand along the back of the seat and curled it around her neck, feeling the tension in it.

"Jenny?" Sam couldn't tell if she wanted to continue. He waited.

She looked at him for a moment, then seemed to stare into the darkness of the woods that stretched beyond the runs.

He began a light massage at the base of her neck. She gave a little sigh that was hard to interpret. Moments passed with neither of them speaking.

For once Sam couldn't tell what Jenny was thinking. "Come on," he urged finally. "Let's go inside."

CHAPTER EIGHT

JENNY FOLLOWED HIM across the yard and up the porch steps. She opened the kitchen door with her key. When he moved to turn the lights on she caught hold of him.

"Don't."

Sam turned toward her, puzzled, and she moved into his arms, eagerly, frantically, exposing the emotions that her silence had concealed.

As Sam enfolded her into his embrace he understood her mood, and for an instant he knew how she must have felt when Richard rushed to her for refuge.

Except this was more than a child he held. Sam could feel the soft curves of Jenny's body as she pressed herself against him. And if she did seek solace in his arms, this need was mixed up in a jumble with everything else she needed from him.

There was a kind of frenzy about her as she clutched his face with her fingers and kissed him urgently, her mouth hot and seeking. When his lips opened in shock and immediate desire, her tongue darted against his in an erotic movement.

Her hands threaded through the silky strands of his hair as though she couldn't get enough of his tactile presence. Then they slid down his neck and into the collar of his shirt, heating his skin with their sensual need.

"Jenny," Sam gasped, not sure how to respond. Knowing that soon his response would be beyond volition. His hands had already begun an instinctive journey of their own down the slope of her back and over the gentle swells below her waist. He fought for sanity. "Jenny, wait..."

"I thought you wanted me."

"I do want you. But I need to know what's going on here."

"I want you, too." Her voice was a husky invitation. He might have been fooled except for the slight catch he heard.

Sam made himself pull away so he could study her. "The question is, why do you want me? Maybe we should talk."

"Talk? Dammit, Sam!" Jenny's voice changed sharply. She fought frustration and sheer terror brought on by her impulsive seduction. "What do I have to do? Climb all over you to get a reaction?"

Staring at him, recklessly ignoring the caution lights flashing in her brain, Jenny rubbed her breasts over his chest and made a similar provocative movement with her lower body. She gave a faintly shocked gasp when she encountered the hard evidence of his desire.

"Find out what you wanted to know?" Sam asked in a rasping voice. "Lady, I'm hot as hell, in case you care."

He closed his eyes with a shuddering sigh, cupped her buttocks tightly and ground himself against her, his face lost for a moment in a kind of remote passion.

With another shudder he seemed to pull himself together, took hold of Jenny's shoulders as though bracing himself and finally broke away. Without speaking, he led her into the living room and toward the lamp beside the couch, flicking it on with a touch. He must have understood she couldn't stand the revealing glare in the kitchen.

Jenny was grateful for that small consideration after what she'd just done.

Sam turned to face her, and she saw that his movements were stiff and jerky. Somehow his features had settled into a more recognizable pattern, however, for a weary patience lined his face.

"I'm ready to make love as soon as you are, Jenny. More than ready. I'm hot and hard just thinking about you."

His strained admission held utter frankness. The soft glow of the lamp washing over Jenny's face revealed her blush.

Sam laughed wryly. "My dear novice temptress, haven't you realized by now how your body excites me? It's been all I could do these past few weeks to keep my hands to myself. To wait until I knew you wanted me as much as I want you."

He searched her face, trying to see beyond the blush. "But that's not what tonight is all about, is it?"

She tried to answer him but the words lodged somewhere in her constricted throat.

He sighed. "Comfort and sex are very different, Jenny. One can lead to the other. But I don't think making love with me would have brought you comfort. I think it would have just added to your guilt."

"Added?" This time she managed a squeak.

"It's been a long evening," Sam said rather tiredly. "I'm not sure we need to get into guilt, either yours or Bob's."

"It doesn't excuse her, you know." All at once, the words burst out, like floodwaters ripping through a dam, as if Jenny could guess what Sam had left unsaid. "I mean, that Annabelle was so young when Daddy died. It doesn't excuse her from all that came later."

Sam didn't pretend to misunderstand. "I wasn't set up to be Annabelle's judge."

"Implying as her daughter I haven't the right to judge, either?"

"No. I'm not set up to judge your feelings, Jenny, any more than I am your mother's. But I think tonight, for the first time, you saw her tragedy through an adult's eyes. There was compassion in your eyes tonight, Jenny. Not only for Bob but for Annabelle. What is upsetting you so much you were willing to use sex as an escape? Why are you running away from the empathy and pity you feel?"

"Because..." Jenny held up her hands in futility. She turned her back abruptly, just as abruptly turned toward him again.

Sam understood the struggle she was having. He could feel it inside him, tearing at his heart.

"Because..." Suddenly, Jenny's fragile barriers collapsed. She stared at Sam in bewilderment. "Because I don't know what I feel. About anything. About you...about Annabelle...about Bob or Richard. Not even about myself. It's like I've...lost my way. My life was set. I knew where I was going. Now I don't. And it's...dark everywhere."

Tears sprang into her eyes. Unexpected, unwanted. Yet entirely necessary. And more useful than Jenny could know. As they began to fall down her cheeks, she looked at Sam as a child would. One of her hands reached up and wiped at her face. She stared at the wetness.

"See. I'm crying again. I can't remember when I've ever cried so much. I'm falling apart. All I wanted you to do," she whispered at last, plaintively, "was to hold me."

He immediately wrapped his arms around her and tucked her head into the crook of his shoulder. "Shh," he soothed, "I'll hold you. The rest of your life, if you'll let me. All you had to do was ask."

"I . . . wasn't sure how to."

Sam chuckled softly, holding her solidly against him. "Well, now you know how."

They stood together for timeless moments, Jenny weeping, Sam comforting. Until the tears stopped flowing, the sobs grew fewer and quieter. Finally Jenny hiccuped, laughed weakly and raised her head to peer into his face.

Every word that came to mind seemed inadequate. She settled on, "Thanks for lending me your shoulder."

"I didn't lend it to you. It's yours as a present."

Jenny heard a hint of Sam's former intensity. Her look fled from his as she remembered her foolishness.

"I—I'm sorry about what happened earlier. It was just my feeble attempt to ask for help." Jenny's lashes dropped. "You've probably guessed by now I'm not very good at that."

"I'm not sorry," he came back promptly. "And your request was far from feeble. And, lady . . . you're getting better at a lot of things all the time." His low tones sent tremors through her.

Sam felt them and cupped her face with his hand. With lingering care he brushed the last tears from her cheeks and gazed at her with a controlled hunger.

"You have passion in you, Jenny. When you're ready to share it—" his lips quirked in a smile "—all you have to do is ask."

Jenny could feel the passion in her, rising, though she dared not give in to it. "How will I know when I'm ready?"

She saw desire flare in Sam's eyes. But his voice was controlled as he answered, "You'll know it."

Jenny smiled, a slow, intriguing smile, which was almost Sam's undoing. "When I know it, I promise, Sam, you'll know it, too."

HOW WILL I KNOW?
You'll know it.

Their words became a round, circling Jenny's mind. The implied promises heated her thoughts. Her need for him on every level had grown into a hunger. A yearning hunger like she'd never known before.

She found herself longing for the touch of his hands on her body. She longed to lingeringly explore his body with her touch, to know a man as she'd never known one. She wanted to lie with him, length to length. To experience the fit and feel of two bodies locked in the ultimate embrace.

For the first time in her life, Jenny felt more than curiosity about the sex act. Sometimes her thoughts shocked her, and she'd rush into an activity or chore to hide from them. But at night, during the dark, restless night, she couldn't flee. She didn't want to. And fantasies fed her hunger until it became an ache permeating her body.

Now she understood the potency of sexual attraction. The way it could control, absorb, take over someone's thoughts. The way it could subvert conscious will or design.

Her absorption with Sam and her burgeoning sexuality made the other activities of her life seem extraneous. Her work suffered. She knew it, yet she couldn't seem to care. The dogs Jenny trained sensed her abstraction and tried her patience. The evening class she gave on Wednesdays went poorly, because she couldn't concentrate on the task at hand.

Sam noted Jenny's dilemma and had a fair understanding of its source. At first she thought he meant to
ignore it. Until she snapped at him one day in sheer sexual frustration. The gingerly way he deflected her ire
alerted her that Sam was handling the volatility between
them with asbestos gloves. She also noticed, over the next
several days, that he seldom touched her except with his
smile. The time was over for careless caresses.

It didn't help that she was facing Sunday at Annabelle's and Lloyd's with growing dread. She couldn't hide
that dread, and Sam decided it was one issue that should
be brought into the open between them.

He carefully chose the time and place for their discussion. An evening over supper on neutral yet friendly turf.
Their accustomed booth at the diner. A sprinkling of
other diners lent an illusion of safety. When Jenny gazed
out the plate-glass window into the street for the third
time in as many minutes, her face wearing a familiar
strained expression, Sam saw the moment had come to
speak.

"Why are you worried about Sunday? The worst is
over. Your mother and I met."

Sam's question jerked Jenny's startled gaze to him.
"How did you know what I was thinking?" She grimaced resignedly and said with a sigh, "Why does your
ability to read my mind continue to surprise me? I should
be used to it by now."

Sam ran his fingers over Jenny's hand as it lay on the
table. He traced the delicate pattern of the veins under
her skin, sending a current of awareness through them
both.

"I don't think I'll ever get used to it," he murmured.
"Sometimes I look into your eyes and know you're
thinking of me. And I know what you're thinking. At

night, I lie in my bed and imagine you in yours, and I can feel our thoughts coupling.''

Jenny sucked in her breath and felt a blush rising up her throat and over her face. As though he couldn't help himself, Sam reached out and followed the line of color up the delicate column of her neck. For a moment, his thumb played against the jump of her erratic pulse.

Then he sighed faintly, pulled his hand away and made a momentary fist before consciously relaxing his palm on the Formica tabletop. He slouched against the cushions and said wryly, ''I just walked us into a mine field, didn't I? Pretty soon there's going to be no place for us to hide.''

As they gazed at each other, reading the other's thoughts, Jenny realized clearly for the first time and with a kind of fatalistic detachment that the sexual tension between them had become a magnet so powerful they were fast approaching the point where they could not pull away. Which made the luncheon Sunday even trickier.

Sam would get back to that.

He did. ''Sunday. What has you so edgy? Is it Lloyd?''

Jenny chose the path of least resistance. ''I don't care for Lloyd. He's not like Gordon was, but he's a cold fish. He doesn't particularly care for me, either. It's always tense when we're together, although Annabelle refuses to admit it.''

She stopped for a moment and shook her head. ''No, that's not true. She just keeps hoping our mutual antipathy will go away. More of Annabelle's wishful thinking, since we haven't gotten along with each other for over fifteen years.''

''From the very beginning?'' Sam rephrased her statement with an odd inflection. ''That's a hell of a long time to be caught in the middle of a family feud.''

The muscles in Jenny's face tightened ominously. "Annabelle brought it on herself. She didn't love Lloyd when she accepted his proposal. She rushed into marriage with him for financial security and respectability, both of which she craved."

"Did Lloyd love her?"

"He...coveted her. The beauty, the femininity, her spontaneity. Lloyd's very controlled. They say opposites attract. Well, he was drawn to Annabelle like the proverbial moth to a flame. He didn't approve of her. Or me, either. I was the obligation he took on, along with his flight of fancy. Lloyd's a big one for obligations."

"You were a teenager when they married?"

"Yes."

Sam's faint smile held irony. "I can imagine how hard it must have been for him to fulfill his imagined duties to a hostile adolescent."

Jenny had to smile, too, although it was with great reluctance. "You're right. It was hell for us both. He was determined to discipline me, to make me conform to his ideas of proper conduct."

"I have a feeling he didn't succeed."

This time Sam managed to draw a laugh from her. "You're right. We fought constantly, but nobody won. There was a collective sigh of relief when I moved out after my high-school graduation. If the Caneys hadn't been nearby for me to escape to, I'd have run away before then."

"And Annabelle? How did she feel about your leaving?"

"As you say—" her gaze met his "—Annabelle was caught in the middle."

"Are they happy now? Has Annabelle grown to love Lloyd?"

"I can't answer that question," Jenny responded shortly. "Annabelle and I don't talk about their marriage. You can understand why."

"Yes, I can."

"You're doing it again." Jenny's words held a faint edge.

"Doing what?"

"Making me feel like a childish, judgmental clod."

Sam's hand covered Jenny's, this time with solid warmth. "Then I'm a clod, because you're none of those things."

"Aren't I?"

"No. You're a very brave, very desirable lady, who's learned to survive everything life dishes out. Well, almost everything. You still have to learn to cope with happiness. But I have every confidence you'll master that, too. Given the right teacher."

Jenny's hand turned upward and her fingers linked with Sam's. He could feel her need communicating itself and his grip tightened.

"Are you the right teacher?" she asked with a peculiar intensity, which belied the lightness of her words. "Do you have an advanced degree in the art of happiness along with your engineering diploma?"

Sam took his time before he spoke. "I know a thing or two. I think I recognize it when I see it—" he smiled crookedly "—which is something of an art. I know that ultimately happiness is something you create with heart and hand." He raised her hand and brushed his lips against the back of it.

For a moment, Jenny let herself revel in the feelings Sam evoked as his mouth moved along her skin. Then she asked with more than irony, "Is happiness like a building, Sam, or a machine?"

Sam caught her meaning, but refused to back down. "Something like that. Depends on the mood and skill of the creator. It can be a haven, a monument, a temple, a space shuttle. And of course, a good engineer or architect builds flexibility into his basic design."

"I'm not very flexible. I'm learning that about myself."

"Scar tissue. Nothing a good surgeon couldn't repair."

"So now you're a surgeon."

"I'm anything you need me to be."

"It hardly seems fair," she said softly.

"What hardly seems fair?"

"You teach me happiness. I teach you pain. I've already caused you pain, Sam. I'll cause you more. That's what I'm good at."

Sam leaned back and studied her with amusement. He refused to break their physical contact, although she'd tried to pull away.

"You know, you surprise me, lady."

Her brows shot up. "How?"

"You told us at the first class I went to that there was no dog you wouldn't accept to train, no breed you couldn't work with."

Jenny raised her brows. "Are you comparing me to a difficult pet?"

"It seemed an analogy you would understand."

"Meaning I can be trained?"

His lips quirked. "To love me."

Her mouth curved as well. "With kindness?"

"And firmness."

"Don't forget consistency."

"Don't you forget training works better with frequent rewards."

WHICH WAS ALL WELL AND GOOD, Jenny thought, remembering their conversation the next day. The analogy Sam made was not so inaccurate. Indeed, there was no trait she couldn't reshape or diminish in a canine. Timidity, stubbornness, even cowering fear.

As much as Jenny hated to admit it, she recognized those traits in herself. She also suspected she had a vicious streak, which might come out if she were cornered.

Cowardice was what it all boiled down to. Fear of what Sam was doing to her, of what she was doing to him. Of where this relationship was leading.

When Jenny met Megan, she knew Sam's sister was afraid. For Sam. Because of Jenny.

SHE SUSPECTED Megan's identity the moment she saw her, and Jenny decided the fates were unkind. Megan had caught her at a horrible moment. Wet and dirty, Jenny was cleaning out a run.

Megan smiled as she came forward. It was a tentative smile that reached out and retreated. A smile compounded of goodwill and wariness.

Jenny sensed Megan hadn't come to judge.

But she had come to see Jenny for herself. To meet the woman who was bewitching Sam.

"I guess I don't need to introduce myself, except to say I'm Megan, Sam's youngest sister." Megan must have seen the recognition flicker in Jenny's eyes. "And you have to be Jenny."

"Have to be?"

"For it to make any sense. Sam's under a spell, and you are enchanting. Ergo, you must be Jenny Hunter."

Jenny managed a laugh. "Thank you. I'm flattered. Especially with the way I look right now. Except you make me feel like Morgan le Fay."

Megan laughed along with her. "Oh, no, that's my department. Morgan is said to have had a touch of Irish in her, and our family claims to have second sight."

"Is Sam—your family Irish?" Jenny rinsed her hands with the hose and surreptitiously wiped them on the back of her shorts.

"My mom's second-generation Irish, from Boston. When she's angry you can hear a hint of the old sod." Megan grabbed the towel hanging on the fence and handed it to Jenny without pausing. "Sam and I get our coloring from her, which is why we look so much alike. Risa and Carol take after Dad."

"Sam said Risa was more like your mother."

"Their personalities are a lot alike. Risa's a typical oldest child. Wants to boss everyone around her. She and Sam fought like cats and dogs when they were young. Fortunately for the rest of us, Risa now has a husband and three children to manage."

Jenny discovered she was fascinated by Sam's relationship with his siblings. "Did you and Sam fight very much?"

"Oh, no! I thought he was wonderful!" Megan rolled her eyes. "My very own gorgeous big brother. All my girlfriends had crushes on him, and I wasn't above displaying him on special occasions. I'm not sure he ever caught on to the troop of giggling females who used to parade by." Her look grew tender. "Actually, I think he knew and was just being kind. He certainly protected me enough times from Risa's wrath." Megan grinned. "Just one tiny flaw mars Sam's perfection. He lectures me constantly. It's the ten years' difference in our ages. Sometimes he forgets I'm no longer an idiot child."

"And Carol? Where does she fit in?" Jenny asked, not wanting the flow of information to stop.

"The family's not sure. We think she's a changeling. The rest of us are roamers, but she's the hearth-and-home type. World events come and go. She never notices. All she wants is her cookbook library, *House Beautiful* and *Baby and Child Care*."

By this time, Jenny had a fair idea Megan sensed her curiosity and was eager to satisfy it. Unfortunately, after Sam's earlier descriptions, Megan's characterizations of the Grants confirmed her worst fears.

She tried to keep her tone light as she commented, "I get the feeling from both you and Sam your family's very close."

"Oh, we are. Luckily, everyone lives in Austin. We get together once a month to catch up on family gossip. Mother likes to keep a close eye on her various offspring."

Jenny would have bet on it.

Something about her expression must have alerted Megan to what Jenny was thinking.

Her flow of chatter ceased. There was an awkward moment before she changed topics abruptly. "Listen, I wanted to tell you how impressed I was with Zeppo. If his new behavior is an example of your technique, then you must be a miracle worker."

Jenny wasn't at all sure she wanted to be the next subject of discussion, but she answered easily enough, "I've made Sam do most of the work. That's the secret of my success. I train the owners. They train the dogs."

Another lull. Both women felt awkward, and Jenny wondered when Megan would come out with the ostensible reason for her visit.

She searched around for something to say in the meantime and decided on a safe topic. "Do you have a pet? A dog you need help with?"

"Oh, no. My ex-landlord would have had a cat if I'd brought a dog on the place." Megan grimaced. "Sorry about that. Actually, it's just as well. I'm currently dispensing with all my worldly possessions. I'm due to leave for Europe in less than a month."

"Sounds lovely. How long do you plan to stay?"

Megan flung out her arms expansively. "For one glorious, decadent year. My college major is in European art, and I intend to wander the continent, wallowing in beauty and culture. Luckily, I have friends in England, France and Italy I can stay with along the way."

As Jenny listened, she realized it was impossible not to be taken by Megan. She was lovely, open and supremely self-assured. Impossible not to be intimidated, as well. All that charm. It must run rampant in the Grant family.

Jenny felt anything but charming. She felt disheveled, off-balance and defensive. The last thing she wanted to do was deal with Megan's concern about her adored older brother.

What she wanted, childishly, irrationally, was for Megan to go away.

CHAPTER NINE

MAYBE IF JENNY USED the magical powers Megan had alluded to, she could close her eyes, click her sneakers three times, and Megan would end up in Kansas.

Jenny refrained from doing this only barely, to comment instead in a formal tone, "Your trip to Europe sounds wonderful. How nice you can take it." She turned away as though needing to get busy again.

It wasn't as though Jenny begrudged Sam's sister her freedom, or the rich and varied life before her. The luxuries of time and money. Jenny didn't begrudge her much, anyway.

No, what Jenny really envied was Megan's blithe assumption such a life was due her. Still, she realized immediately Megan had misinterpreted her withdrawal. A less sensitive person might not have noticed the retreat. Jenny should have known Megan would be as perceptive as Sam.

When Megan spoke again, her voice faltered. "S-Sam tells me your work keeps you busy. It must be hard to run a business by yourself."

Don't tense up, Jenny. Don't get more defensive.

"It can be hard," she said evenly. "But I don't mind. It's been my dream to own a kennel and to be self-sufficient. I'm willing to do whatever it takes to keep that dream alive."

"You must take a great deal of pride in what you've already accomplished."

Megan's graciousness made Jenny feel petty. "I do. Of course."

"I envy you."

"Me?"

"Yes. I still haven't found the direction I want my life to take. In some ways this trip is a way of avoiding a decision. Sam says part of my problem is that Daddy and Mom spoiled me, being the baby of the family. As usual, he's right. I'm hoping...well, I'm hoping this year on my own away from everybody..." Megan's grin grew rueful. "Well, I'm hoping to take the opportunity to finally grow up."

How like Megan to be completely open. She didn't seem to have a defensive bone in her body.

The conversation, Megan's honesty, the defensive way Jenny was reacting, all were more than Jenny could take.

She fumbled with the lock on one of the runs. Leaned over to pet Hilde, who shadowed her movements, and tried to dredge up the semblance of a reply.

"Is this Hilde?" Megan asked quickly. "Sam's told me about her."

"Sam seems to have shared quite a lot with you one way or another."

The minute Jenny said the words, she could have bitten out her tongue. Because when she glanced up to estimate the damage, she caught Megan's stricken look.

Suddenly, Megan's reasons for being here became clear. She'd come because she loved Sam. She'd come hoping to be reassured. And Jenny had failed miserably to reassure her.

"I...I'm sorry, Megan." She spoke impulsively. "I didn't mean to be snide."

"I shouldn't have come."

"No, don't feel that way. I understand why you're here. I don't blame you for coming. I'm just uncomfortable because this thing between Sam and me is very uncertain. That makes it hard to meet any of his family." Jenny took a deep breath. "You know, I envy you."

"Me?"

"Yes, you. Probably not for the reasons you think. No, please, don't be embarrassed. I know I acted like a jealous snit."

Jenny reached out for Megan's hand, then withdrew her hand hastily. "I really wouldn't want to change places with you. I'm happy with who I am and what I've accomplished. And I love my work. But well, if I seem single-minded, it's because I've had to be. It's the only way I know to survive. I need direction, it gives me peace and order. It helps me know who I am. Now Sam has breezed into my life, scattering my order to the winds. It's disconcerting. To say the least."

As Jenny searched Megan's face to see how she'd taken this surprising confession, she saw the beginnings of comprehension if not complete understanding. She smiled hesitantly, not knowing what else to say.

Megan continued for her, reaching out as Jenny had. Completing the contact as Jenny hadn't dared. "And Sam's so damn sure of himself. That makes the going rougher, doesn't it?"

"Yeah. You Grants must have a gene for self-assurance."

Megan looked chagrined. "I'm afraid we Grants tend to be a smug lot."

"Don't get me wrong. It's a very attractive quality. Just a little overwhelming."

Megan laughed. She sounded more relaxed than before. "Meaning Sam and I are already more than you can handle, and you're not ready to meet the family en masse."

Jenny visibly paled. "Good Lord, no. We haven't faced my mother and Lloyd yet. Is that why you're here? As Sam's deputy? To issue an invitation?"

"Sort of. We're having a family get-together a couple of weeks from now at our cabin on Lake Travis, and Mom wanted you to know how much we'd love to have you. Has Sam mentioned the invitation?"

"He didn't dare."

Megan groaned. "Then he'll probably have my head." Her tone changed abruptly. "Jenny, I want you to know I didn't come here today to..." Suddenly it was Megan who was at a loss for words.

"I know you didn't. I think I know why you're really here. And I wish I could tell you what you want to know." Jenny leaned down once more to stroke Hilde's ears in a revealing gesture. "I can't."

"Jenny, listen." Megan's voice held a new intensity. "Don't feel you have to make things easy for Sam. It's not your job. You have to do what's right for you, and the devil take the hindmost. A little suffering won't hurt Sam. He'll survive."

"Those were almost his exact words."

"Believe him. Adversity is the best thing for people like Sam and me. It's good for our souls and keeps us humble."

Something, the faintest something, in Megan's voice led Jenny to ask curiously, "You sound as if you've been hurt once or twice."

"Let's just say I've wanted something very badly for a very long time. And I have a suspicion I'm not going to get it. This year in Europe is my way of coming to grips with that fact."

"Part of your growing up."

Megan smiled painfully. "Exactly."

Jenny clasped Megan's arm in a spontaneous gesture of kinship. They met each other's gaze, and there was a feeling of mutual empathy that Jenny found astonishing.

"Now don't feel bad for me," Megan said at Jenny's sympathetic look. "I'm not sorry it happened. I've learned a great deal. And Jenny," Megan said with firm resolution, "don't worry about Sam, either. Whatever happens, I promise, he won't have any regrets."

EVENING CHOW TIME WAS OVER. Jenny's spaniel boarder had gotten a bath in preparation for going home the next day. Leia had left, and Jenny knew she wouldn't be seeing Sam for supper. He'd called to say he and Nate were working late on a production problem. Dagwood was off on one of her hunting expeditions and hadn't been seen since early that day.

Jenny was alone except for Hilde, who snored gently at her feet. She sat in her rocking chair on the porch, cool for the moment after a refreshing shower, feeling the day fading around her.

There really was a hush to a summer's evening. All the animals of the sun were gone to ground, and the nocturnal creatures had yet to scurry out on their errands. Only the fireflies were out in force, their blinking points of light like fairy beacons through the leafy tree limbs.

They lent an air of enchantment to the woods close by.

At one time, Jenny would have considered this private moment, this quiet time, as an interlude to be savored.

Before Sam.

That's how Jenny characterized her life these days. Before Sam and After Sam.

Alone. She hadn't been alone much lately.

Before Sam, solitude had been a common commodity, with Jenny's private life remarkably uncluttered. In fact, she was beginning to realize that outside her business contacts she'd lived somewhat like a hermit.

Now she felt as though she was standing in the middle of a freeway exchange. Sam crowded out solitary evenings. Relatives, both hers and his, dotted the landscape. Richard haunted Hunter's Kennels much as Jenny had haunted the Caneys' place long ago.

Well, she was alone now. And always before at times like these peace dropped in to pay a social call. She hadn't seen much of peace lately. He must have gone north for the summer, leaving only swarming thoughts buzzing around her mind like flies.

Jenny sighed. She knew her problem. She was avoiding thinking about Megan's visit. Avoiding grappling with its implications. Avoiding facing the fact that soon she would have to meet the whole Grant family. If today was any indication, the meeting would be a fiasco.

Jenny pushed that particular buzzing thought away and permitted herself a smile. Sam's sister really was quite lovely. And utterly natural. Impossible not to like her. Impossible not to appreciate the motives that had brought her here.

In other circumstances, Jenny felt the two women might be friends. Megan probably offered her loyalty with a rare generosity. They might be friends without Sam as an issue. Without Jenny's inevitable defensiveness.

Instead, she'd curled up like a hedgehog, all prickly quills.

How could she possibly meet the Grants, fit in with them and enjoy the kind of people they were? How could she watch them watching her, loving concern for Sam evident in their eyes? And know they were wondering how she could measure up to the love Sam had within him.

Jenny sighed again and the sigh became a moan.

Sunday. Two days away. An intimate luncheon. With Annabelle...and Lloyd...and Sam...and Jenny. The perfect foursome.

Jenny could hardly wait.

"MEG TOLD ME she came to see you Friday."

"Did she?"

The two words were almost the first Jenny had spoken since Sam picked her up for the drive to her mother's. Sam knew Jenny was tense about the upcoming visit. He suspected she was tense for other reasons, as well.

"Yeah," he went on. "She wanted to be the one to confess before I heard it from you."

"There's nothing to confess," Jenny said evenly. "Megan's delightful. I didn't mind her visit."

"I did, and she's a pest. Which is what I informed her."

"One of your brotherly lectures?"

"Hell, no! I was too angry for that."

"Why were you mad?" Jenny turned in her seat and gazed at him somberly. "Because she adores you? Because she wants the best for you?"

Sam glanced at her face before he gave his attention to the road. "Because," he said tersely, "she interprets her love as the right to interfere."

"She wasn't interfering. She just came to meet me."

Her flat tone made Sam come back roundly. "What? Just like that? You two had a pleasant chat with no harm done? I don't believe you."

"Believe what you will."

"Megan felt she'd upset you."

"All right then!" Sam had finally goaded her sufficiently. Jenny's control vanished into the air. "I was upset! Is that what you want to hear? And how do you think I feel about meeting the rest of your relatives?"

"Megan's sorry she spoke out of turn. She realized I'd wanted to talk to you first."

"To prepare me? How are you going to prepare your family? 'Mom, Dad, I want you to meet Jenny, my latest reclamation project'?"

"For God's sake, Jenny, you surely don't think my parents won't like you? That's an insult to them."

"Sam—" Jenny's voice wobbled despite her best efforts "—have you ever thought I might screw up the introduction? I wasn't exactly charming with your sister. In fact, I was something of a bitch."

"That's not the way Megan saw it. She felt she'd cornered you. Laid a trip on you was how she put it."

"She didn't lay a trip on me. She didn't have to. I laid it on myself."

"Jenny, honey...listen." Sam laid a comforting hand on her knee.

She edged away and stared out the window. "Please, I don't want to talk about this any more. We're almost there. It's going to be hard enough..." Her voice trailed off.

"I'm sorry." He was instantly contrite. "You're right. We'll discuss this later. Hey, are you okay?"

Sam pulled off the road to give her his full attention. "Jenny?" He lightly rubbed the side of her face with his knuckles. "Look at me."

After a moment she did as he directed, and he took the opportunity to feather her lips with his.

"This is not going to be the ordeal you think it is. I'll behave, I promise. Just remember we're a team."

"Oh, Sam." She held his face between her hands and kissed him rather desperately. "It's not you I'm worried about. It's me." She dropped her hands into her lap and shook her head sadly. "That's what you don't understand, and I can't explain it to you. Let's just get this over with. Turn the next corner. You can see the house from there."

SAM WAS NOT SURPRISED to find the Jarvis home attractive and substantial. Remarks Jenny had made earlier had indicated to him Lloyd Jarvis was successful, and the neighborhood they'd driven through was one of Austin's best.

What he hadn't expected, at least on the basis of his meeting with Annabelle, was the tastefulness of the decor. Muted greens and grays. Comfortable furniture with subdued upholstery. Numerous decorative plants and wall hangings. Annabelle evidently knew how to dress up her surroundings better than herself.

His next surprise was Lloyd.

Sam could see the austerity Jenny had described. Stern lines were etched deeply in Lloyd's weathered face. His greeting to Sam, however, was genuinely welcoming.

Yet as soon as Lloyd turned to greet his stepdaughter, Sam felt the tension mount. He could see Annabelle brace herself, and he fought the urge to brace himself as well.

"Hello, Jenny," Lloyd said a little stiffly. "You're looking well."

"Thank you, Lloyd."

There was a small pause.

No polite kiss. No obligatory hug. Not even a handshake.

Still, their interchange must have exceeded Annabelle's expectations, because she broke the pause with a trilling laugh.

"Lloyd, dear, you're so right, she is looking well. It must be your influence, Sam. I do believe you're fattening her up."

Jenny stiffened. "I wasn't aware I needed fattening. You make me sound like a Christmas goose."

Sam stepped in hurriedly before Annabelle dug herself in deeper. "It's our high living. With the extra work we've been faced with, we're single-handedly supporting Charlie's Diner."

Annabelle's need to play to an audience came to the fore. "Jenny, dear. Haven't you offered Sam any home-cooked meals? Shame on you!" She smiled coyly at Sam. "I'm afraid Jenny takes after me. Neither one of us has the talent to be a very good cook." Her look invited him to appraise what talents she did have.

Sam was ready to do so gallantly.

Jenny didn't give him the chance. "I have a business to run. I don't have time to cook." Sam wasn't sure, but he suspected she was gritting her teeth. "If Sam wants a home-cooked meal he can fix it. He's more than capable of looking after himself."

"How is business coming, Jenny?" Lloyd asked, surprising Sam. "This local economy isn't getting any better. My north store barely breaks even."

It seemed to Sam that Lloyd was trying to defuse the situation. Ultimately his efforts were a failure, because he went on to say, "Your mother tells me your finances are shaky."

Jenny whipped around to face him. "Whatever Annabelle told you, my income is fine."

By this time, Sam had an excellent picture of the joys the afternoon held in store. He felt a brief impulse to throw up his hands. Instead, he took Jenny firmly by the elbow and marched her into the living room.

"Your north store?" he asked Lloyd pointedly. "Now I know why your name sounds familiar. Jarvis Hardware. I'm sure you know my brother-in-law, Gary Mason."

"Mason's Dry Cleaning," Lloyd guessed, and his smile grew approving. "Of course. Gary's done a fine job taking over for his father. I hear he's opened up four new locations. He and I served on a chamber committee one year. We hometown businessmen have to stick together."

Annabelle trailed them in, momentarily recovered from her skirmish with Jenny. She beamed. "How nice, Lloyd. You and Sam practically know each other. I'm always struck by how small this city really is."

"And you," Lloyd said, clearly attempting to ascertain Sam's credentials, "I understand you're half of Grant and Kittridge Engineering. I've heard very favorable things about your firm."

"Thank you." Sam smiled.

Jenny glared at all of them. "He's house-trained, too, he doesn't shed, and he's almost as good a companion as Hilde."

Annabelle twittered nervously, while Lloyd's expression stiffened. Sam had a suspicion that at one time, during the stormy years of Jenny's adolescence, Lloyd would have felt an obligation to rebuke her for her rudeness. Certainly, Jenny's chin jutted defiantly, as though Lloyd's look was rebuke enough.

This time Annabelle moved to break the tension. "Dear—" she moved to her husband's side and patted his arm entreatingly "—hadn't you better check the fire?" Her anxious smile encompassed them. "Lloyd's the chef today. He's grilling steaks on the patio. He wanted to spare you that terrible cooking I warned you about."

"You're a good cook, Annie," Lloyd said indulgently, "when you're not in a stew. I just thought you'd like to play hostess today." He covered Annabelle's hand as it clung to him tightly.

A look of tenderness passed between them, providing Sam with another shock. Whatever had been the original terms of this marriage, the bond between these two people now was strong and secure.

When he glanced Jenny's way, however, he caught a look of distaste. And for the first time since he'd known her, Sam had the urge to yank Jenny up and offer her some unwelcome truths.

His pointed stare was probably as unyielding as her stepfather's. A faint stain colored her face. Sam waited for her chin to challenge him. He was faintly amused when she offered him an apologetic grimace, instead.

Certainly for the rest of the afternoon Jenny made a point of being civil, even pleasant. Her good behavior came in spite of the fact that Annabelle and Lloyd kept antagonizing her, albeit unintentionally. Sam couldn't remember when he'd ever met a group of people who misunderstood each other more.

Mother and daughter would tangle and daughter would bristle. Stepfather would intervene, doing more harm than good. Then the boyfriend—Sam—would wade in and complete the cycle.

Sam began to fear that if he didn't do something to break that cycle, he'd become a permanent loop. This afternoon was too soon for intervention, however. This afternoon was the time to observe.

He already knew that despite Jenny's disdain for her mother's marriage, it was a comfortable, even a loving one. Annabelle's flamboyance made a perfect foil to Lloyd's severity. He indulged her helplessness, and she looked to him to provide emotional support. Only Jenny's presence ruffled the calm.

Sam might have concluded that Lloyd and Annabelle resented Jenny's existence. But the tangled relationship between the three of them was far more complex than that.

Sam's most profound observation occurred after lunch.

Good food and drink had eased the tensions. The Jarvises certainly knew how to lay on a feast. Lloyd became somewhat expansive. And Annabelle's fluttery manner seemed to develop style as she relaxed.

Actually, Sam gave himself credit for the atmosphere of harmony. He'd gotten Lloyd to recount strange requests he'd received over his years in the hardware business. Then Sam recounted some of the bizarre requests his firm had filled. He slid smoothly into a description of his inadequacies as Jenny's assistant and drew her out about some of her wackier clientele and their pets.

"You have to tell them about Mrs. Wakefield."

"Oh, Sam."

"Come on, Jenny. She's a dear, eccentric woman, and she deserves her own story."

"Yes, dear. Do tell us. You hardly ever let us share what you do."

Jenny rolled her eyes but obediently launched into a narrative of her first meeting and subsequent work with Mrs. Wakefield. As she got into the story, Sam could see she was enjoying herself. For once, Annabelle was content to allow her daughter the spotlight.

Presented center stage, perform Jenny did. Jenny had a knack for the dramatic, Sam decided happily. As well as a sense of humor and an innate kindness. She presented the characters of her tale in a sympathetic light.

"Both Mrs. Wakefield and her menagerie have come a long way. The last time I was over, Muffin had ventured out from under the bed, and Sparky has stopped marking every stick of furniture in the house. We were working on having a group therapy session. In case you wondered, that translates to getting all the darlings in the same room at the same time." Jenny sighed dramatically. "There's a new crisis, however. This week her son called me in desperation."

"What?" Sam raised his eyebrows. "A new plague of fleas?"

Jenny shook her head sadly. "Worse than that. Mrs. Wakefield has found another stray. This last addition bears a distinct resemblance to Attila the Hun. He's apparently lived life on the rough, and we suspect he's the don of a canine mob. At any rate, he's terrorizing everyone, including Mrs. Wakefield. Muffin's disappeared, and they're not absolutely sure she wasn't rubbed out."

"You don't mean . . ." Annabelle was horrified.

Jenny chuckled, enjoying the reaction. "Not really. They think she's in the guest room. They can hear noises.

And when they put food in for her, it's gone the next day."

"But still..." Annabelle considered the implications with great trepidation.

Sam asked Jenny, "Why hasn't Mrs. Wakefield called you?"

"She's afraid to. And ashamed. She knows what I'll say. Especially after everything we've accomplished."

Sam smiled at her teasingly. "Have you finally found a dog even you can't cope with?"

Jenny's retort held supreme assurance. "Oh, I could cope with him. But Mrs. Wakefield and Muffin can't."

Annabelle asked Jenny something about Mrs. Wakefield's son. Jenny explained his dilemma.

Sam listened to them chatting easily for once and was pleased with his efforts. Then he happened to glance Lloyd's way, and his attention was arrested by the look on Lloyd's face.

He watched his stepdaughter with a strange intensity.

Sam couldn't blame him for his interest. At this moment, Jenny was at her best. Her delicate features were positively glowing. She was laughing, animated and speaking with authority about the work she loved. Sam knew this was a Jenny Lloyd and Annabelle rarely saw and barely knew.

Still, Sam couldn't interpret Lloyd's expression as astonishment at the lovely young woman who'd suddenly appeared in Jenny's place.

It was more than curious bewilderment he saw in the older man's expression. It was a kind of yearning regret and tenderness. Not entirely different from the tender look he'd earlier shared with his wife. Sam suddenly recognized the subtle blend of emotions.

Lloyd loved Jenny. In his own austere way. He would have liked to have been a father to her. The idea flashed through Sam's mind with certainty.

The twin revelations struck him with such force that he almost gaped.

Lloyd sensed Sam studying him, and his face tightened with an effort at control. But Sam wasn't fooled. And he had a feeling Annabelle hadn't been fooled all these years. Which gave her ineffectual efforts to draw Jenny and Lloyd together a new poignancy.

Sam turned his thoughts to the object of Lloyd's feelings. If Jenny would only let Lloyd love her. If somehow the distrust, the old anger, the misunderstandings could be resolved. If only a rudimentary communication could be established between the three of them.

"Sam?"

He came to and found Jenny staring at him oddly.

"Did you hear me? I said it was time to go."

"Oh, Jenny, dear, won't you please stay a little longer?" Annabelle's voice held supplication. "I was so enjoying your stories. Lloyd, aren't you enjoying them, too?"

Jenny turned a vaguely haughty look in his direction, as if wondering what he could possibly say to convince her to stay.

Lloyd read the plea in his wife's face before saying stonily, "Jenny, you know your mother doesn't get to see you often enough."

Jenny raised a brow at his efforts to make her feel guilty. Other than that, she chose to ignore him, turning to her mother. "I said we couldn't stay long when you invited us. You know every Sunday I go over the books."

"Sam," Annabelle asked, "can't you persuade her?"

There was a militant look in Jenny's eye as she faced him.

"No, Sam can't," she assured them all. "And he'd better not try."

CHAPTER TEN

"SO WHY DIDN'T YOU?" Jenny asked with a hint of belligerence moments later as they drove from the house.

Sam feigned innocence. "Why didn't I what?"

"Try to get me to stay? My mother was being very persuasive."

But Sam had decided as soon as he saw the militant look on Jenny's face that he wasn't going to be drawn into an argument.

Instead, he drawled, "I was tired of crowds. We haven't been alone in almost four days."

"You can make that five. I meant it when I said I had to go over the week's accounting."

His mouth quirked. "Did you?"

"Yes," she snapped, aggravated by his impassive manner. "So you might as well be on your way when we get to my house. I don't have time to entertain."

"Don't you?"

"Will you stop that?" Jenny shouted. "And don't you dare say, 'Stop what?'"

He didn't say a word.

It was Jenny who was forced to break the silence. "Sam, what's going on? Sam!" She'd suddenly taken notice of the direction they were heading. "Where are you going? This isn't the way."

"To my house, it is."

"Your house?"

Sam sighed elaborately. "Jenny, have you noticed the repetitive nature of this discussion?"

"Have I noticed?"

He chuckled.

Jenny took a steadying breath. She barely restrained herself from making a childish face. "I would like to know why," she began with deliberate calm, "we're going to your place when you know I have to work."

"Later."

"But I have to feed the dogs."

"Later."

"Sam, will you please provide me more than one-word answers?"

"I will if you choose the right topic."

"And what topic is that?"

"Us." He dropped one hand over hers where they lay in her lap.

The sudden contact jolted Jenny and left her momentarily speechless. By the time she'd regained enough poise to resume their ersatz conversation, Sam had pulled into his parking place at the town house.

He turned to her, his humor obscured by a serious look. "Listen, Jenny, we've both been working too hard. I'm tired of dogs, ice-cream machines and relatives, not necessarily in that order. I figured we could use a break from all three."

Sam studied Jenny's face as he offered his explanation. He wondered if she had any suspicion of what he had in mind.

When he'd awakened this morning, Sam hadn't consciously decided on taking Jenny to his bed, but he'd known for weeks their relationship needed the strength of a physical bond. He was also convinced their lovemaking would give her confidence and self-assurance enough to face any number of relatives. Only he didn't want this to be a one-way seduction.

Evidently Jenny hadn't caught on to his intentions, because she continued to brood over the early afternoon. "You're the one who was dead set on this lunch with Annabelle and Lloyd today."

"Yes, I was, and it was most instructional. Now it's over and done with, and I want to concentrate on you."

"Instructional? How am I supposed to take that?"

He ignored her question completely. "I thought," he said softly, running lazy fingers down her arm to capture her wrist, "this would be a good time to hide out, unplug the phone and say to hell with the world."

Jenny's accelerated pulse against Sam's sensitive fingers spoke volumes. He brought her wrist to his lips and brushed the skin lightly. Another erratic jump told him she'd caught on at last to what was on his mind. He could sense the instant when her mood altered.

An elusive smile played around her lips. Still, she asked, "You don't want to lecture me on how badly I acted?"

"I'm much more interested in how you act now."

"You…" She cleared her throat. "You don't think we ought to clear up any misunderstandings about Megan's visit?"

"I have an excellent suggestion for clearing up misunderstandings."

"I see."

By this time, Sam had propped Jenny's curled hand on his shoulder and was nibbling his way up the inside of her arm.

He knows how sensitive I am right there…

"Sam…" Jenny barely managed to get the words out. "Are you planning on seducing me when we go inside?"

Sam laughed softly. "Well, I certainly don't intend to make love in the car. Although—" he'd reached the rounded collar of her sundress "—I wouldn't mind a few preliminary kisses." She tilted her head to give him access to the curve of her neck. "As for my plans, mmm, I hoped they'd be mutually agreed on."

Without preliminaries, it was out in the open. The question between them. And it was up to Jenny to answer yes or no. If she said no, she knew Sam would back the car out and drive her home without anger and without argument. And she could work on her accounts in splendid isolation.

But there would be no more kisses, no more of his lips brushing the line of her throat, driving her wild. They were in too deep to dally with desire.

"Sam, you're not playing fair. I can't think when you touch me."

Reluctantly, he pulled away to stare at her, arousal slumbering in the depths of his eyes. "I can't think, period. I want you so much."

"I want you, too."

"I know. You've been telling me for days."

"So you do believe I'm ready?"

"Yes. You just need a little courage. I know of only one way at this point to help you find that courage. I promise you'll enjoy my methods."

Jenny's lashes fell. "You don't think we'd be making love for the wrong reasons?"

Sam's low chuckle drew her gaze to his. "Reasons won't matter once we're in my bed lying naked together."

His words flashed vivid images through her mind. Images that made her stutter. "Th-that's not w-what you said before."

"Jenny..." He took hold of her shoulders and caressed them. "I just didn't want us to play games with sex. But I don't believe there will be any game playing now if we make love. We'll be creating a beautiful moment together."

Something about the way he said the last caused a bleak look to flicker across her face. "Are you sure of that? You don't know much about this side of me."

"I'm sure. Jenny, trust me. Come inside." He opened the door, but his look stayed on her compellingly. "We'll take it slow and easy, and I'll slay any dragons I need to along the way."

Sam knew, somehow he knew, in the way he knew so many things, that her hesitation was more than virginal reluctance.

And Jenny knew if she did say no and went home to lie restlessly in her bed alone that her anxiety would grow and gain more control over her. Sam was surely the one man she could trust to help banish her anxiety for good.

She opened her door and climbed out of the car, speaking in an airy tone that fooled neither of them. "I'm a little rusty on seduction. If you want this to be mutual you'll have to provide pointers." She walked rather hurriedly toward his back door.

A tender smile tugged at Sam's mouth as he caught up with her. Pulling her torso against him, he whispered provocatively, "You're quick on your feet, you'll catch on right away."

Jenny grimaced wryly. "Quick on my feet, maybe, but not on my back."

She felt his muffled laughter against her hair.

Fun? Was this thing called sex supposed to be fun?

Evidently so, because when Sam gazed at her intently, a hint of mischief lurked in his eyes. Intuitively, Jenny knew he wasn't laughing at her but inviting her to join him. As if he was privy to a marvelous secret and soon she would know it, too.

In fact there were any number of promises to be found in his expression. Jenny had trouble breathing as she read them all.

Sam unlocked the back door. When he did so, the memory came to him of the last time he'd brought a woman here for amorous purposes. He smiled inwardly. What a difference the woman makes to the mood.

As before, he switched on the kitchen light.

And as before, a spotted tornado advanced upon them from the gloom of the living room.

Déjà vu.

Except this scene veered sharply from the former. For one thing, there was a semblance of order to Sam's house, despite his absence.

And when Jenny commanded firmly, "Off, Zeppo! Off!" the canine cannonball faltered in his leap into her arms. He fell to earth like a spent rocket and crouched on the floor, shaking with excitement, barely containing himself to receive his reward.

It was swift in coming. "Good, Zeppo!" Jenny crouched. "What a smart baby! Isn't he a sweetie?"

Sam winced at her choice of words but bent to scratch Zeppo fondly. A look of beatific joy spread over Zeppo's shaggy face.

Sam could tell when Jenny rose, smiling, that she had begun to relax.

"Can I get you something to drink?" he asked, heading for the kitchen.

"What do you have?"

"Sparkling water, soft drinks, white wine, rum and mixers, and—" he held up a bottle "—about four fingers of very expensive Scotch."

"Is plying me with liquor part of your strategy?" she asked, striving for the light touch.

"On the contrary." Sam turned from his examination of the liquid refreshments to smile at her. "Your limit is one drink. I don't want to dull your senses."

At his smile, Jenny's heart seemed to flip-flop in her breast. "In that case, I'll have sparkling water, please." To try to control the hammering inside her, she asked mockingly, "Where would you suggest this seduction begin?"

"Couches have been known to serve the purpose."

"You're speaking from vast experience, of course." Jenny tried to make the comment casual, but she didn't succeed. She started for the living room, not wanting to meet Sam's look.

He came up behind her, cupped one shoulder lightly, placed her drink in her hand and assured her gently, "Not vast. I am, however, a normal, healthy male of thirty-four who enjoys sex."

"What does that make me?" she asked, her tone wistful.

By this time, Sam could read every nuance of her expression. "You are," he stated calmly, "a normal, healthy female of thirty who's about to lose her inhibitions. But you only have permission to lose them with me."

"You make it sound so easy."

"It is, between the right two people. Come." Sam led her to the spacious sofa. He pushed her down gently and followed so that they sank into the cushions together. His arm slid along the back of the couch to toy with her curls.

His other hand took one of hers and spread it over his thigh.

"I love your hands," he said quietly. "They're slender and delicate just like the rest of you." He began to stroke from her wrist to each nail as if he was on an erotic inventory.

The heat from his leg scorched her bare skin. Jenny made a jerky fist and protested, "Oh, no, Sam. They're rough and callused. I despair of them."

"That's because they know how to work. You have sturdy hands, graceful hands. Hands that could learn to give a man pleasure." He spread out her curled fingers methodically so that her palm was once more against the cotton fabric of his slacks.

"I've dreamed at night of your hands roaming my body."

Jenny's breathing grew shallow. "I've dreamed that, too."

He turned and leaned toward her so that they were facing each other. "Just as I've dreamed of roaming your body with my hands and mouth. Learning the ways to give you pleasure." He punctuated his words by moving his hand over her thigh, then spreading his palm so that his hand mirrored hers.

Jenny swallowed hard. "I've dreamed that, too."

He smiled whimsically. "Sounds like our dreams are a step ahead of us."

"Sounds that way," were the only words Jenny could find to say.

Sam leaned closer until his lips brushed the side of her mouth. "What are we going to do about that?" His question sent warm breath against her skin.

"I don't know," Jenny whispered. "You're the expert. I thought you were in charge here."

He chuckled and dropped a kiss on the other corner of her mouth. "That's what you think."

Sam took her hand and swept it up his torso until it was centered on his chest. "Do you feel my heart?"

It beat like a hammer. Jenny nodded mutely.

Sam placed his hand in the valley between her breasts. Her heart responded with a wild tripping.

"Oh, Jenny. What magical things we do to each other." He stroked one of her nipples ever so lightly, covered her mouth and spoke against her lips. "Don't you know, lady, this is new for me, too? I've never experienced this kind of loving."

As he murmured the words, his thumb made wanton forays over her breast, until her tip hardened to a nub and sent an aching heat through her body.

Her hands developed a will of their own and moved up the hard musculature of his chest, over his shoulders and into his hair. Suddenly, she strained against him.

"Don't tease me, please. Kiss me."

"How would you like to be kissed?"

His lips whispered over her cheeks, her brows, her closed eyes.

"Every way," she breathed raggedly.

"Like this?" He tugged at her bottom lip and bit it delicately.

"Yes..."

"Or this?" He ran his tongue lightly over her teeth and gums.

"Oh, yes..."

"Or this?"

He pulled her into his arms until they were breast to breast and delved into her mouth.

Instantly, passion flamed between them. He slanted his head and the kiss grew insistent. Hot and wet and seeking. Her tongue sought and mirrored his actions, eliciting a groan.

Subtly and expertly he changed their position. Jenny found herself lying against the cushions, Sam stretched out over her so they were length to length.

She felt the full heat and pressure of his arousal. His hips began to make erotic movements as he slid one of his legs between hers. His hand found her thigh again and began to circle higher, finding its way under her flared skirt.

Without warning, panic struck her. Sudden. Immediate.

Where pliant womanhood had lain beneath Sam, he felt her stiffen in shock.

"Jenny, what's wrong?" He raised his head to search her features. "Am I moving too fast?"

"It's not that." Jenny turned her face into the pillows, feeling ridiculous. She was ashamed of her panic and hesitant to explain its source.

"Have we come upon the lair of a dragon, Jenny? Shall I unsheathe my trusty sword?"

Something about the way he said it made her giggle absurdly. "To what sword, kind sir, were you referring?"

"Ah, Jenny." His voice was a rumble deep in his chest. "I told you we'd have fun together."

"Fun? You call panic fun?"

"I didn't say the road wouldn't have detours. That's okay, if we can laugh along the way. Now." He settled his length to one side, propped his head on his hand and assumed a serious expression. "Panic. Yours. Why?"

"Because..." Jenny hesitated, then the words came out in a rush. "There's something you ought to know, Sam. Something I need to tell you."

"There are no oughts between us," he corrected. "But if you need to tell me what's standing in the way of your pleasure, then go ahead."

"Sam . . ." She steeled herself for the admission. "I'm not a virgin."

"Jenny..." A dear smile came and went on his lips. "I assure you, love, it's not required."

"That's right, laugh," she admonished shakily.

"I'm not laughing." He buried his face for a moment in her curls. "You're just so cute when you confess."

She fought an answering smile and scolded him. "You think this is some kind of maidenly confession? I'm trying to explain to you . . ."

"I know, love." He kissed her lightly. His expression as he gazed at her was as serious as she could have hoped.

"There was this man," she began determinedly.

Sam's brow raised ever so slightly.

Jenny fought the urge to giggle again. This revelation was not proceeding as she'd expected.

"I was twenty-three and I *was* a virgin. And, well, I was beginning to think my virginity was a permanent state. I'd never gotten a serious proposition, and I . . . I wondered if there was something wrong with me. I mean, I was curious. Who wouldn't be?"

"Who wouldn't be?" he repeated with just the faintest gleam in his eye.

"I mean, I'd been kissed here and there and fended off a few gropes in the front seats of cars. But I never dated much, even in high school. I'm aware of the fact I'm no femme fatale."

"I'd have to disagree with you on that point," he remarked thoughtfully.

"Oh, Sam." Jenny's look was ever so slightly imploring. "You're the only one who would."

"The only one who matters. I'll see to that." This time he moved his hand over her waist possessively and discovered he liked the feel of her skin through the thin material. His touch became a caress.

He could make her tremble at the lightest touch.

"I think we've just changed the subject," she murmured.

"I think I want to hear how this story ends."

"What I'm trying to tell you is, this man Milton—he was a dog trainer I met at one of the shows..." She floundered for a moment, took a deep breath and tried again. "What I'm telling you is that Milton thought he loved me. He wanted to marry me. I went to bed with him because it was my first real offer, and he went to bed with me because he cared. I was naive, I didn't realize what I was doing. But the fact is, I used him and made a mess of things. I hurt him. I'd thought...his kisses were okay...I thought I'd enjoy it. But the first time was terrible. We tried again, but it wasn't much better. He was disappointed and I was humiliated." A shudder went through Jenny. "I—I just don't want the same thing to happen today."

"It won't." Sam sounded very confident.

Jenny wasn't convinced. "How can you be sure?"

"How attracted were you to this inept deflowerer of virgins?"

Jenny hid a smile. She did indeed detect the faintest note of hostility behind his drawling question. It cheered her inordinately.

"I thought I was—mildly. But it was nothing like the way I'm attracted to you." The admission she made was only the truth, and Jenny was finding that perhaps she did have a bit of the vamp in her. They say confession is good for the soul. She discovered it worked wonders for the more corporal elements.

Especially when Sam's hand resumed its meanderings, and he smiled knowingly at her expression. "You see, I said you'd catch on quickly."

"Oh, Sam." She chuckled softly. The laughter caught in her throat when, in the midst of its wanderings, his hand happened on the swell of her breast. "I have another confession to make."

"And what's that?" he asked from the base of her throat where he'd begun to do wild and wonderful things with his lips and tongue.

"I enjoy flirting with you. I'm not sure my feminist soul approves."

"Just consider it part of the mating ritual and give in to the inevitable." Without perceptible motion, he'd insinuated a leg between her thighs and had begun to press erotically against her.

"Are you the inevitable?" Jenny's voice was smoky. She felt no panic now, just a restless lethargy.

"What's happening between us is. As inevitable and natural and as old as time."

He stared at her intensely, then his lips met hers. It was an urgent kiss. They both strained into it. The interlude of moments ago had only banked the fires of desire and heated them. Passion flared anew with a red-hot flame.

With sudden urgency Jenny's hands began a restless pattern up and down Sam's back. She shaped his tapering waist then wandered down to cup his buttocks, so tight, thrusting against her.

Sam found the sensitive flesh where her skirt had ridden high and he began a tantalizing journey upward with the tips of his fingers.

There was no panic this time, only a rush of animal need.

Jenny moaned deep inside her throat. Her hips began an instinctive rotation.

This time it was Sam who stopped them abruptly. "I think," he said raspily, "the couch has done its duty. I vote we move to the bedroom and get comfortable."

Which meant taking off their clothes. It wasn't panic now that made Jenny hesitate, but pure shyness. He picked up on it and hoisted her into his arms.

"My dear modest semi-virgin." His voice was a teasing murmur against the shell of her ear. "I am about to initiate you into the pleasures of getting 'nekked' with a man."

She wound her arms tightly around his neck and burrowed her head into the warmth of his throat. He could barely hear her admission when it came. "I've never undressed in front of a man before."

"What?" Jenny could tell by his tone Sam was genuinely startled. "How did you and Romeo manage that?"

"Well, we did it in the back of his trailer after the shows. We were always afraid someone would catch us."

"Heaven give me strength," Sam muttered as he carried her up the stairs.

He walked into his bedroom and kicked the door closed. "I'm not ready to have Zeppo for an audience," he offered in explanation.

Jenny giggled into his shoulder.

He stopped for a moment by the bed to stare at her flushed, laughing face.

"You are going to find," he said after a moment of deliberation, "that 'doing it' is much more enjoyable in the privacy of a bedroom, on a nice, soft bed, without encumbrances. You really are inexperienced, my love, in every way that counts.''

A slow, lazy smile appeared. Jenny's five senses were dazzled.

''Not to worry, however,'' he went on in a murmur. ''We'll remedy the situation.''

He laid her on the bed, switched on the mellow light of the bedside lamp and allowed his eyes to roam freely over her prone body. Jenny could almost feel their touch.

She sat up on one elbow and attempted a certain boldness. ''Talk, talk, talk, Sam. All I've heard is talk. Where's the action?''

''The action usually begins by removing the clothing.'' In a smooth movement that caught her unawares, Sam straddled her, capturing her lower body between the calves of his legs. He sat back on his heels and smiled provocatively while he unbuckled her belt and slipped it slowly out from under her.

Jenny fought a blush, and her lashes drifted downward. Her look slid over the planes of his body and she could see the bulge near the crotch of his slacks.

By this time he'd begun to unfasten the buttons running the length of her bodice. He divided the dress with his hands and smoothed the edges over her skin, exposing her lacy bra, one the gypsy had purchased.

''Mmm. Nice, very nice.'' With a deft motion, he reached under her and unsnapped it. ''Very, very nice.''

He cupped her bare breasts and in a sudden maneuver, flicked one of her nipples with the tip of his tongue.

''Oh.'' Jenny's moan was a convulsive sigh of pleasure. She was totally unaware she'd made it. All her senses were concentrated on the nuances of his touch.

He flicked the other breast. Then settled his mouth over it, beginning a suckling motion that left her feeling as if she was flying apart.

"Sam...Sam." His whispered name became a rhythmic cry of need.

"Hmm?" His hands slid down her rib cage and over her waist, then found the elastic of her panties. His fingers slipped beneath the stretchy material and touched her ever so slightly where she was wet and throbbing.

"Sam!"

"I know, love, I know," Sam whispered raggedly. He slipped away from her and in a moment had rid her of everything she wore.

He began to unbutton his shirt. Jenny stopped him. Pushed him into the mattress.

"Let me," she commanded. Her fingers worked busily, as Sam's had done.

Jenny's modesty had long since been forgotten as she crouched beside him. Now she had the need to measure his body with her hands. She wanted to learn the angles and texture of him. With her outstretched palms she molded his chest with an upward motion. Her fingers tangled in the soft tuft of black hair. She discovered his nipples and was delightfully surprised when her teasing play over the nubs elicited a moan.

"Jenny..."

"I know, love, I know," she murmured, intoxicated with her newly discovered power.

Her fingers wandered downward and found the waistband of his pants, hesitated for a moment over the stressed material of his zipper. This was dangerously exciting territory. Jenny wasn't sure what was called for.

Sam showed her by pressing the entire length of her hand over the object in question.

"Oh, yes, Jenny, yes," he sighed and raised his hips against the pressure of her palm. Then he fell back against the pillows and stroked her cheek, her throat, the curve of her arm.

"Jenny," he said with a husky tenderness. "I want to protect you."

Her look slid from his. For the first time since he'd undressed her, Jenny blushed. "That—that won't be necessary," she confessed. "I made a doctor's appointment and went on the pill."

"Hot damn," Sam crowed in exultation, grabbed her to him in a bear hug and tumbled them over on the bed. "That's my Jenny. Full of surprises."

As if her admission made him suddenly impatient, Sam let her go and stripped hurriedly. Once done, he was content to lie back and gauge her reaction to his jutting arousal. She saw in his eyes a residue of laughter. Yet there was more, much more to his look as he lingered over her curves.

Was her look as hungry as his as she allowed herself to take in all of him? Every splendid inch of him. And he was hers, all hers, to touch and fondle and explore.

Her hunger must have shown because after a long, silent moment, he growled softly, pulled her down beside him and covered her mouth with a searching kiss while their bodies found a fit.

His hands roamed over her as his eyes had done. Her breasts, her tapering ribs, the dip of her waist, her swelling hips, her thighs.

Everywhere but . . .

Close, closer, his touch drew closer . . .

"Sam, please! Ah!" Jenny stiffened for an instant with jolting pleasure as he found her, then melted around him when he dipped inside.

Suddenly it seemed as if he was everywhere, his body heating her skin, his touch invading every sense, evoking an awareness she couldn't have imagined.

His mouth moved over her breasts to resume a familiar torment. She writhed beneath him beyond will or control. Her body yearned for an elusive satiation.

She needed...she wanted...she must have...

"Oh, yes, love...let it come...let it come."

"Oh! Oh..." Jenny's cries were a blend of surprise and wonder. The world, even Sam, faded as her body was seized with throbbing ripples of intense satisfaction. There was an inward moment beyond time or place.

Then, just as the waves of contractions began to diminish, Sam moved over her, his mouth found hers in a seeking kiss and Jenny felt his fullness as he buried himself inside her.

Their bodies coupled and tangled, all hardness and softness and curves and hollows, and she fit his hard length like liquid satin.

Jenny arched at the new sensation of Sam being in and above and around her. Her arms encircled his back to urge him closer as an exquisite pleasure overtook her.

He filled her, he completed her, his hips and tongue spoke an unwritten language that hers understood. She answered him and they began the timeless duet. The rhythmic accompaniment to love.

"Oh, Jenny, Jenny, it's good, so good."

With his words, his guttural sighs of pleasure, Jenny felt a wild exultation sweep through her. This man, this wonderful, marvelous man was losing himself in their shared passion.

Their passion grew urgent and searching and more demanding.

Their tempo quickened and quickened more. Jenny felt that same tantalizing moment of anticipation. She gasped in wonder as the pulses seized her, rippling over Sam who was deep inside. Sending him beyond desire.

His muscles tensed, he stiffened above her and cried out as his thrusts answered her completion.

It was moments or an age before the tension left their bodies and they relaxed in a sprawling mix of arms and legs.

CHAPTER ELEVEN

"SO THAT'S HOW IT'S DONE." Jenny's dazed comment minutes later held a curious touch of astonishment.

Sam's humorous rumble vibrated through her. He raised himself to gaze at her face.

"Yeah," he said, his voice lazy with satisfaction, "that's how it's done. If you're fortunate."

Jenny ran her hands up and around his back, luxuriating in the muscular definition she found there. "You think good fortune had that much to do with it?" she questioned, still inordinately pleased with them both.

He dropped a kiss on the slope of her shoulder. "Well," he conceded, "natural aptitude played a large part."

"So you don't think it was beginner's luck?"

Sam seemed to find that question so endearing he responded with a series of achingly tender kisses. Then he rolled onto his back, carrying Jenny with him, so that her arms were criss-crossed on his chest. Now one of his hands was free to make ambling journeys wherever its inclination led it. The other moved to her hair where his fingers plucked at the abandoned curls.

"Making love isn't like gin rummy, sweetheart," he said finally, his lips curved in amusement. "It just gets better the more times you do it. If you've found the right person."

"How could it get better than what just happened?" Jenny's eyes widened in amazement.

"The only way for me to answer your question—" Sam took his time in responding, having discovered that the swell of her backside held infinite charm "—would be to show you." He cupped one hip and insinuated it closer.

"Now?"

Sam laughed ruefully. "Not *right* now. And not in one day. We need many, many days and many, many nights and soft-lit bedrooms and velvet darkness and scented meadows washed with sunlight and..."

"I—I think I get the picture," Jenny interrupted breathlessly. "You have a talent for explaining things."

Sam's thigh nudged hers provocatively. "Hmm, you ain't seen nothin' yet."

Then a thought struck him, his expression grew serious, and his fingers moved to frame her face. "I don't think I have really explained what's happening. This attraction between us, the physical passion we share, is very, very special. I've never experienced it before. This is as new for me as it is for you."

"You mean our making love just now?" He could hear her doubt intruding.

"I mean loving, creating love, physically and in every other way. I'm in love with you, Jenny. That's why it's new and why it's so special. And I believe you're in love with me."

Jenny tensed. She would have moved away from him awkwardly, if he hadn't anticipated her actions and countered the withdrawal. Instead of separating from Sam, emotionally and physically, she found herself lying on her back, captured by his body, held in his embrace.

All she could do was turn her face away. Her voice wobbled as she stared at the wall. "Don't talk like that. Please. Don't spoil the moment. Isn't sexual compatibility enough for now?"

Sam sighed but leaned close to brush the corner of her eyelid. He thought for a moment he tasted a tear.

"For now," he soothed her. Then he dropped butterfly kisses in a trail leading to the shell of her ear.

His body whispered a sensual message when he settled over her. Jenny felt herself melting as she heard him say, "We'll call it sexual compatibility or anything you like. What's important is that we learn from it. Let me teach you more of the delights of mating."

And he proceeded to make sweet love with her.

Languorous love. Slow love. Love that searched out and discovered.

Love that lulled her doubts and stirred the many facets of her desire.

Tender love. Caring love. Love that beguiled her every sense. It was as though his wandering lips and hands possessed her body and her will.

When she reached out to give Sam pleasure, he took her hand and nibbled the tip of each finger. Then he held her wrist against the pillow by her head.

His other hand moved between her legs. She was hot and sweet and ready and arched to meet his touch. In a blazing instant, release throbbed through her. She gasped out his name.

And he came into her as though claiming her soul. His hands spread her thighs and lifted them to meet him. And as his long, rhythmic thrusts began, they stoked her desire over...and over...and over again.

As he stroked, he studied her face intently, her lost expression, her restless tossing from side to side. Her skin flushed with a sheen of sweat, her lashes sooty against her cheeks and her lips opened in wanton abandon. As wantonly open as the moist lips below, which he breached again and again.

He leaned down and darted his tongue into her mouth, then commanded her with a soft urgency.

"Open your eyes. Look at me. Look at us. See what we're making together."

Jenny's lashes flickered open. She saw Sam's face intensely tender. The shuddering breathing in his chest. The insistent, pulsing union between them.

She moaned deep in her throat. Her lashes fluttered.

"No, Jenny. Stay with me. Stay with me, lover."

And her look sought his once more. She found the love they shared etched in his face. And she had no will to deny it.

As they stared into each other's eyes, Sam carried them at last over the final precipice, then slowly, tenderly home to rest.

IT WAS TUESDAY AFTERNOON and Richard skipped along beside Jenny as she exercised the dogs before their evening feed.

Jenny was glad for Richard's company. Sam had phoned Monday morning to say he was booked on an emergency flight to Atlanta. He wouldn't be back till Thursday, and Jenny was feeling bereft—in spite of the satisfying long-distance call late last night.

Richard was acting particularly cheerful today, which raised Jenny's spirits. In some ways he wasn't the same little boy she'd been introduced to. At least with her he wasn't. Jenny still sensed the gulf between father and son.

"How's Albert?" she asked, while she unhooked the leash from the collar of a soulful-looking basset hound and shooed him into his run. She knew the search for Albert's home had proven futile, and Bob had consented to his staying.

"Albert's great," Richard said, paternal pride evident. "He's got his shots and everything. You wouldn't believe how fast he's growing."

"How are he and Arnie doing?"

Richard giggled. "You know what Albert does? He waits till Arnie's asleep then stalks up to him and pounces on his nose. Sometimes when Albert starts meowing, Arnie gets all upset and goes over to snuffle him."

Jenny smiled at the picture Richard had drawn. Without conscious thought, she lay an arm across his shoulders and gave him a quick hug. He leaned into it. One eye peeked up at her through incredibly long lashes.

If he ever grows into those lashes, Jenny thought, he'll be a lady's man for sure. Richard sidled a hand into hers and began to swing them both with a bouncing motion.

"Dad called you Sunday to see if I could come by, but you were gone all afternoon."

Checking up on her, was he? "Sam and I went to eat at my mother's house," she explained.

"Sam? Do you see a lot of him?" He glanced at her again with a sideways look.

It was all Jenny could do not to grin openly. Richard was jealous, or she missed her guess. Sam would be amused to see where his competition came from.

"I see quite a lot of him. We're close friends." Which was a euphemistic description if she ever heard one.

"Are you and Sam getting married?" Richard blurted out, his good humor fraying.

"Married? Why, no, of course not. I mean..." Jenny backpedaled furiously, realizing these matters were black and white for a child Richard's age. "It's too soon to think about that sort of thing." She gave him a mildly admonishing look. "You know, Richard, that's a very personal question." At least she didn't have to worry that he was being preternaturally polite. These past few weeks really had made a difference.

How much was evident. "Yeah, I know," he said, grinning, not a bit intimidated by her look and obviously pleased with her answer.

He swung their arms wider. "Dad's going to call you."

"He is? What about?" Jenny was intrigued by Richard's little-boy look of slyness.

"He's going to ask you to go out to dinner with him." He watched her carefully as he spoke.

Jenny felt the first twinge of alarm as she recognized Richard's true intentions. "Well, that's very nice of him," she responded carefully. "I'm awfully busy, you know. I might not . . ."

Richard's face fell. She felt her resolve slipping. "But I'll—try to rearrange my schedule, depending on yours and his. Where would you like the three of us to go?"

"Oh, no, it'll just be you and Dad. He'll get a baby-sitter for me and everything. He doesn't want you mad at him like you were the other night. You'll go, won't you?"

"I wasn't mad at your dad, Richard," she said, feeling her way.

"Then you will go, Jenny, please?" His anxious pleading was effective.

"Well," she murmured helplessly, "your dad and I'll talk about it when he calls."

Bob did call that evening after he picked Richard up. Jenny had a suspicion Richard had coached him.

Great. The gulf between father and son was narrowing. Only she hadn't intended to be the bridge.

Jenny had not been surprised that Richard was jealous of Sam. Now she realized his motives were more complex. He'd apparently set himself up as matchmaker.

Jenny was certain she was in over her head.

However, she didn't have the heart to refuse to go out with Bob. If for no other reason than to clear the air. And the date was for Wednesday, the day before Sam came back.

Jenny quashed feelings of guilt and betrayal and tried not to think of the lecture Sam would deliver about the mixed messages this date might produce.

When Bob arrived the next evening, he was dressed in a fashionable suit and tie. A handsome man, Jenny decided dispassionately, if you liked the executive type.

She wore her only conventionally dressy outfit, the one she'd bought to impress her banker. Cool and professional hit the right note. Jenny's gypsy wasn't the least bit interested in Bob Ingram. The gypsy intended to stay home tonight.

Bob took Jenny to an expensive restaurant, wined and dined her, and for the most part steered the conversation to their respective work. He made a pleasant, attentive companion. Except that the occasional glance, as well as the same questioning look she'd seen Richard give her, told Jenny Bob had more on his mind than a pleasant date.

"You know, Jenny, you're quite impressive." Bob toyed with her fingers as they lay on the tablecloth.

"Me? Why do you say that?" Jenny smiled nervously and untangled her hand to take a sip of wine.

"You're young—"

"Not that young—"

"Yet you have your own business, you're successful. You've achieved an excellent reputation in your field. I know, I checked around."

"You did?" Jenny said, startled.

"Well, yes, I . . ." Bob had the grace to blush. "That is, I checked before we came to you with Arnie."

"I see."

"What I'm trying to say is, I admire your hard work and dedication. I know what it takes to succeed on your own."

Single-mindedness. Obsession. Loneliness.

"Thank you, Bob," Jenny murmured, not sure how to respond to his misguided paean of praise. "It's sweet of you to say all that."

"Oh, no, it's not," he said earnestly. "I've admired you since we met. You're so well put together, so sure of yourself. I can't imagine you failing at anything."

Jenny attempted a smile as she tried to suppress acute discomfort. Here was a man who'd bought her facade with a vengeance. So why was she suddenly fighting a claustrophobic alarm?

"You know, I'm really not all that well put together, Bob. There's a dark side to me." She grinned faintly. "I have my moments."

"We all do," he assured her. His eyes skidded away. "I certainly haven't presented myself in a very attractive light."

"It wasn't necessary," she assured him kindly.

"Wasn't it?" A wry look came and went. "A man always likes to impress a beautiful woman."

Jenny laughed, hoping to keep the conversation light. "Well, your compliments are impressive. I'll say that for them. Even if they are a bit extravagant."

"Extravagance is licensed in certain situations." Bob Ingram's eyes held a recognizable gleam. If Jenny still had doubts about the direction he was heading, the next words disproved them. "Richard tells me you and Sam aren't serious."

Jenny opened her mouth to speak.

Bob interrupted hurriedly. "I know, I've already spoken to Richard about impertinent questions. But I'm glad he asked the ones he did."

"Actually, Bob..." Actually, Jenny wasn't sure exactly what she planned to say.

It didn't matter. Bob rushed on. "You and Sam aren't engaged to be married, are you? Was Richard wrong?"

"No..."

"Then," he said, smiling happily, "we have a chance."

"We?" Jenny was floundering. She couldn't think of a way to stop Bob's words.

"Richard and me," he clarified quickly. "Oh, Jenny, I know it's too soon to discuss this. But I can see how much you mean to Richard. And I think I know how much Richard means to you."

"I am very fond of him, but..."

"And you've done so much for him. I know, I've said this before, but I can't tell you how grateful I am for all the time you've spent with him."

He took hold of her hand so she couldn't free it easily. She felt invisible tentacles coiling around her.

"Bob." She tried to speak calmly. "No relationship should be built solely on gratitude."

"I agree." He nodded, capturing her other hand. "I feel it's much more than that. Can't you see? Richard has changed. He's opened up to you. You've managed to reach him in ways I can't seem to. He needs you. I need you." For an instant there was a frantic edge to his voice.

Jenny decided against struggling to free her fingers. Instead, she let them lie passively within his grip and gazed at him directly. "How do you need me, Bob? We hardly know each other. I told you, I'm not the woman you think."

"We can get to know each other. Tonight's dinner's a start. I've said already I'm acting prematurely. But with Grant in the picture, I just wanted you to know my intentions now."

"And they are?" Jenny asked, deciding she needed to hear the worst.

"Why, I . . . I want to marry you, Jenny, at some point in the future. I'd like you to become Richard's mother and my wife."

For the third time, Jenny said in as many words, "We hardly know each other." She succeeded in freeing her hands to pat his arm while she went on patiently. "I don't really think you'd like knowing the complete Jenny Hunter."

"Of course, I would," Bob disagreed adamantly, then went on to the crux of his argument. "Besides, the important thing is, we both love Richard. That can be the basis for everything else."

"Are you saying Richard would be the glue that holds us together? Because that's too much to ask of a child."

"No, I don't mean that. I need you, too." At her skeptical look he went on blindly. "To give balance to my life. I've been so alone. I've missed Doris, and the home we shared."

Jenny sighed. "From your description of Doris, I don't think I'm at all like her, Bob." Jenny called his attention when it slid away. "I wouldn't make a very good replacement."

His mulish look reappeared. "I think I can be the best judge of that." As soon as he said it, he realized his mistake. "Besides, I—I'm not looking for a replacement. Richard loves you because you're you, not because you remind him of his mother. I'm sure I could, too. I'm already half in love with you." He spoke the last defiantly.

"You want to be. It's not the same. No, listen, Bob." She stopped him when he would have interrupted. "There are some things I need to say. It's true, Richard cares for me. I care for him. And I want you to know his love is very important to me. Richard's taught me a great deal about myself. But what's between Richard and me isn't enough to support a permanent relationship between the two of us. I care about Richard and you, but I'm not in love with you."

Bob heard only what he wanted. "Your feelings can change, if you'll give me a chance." His words were almost frantically eager. "You say you care for me. Let's build on that."

"No, Bob." She kept her patience with difficulty. "Because you see, I don't think I could ever fall in love with you. I think I know what love is. And I don't believe we'd find it together."

"Are you talking about passion? Jenny, don't you realize I want you? You're a beautiful, vibrant woman that any man could desire."

Jenny's expression was as gentle as she knew how to make it. "Thank you. I appreciate the compliment. But you see—" she reached out and touched his arm lightly, hoping what she had to say next would not hurt him too deeply "—although I do care for you, it's only as a friend."

"That can change... if you'll let me..."

"No, I don't think so."

He started to speak, and Jenny held up her hand. "Bob, wait. I'm deeply honored you would want me to be your wife and Richard's mother. I think at one time I would have been more than honored. I might even have been tempted by this...this pre-proposal, on the basis of how much Richard means to me. That might have been enough once. But it's not now. And it shouldn't be for you, either. I can't be the means by which you find your way to Richard. I can't be the bridge between you. You two must work your relationship out together. All I can be is Richard's friend. And yours."

"Dammit, I want more than your friendship. Haven't you heard anything I've said? I *need* you."

Don't panic, Jenny. Just don't panic.

"But you need me for all the wrong reasons. I don't think I could meet all your needs. Please, believe me. I don't plan on marrying. I'd make a terrible wife."

"I won't let you put yourself down," he said stubbornly.

"But you said yourself, I'm dedicated to my business."

"Yes, of course. Before you had Richard and me in your life. I know you'd be just as dedicated to making a home for the three of us. I told you I didn't think you could fail. Jenny, nothing you've said convinces me we don't have a chance. Just a chance, that's all I ask."

Bob looked at her imploringly, and Jenny knew she had failed. She'd failed to make Bob understand there could be nothing between them. She was suddenly exhausted with the effort. And perilously close to losing control.

"Bob, I'd like to go home."

Something in her tone of voice or her expression must have finally gotten through to him.

"Yes, of course, we'll go right now."

He paid the bill, asked for his car, and they rode away in silence.

"Jenny," Bob said at one point, concerned with her mood, "I didn't mean to badger you."

"Then please don't."

Her bleak request precluded further conversation.

When Bob drove up to her house, however, it seemed he wasn't finished. "What shall I tell Richard? About us, that is?"

"Don't tell him anything. There's nothing to tell."

"Will you let me see you again?"

"No. It wouldn't be fair to either of us."

"I want to see you. And Richard expects it."

With those words, Bob made her angry at last.

She turned to him, her expression formidable. "Don't you dare use Richard as emotional blackmail."

"I wouldn't... That is, I didn't..." He took a shaky breath. "I didn't mean to do that." His fingers gripped the steering wheel and he leaned his forehead on them. "This evening hasn't gone as I'd planned."

When his expression crumbled, Jenny couldn't stay mad at him. He was so helpless, so lost, so unsure of his way.

"I want to say something, Bob, and I think this evening's given me the right to do so." Jenny took a deep breath and began. "You can't love me, or anyone else, for that matter. Not yet. You're still grieving over your wife. You need to reach out to Richard, so you can grieve together. It's very important."

"I don't know how. I hoped you'd help me."

"Have you sat down and talked to Richard about his mother?"

"No, it's too painful."

"Then the pain," Jenny said with somber authority, "the pain is where you must begin."

WHEN THE PHONE RANG, Jenny rushed to answer it.

"Sam?"

His laugh caressed her over the wire. "Is that how you greet all your callers?"

"Who else could it be," she asked breathlessly, "this late at night?"

"I liked the way you say that, lover."

"Oh, Sam, I miss you!" Jenny's voice cracked and she couldn't continue.

"Is this in the way of another confession?" he asked. And waited. "Jenny?" His tone changed in an instant. "Jenny, what's wrong?"

"Everything," she wailed.

Although Jenny had been in control of her emotions when Bob left, in the hour since she'd slowly but surely come unglued.

"Is Hilde hurt?" he asked anxiously. "Has someone died?"

"No. No, it's nothing like that."

"Bank foreclosed on the mortgage?" he guessed half seriously.

"No. It's not about business." Jenny saw no other way but to blurt out the truth. "Bob Ingram took me to dinner tonight."

"Oh."

"Don't you dare say oh to me in that tone of voice." Jenny stopped, appalled at the note of hysteria in her voice. "Sam? Are you there?"

"I'm here, sweetheart." His quiet voice had the ability to calm her. "Why don't you start at the beginning, and tell me everything."

"Sam, you were right. Bob wants to see me. He—he practically proposed."

"I see." His voice was still very quiet. "And how did you answer?"

"Well, I tried to be as kind as I could, but I told him it wasn't possible. He kept using Richard."

"Which doesn't surprise me."

"But what you don't know is, Richard wants it, too. You could say he arranged the evening."

"Now that I think of it, that doesn't surprise me, either. In fact, we should have seen it coming."

"I didn't see it coming. I thought Richard was just being jealous when he asked me how serious you and I were."

"And what did you tell Richard about us?"

"I told him we were good friends. What did you expect me to say?"

She heard him sigh, though only faintly. "Did Bob ask you about us before he proposed?"

"Well, yes, but I didn't tell him anything. It was none of his business." Without understanding her uneasiness, Jenny rushed on. "Sam, it was horrible. Bob thinks I'm some sort of superwoman. He doesn't know me at all."

"Like I do."

"Like...like you do." Jenny suddenly felt a great rush of relief. "That's right. Like you do. I kept trying to explain to him I wasn't in love with him, could never fall in love with him. He just wouldn't listen."

"There's one thing you could have said that would have convinced him." Sam's voice was hard to read.

"What?" Once again, Jenny felt uneasy.

"You could have told him you and I are more than friends. That we're lovers. Bob would understand what that means for a woman like you."

"I couldn't do that."

"Why? Because you can't admit it?"

"Yes. No! I can't think... Oh, Sam, I don't know what to do. Don't be angry with me. I need help. I—I need you."

"Say it again," he commanded softly.

"I need you." The words came out easier the second time.

"Well, it's a beginning, at any rate." Sam's tone was ironic. "Just hold on, lover, I'll be right there."

IT WAS BARELY DAWN when Jenny heard the doorbell. At first she thought it was the alarm clock interrupting her long-awaited sleep. Then she looked at the dial and found it was barely five-thirty.

Was it her mother? Disaster? She stumbled toward the door.

When she opened it, Sam stood before her in a rumpled suit, looking bleary-eyed but very solid.

Sighing his name, she fell into his embrace.

Sam swung her up in his arms and headed toward her bedroom.

"How did you get here so quickly?" she mumbled into his shirt.

"I took the red-eye special into Houston. I'd already called Hobby Airport from Atlanta and scared up a plane and a pilot to fly me here."

"Y-you didn't have to go to so much trouble."

"Didn't I? You said you needed me."

"I do." She snuggled closer. "I do need you."

He kissed her on the lips slowly and thoroughly before saying, "That's why I'm here."

CHAPTER TWELVE

IT WAS THE CROWD SCENE from *Ben-Hur*. Or maybe it just seemed to be, Jenny thought distractedly, as she sat in momentary solitude under an oak tree down the slope from the Grants' lakefront cottage.

Actually, the scene before her could serve as an advertisement for Club Med with its variety of bronzed, athletic bodies. Although the breeze off the water was fresh, the temperature on this late July day hovered in the mid-nineties, and everyone from the oldest to the youngest guest wore bathing suits, ready to run down to the clear, cool waters of Lake Travis for a swim.

Jenny hadn't realized when she'd come with Sam that the family picnic he'd described was doubling as Megan's bon voyage party. Not only had she met Sam's sisters and brothers-in-law, along with his nieces and nephews, she'd also been presented to several stray aunts and uncles, assorted cousins, Nate Kittridge and a sampling of Megan's friends. She was still sorting out the various kith and kin.

Nate she'd met briefly once before, and Megan she knew. All the other introductions of the morning were a blur in her mind. In fact, the whole morning was something of a blur. This was the first time she'd had a moment to rest and reconnoiter.

As Jenny surveyed the activity around her, she realized it was unique in her experience. Never before could she remember being part of such a noisy, boisterous bunch of people, laughing, roughhousing and having fun.

At the top of a gentle rise, about thirty yards from where she was sitting, sprawled the Grant weekend retreat, an unpretentious cabin that had been renovated and remodeled according to the needs of the family. It was now a haphazard collection of bedrooms and baths angling off a large family room and kitchen. Molly, Sam's mother, was in charge of the lunch preparations taking place inside.

Along the back of the house were sliding glass doors that opened up to a shaded stone patio decorated with wrought-iron furniture. One of Sam's aunts lounged there, as did Carol, his pregnant sister. There was a collection of children playing under the women's watchful looks. A large barbecue pit nearby sent out smoky, succulent scents, and a long picnic table had been set up to display the noon meal. Risa, Sam's eldest sister, periodically brought out covered dishes in preparation for the feast to come.

Just below the patio, permanent horseshoe pits had been installed. A cutthroat game of horseshoes was being waged, with Andrew, Sam's dad, and Gary, Carol's husband, pitching against Sam's two uncles. The patio contingent cheered the heated competition.

Closer to Jenny the ground continued its gentle slope, and clusters of lawn chairs were set up under the trees in anticipation of luncheon. Some of them were occupied by couples whose names Jenny couldn't remember. Several hammocks were hung between the trees. They looked perfect for afternoon siestas.

Twenty feet beyond Jenny was a dredged-out boat slip with a powerboat and a sailing sloop at dock. Plans were being made to take both vessels out later.

Right now, however, Jenny was engaged in following a rowdy game of volleyball being played on a section of level ground just in front of her. All ages were welcome to join in. In fact, Jenny had come out of the fray only minutes ago, so Sam's oldest niece, Kelly, could replace her. The young bucks of the gathering tended to dominate the play.

Sam was in the middle of the action, and it was clear to Jenny he was by far the most athletic player. Although Nate on the other team did give him a good game. Sam was also, Jenny decided judiciously, the handsomest man in sight, although again, Nate gave him a run for his money. While the game progressed, she was intrigued by the various displays of kinship and friendship, the camaraderie and bickering.

"Nate Kittridge, stop hogging!" Megan shouted. "That's the third setup you've swiped from me!"

"Start hustling, Megan!" he came back strongly. "This is a volleyball game, remember, not the Brighton ferry waiting to dock at Le Havre."

Megan glared at Nate, then stalked off the grassy court. She stopped by a blond hunk who'd been ogling her form from the sidelines.

"Michael, sweetie, sub for me. You and Nate can fight over the ball."

She slumped down in the chaise longue next to Jenny.

"That man," she muttered darkly. "Why do I let him get to me?"

"This feud between you two." Jenny eyed Megan cautiously. "Is it long-standing?"

"You noticed, did you?"

Jenny grinned apologetically. "It's hard not to."

"Forever, that's your answer." Megan smiled, but she remained disgruntled. "Nate still treats me like Sam's baby sister."

"Your friend Michael doesn't feel that way."

Megan shrugged. "Michael's a prop. I parade him in front of my family occasionally, to remind them I'm past the age of consent. It's hard being the youngest sibling."

"Is it?" Jenny asked, hoping her tone was neutral.

Megan wasn't fooled. "I'm being bratty, aren't I? Actually, I don't know what I'd do without my family."

"There seem to be a lot of you," Jenny commented lamely.

Megan grinned at her mischievously. "There's always room for one more."

Jenny decided not to pursue that line of conversation. "From what you say, I gather Sam and Nate were childhood buddies. How unusual they should go into business together."

"Nate lived down the street when we were all growing up. He and Sam have always been close. As partners they complement each other. Sam's the genius behind the firm's designs. Nate's the one who handles the business end of it. I guess you could say he's a genius, too, in his own way."

"As a pair they're fairly formidable." Jenny hesitated for a second then decided to risk the next. "Especially to female hearts."

Megan grimaced wryly. "How true. For years I had a terrible crush on Nate."

"And now?"

"Why do you think I'm leaving for Europe?" The two women's eyes met in understanding.

"I don't know why," Megan volunteered after a moment, "but Nate brings out the worst in me. It's gotten so bad I don't like to be around him. All I know is I have to get away."

"I think I know what you mean," Jenny found herself saying. "Sometimes it seems like I'm determined to show Sam my worst side. And that day with you . . ."

Megan laughed and waved her hand dismissively. "Neither of us covered ourselves with glory."

"Yet, still it bothers me that I get so defensive. You know how anxious I was about today. Afraid I'd make a fool of myself."

Megan smiled, then settled against the woven fabric. "The day hasn't been so bad, has it, Jenny?"

"No." Jenny discovered she spoke the truth. "The day hasn't been bad at all." And neither had she. In fact, it was amazing how relaxed she was feeling.

No one made a big deal about her. She was here, she was special to Sam, and the family accepted that. Molly had hugged both Sam and her when they arrived, and Jenny had been momentarily startled. Then other people poured in and received their obligatory greeting, and Jenny realized that Molly hugged *everyone*.

She'd been jarred when Andrew called her m'dear at their initial meeting. Later, the endearment became a source of secret amusement to Jenny. Andrew called all females m'dear. Probably because he couldn't remember their names.

The first time Sam had thrown an arm around her and dropped a kiss on the end of her nose, she'd stiffened in panic. Since they'd become lovers, Sam was always touching her in light, casual, unconscious ways. Sometimes she felt like a much-beloved kitten. She was still uncomfortable with public displays. Especially with his family.

As the day wore on, however, she realized Sam's caresses went unnoticed. The entire clan was generous with physical affection. They kissed and touched and cuddled each other in a way Jenny had not experienced before. It was a veritable love feast.

Jenny was struck by the thought that if she and Sam had not gone to bed with each other, if they'd come today as strung out as they'd been two weeks ago, the sexual tension and frustration would have stood out starkly amidst the easy give and take of love.

This realization struck her while they were heading to inspect the lake in midmorning. Impulsively, she'd caught Sam's hand and squeezed it with a kind of inchoate gratitude. He'd turned to her with a questioning smile, seen something in her eyes that told him of her feelings. He squeezed her hand then brought it up to brush with his lips.

No, the day was certainly not going at all as she expected.

Jenny wasn't sure how it happened, but at lunch she found herself balancing a plate heaped with beef slices, coleslaw, beans and potato salad, sitting with Sam on one side of her and Andrew on the other.

"I can't let Sam monopolize a beautiful woman," Andrew said, a definite twinkle in his eyes. "He already has things too much his way."

Jenny suspected she was in love with Andrew. His gallantry sealed her fate. "I know," she said cheekily. "I accused Sam of being spoiled soon after I met him."

"Ah, a discriminating female. How did you find her, son? I was about to give up hope."

"I'm slow," Sam drawled between bites, seemingly unfazed by the conversation. "But I finally caught on to the procedure."

Jenny almost choked on a bean.

"What procedure, dear?" Molly bustled up to them. "Are you getting enough to eat, Jenny? Remember there's plenty more where that came from." She went on before Jenny could answer. "Drew, that's the last helping of potato salad for you today. Too many eggs. Remember the cholesterol. And no more beef brisket, either. Next time, get a nice chicken breast." She patted his shoulder and landed a kiss in the vicinity of an eyebrow.

"Yes, Mol." Andrew's voice drifted after her as she continued her rounds. He turned to Jenny. "Being spoiled has its drawbacks."

Jenny failed to contain a smile.

"Grandpa, Grandpa." It was Sam's youngest niece, Tina. She careened into Andrew, almost unbalancing his plate, which he hastily set aside. Having done so, he wrapped his arms around a miniature version of Sam and Megan.

"What is it, what is it?" he asked her breathlessly.

Tina was about five years old and quite distressed. "Evan said we weren't gonna get to go in the boat after nap time. I told him you promised you'd take me. But he said you'd forget." By this time she'd wrapped her chubby arms around his neck and leaned her head against his shoulder.

They started them young in this family, Jenny thought.

Andrew chuckled. "Well, now, m'dear, your grandpa doesn't always remember everything he needs to. But he wouldn't forget an important promise like that." He smoothed her tumbling black curls. "Especially not for my best girl."

Tina seemed reassured. She found one of Andrew's earlobes and twisted it absently. "You say that to everybody, Grandpa. But your best girl's really Grannie."

"Very true," he said, looking solemnly at her. "A gentleman can have a roving eye, however."

"What's a roving eye?" Tina asked, her own eyes big.

Jenny was interested in how Andrew was going to answer. In fact, she'd been fascinated by the whole exchange, fascinated and moved. This is how Sam would look in thirty years with his own grandchildren.

She got a glimpse of how he'd be with his children, too. Because before Andrew could come up with a suitable reply, Tina had spied her uncle and bounced his way.

"Hi, Uncle Sammy. You goin' on the boat with us?" She snuggled close, obviously expecting a welcome.

Uncle Sammy? Jenny's brow arched in amusement.

Sam grinned then turned his attention to his niece. "Maybe. If Jenny wants to. You remember Jenny," he said, at Tina's questioning look. He turned her Jenny's way. "You met her this morning."

Tina leaned against Sam's leg and eyed Jenny curiously. "Are you Uncle Sammy's new girlfriend? Mama says..."

"Yes, she is." Sam stepped in firmly. "And if you ask her nicely, maybe we can all go on the boat."

"Will you let Uncle Sammy come with us?" Tina pleaded, then as if dimly remembering a set of instructions, she added, "You can come, too."

"Thank you very much," Jenny said. "I wouldn't dream of keeping your Uncle Sammy from going. If there's room, I'll come along."

"Oh boy, oh boy, I'm gonna tell Evan." Tina twirled out of Sam's arms and was on her way.

Jenny was rather sorry to see Tina go. Sam and his niece made a charming picture. One that tugged at Jenny's heart.

Sam seemed unaware he'd been part of a piquant tableau. "Thanks, Dad," he said with a deadpan expression, "for dragging us into this scheme of yours."

"Me? I didn't do it. Seems to me you got in all on your own. Don't you agree, Jenny?"

"I certainly do. And I wasn't about to play the ogre. Looks like you're going for a ride. Besides, I think it's a son's duty to come to the aid of his father."

Andrew nodded and smiled approvingly. Jenny decided she was enjoying herself.

It must have showed, because Sam's eyes narrowed purposefully. "If I go, you go. So wipe that smarty grin off your face. No, wait, I've got a better idea." And before Jenny knew what was happening, Sam had taken her plate, put it aside and scooped her up in his arms.

"Sam!" Jenny struggled against him, hearing laughter around them. "What are you doing? I was going back for seconds."

"Not now you aren't," he said, ignoring her struggles and striding toward the water's edge.

She sent out a mute appeal to Andrew. He raised his hands in a signal of helplessness and sat back contentedly to watch his son's progress.

"Sam!" Jenny hissed at her captor. "Your dad's watching! Everybody's watching! What will they think?"

"They'll think I couldn't keep my hands off you another minute. Which is God's own truth."

He waded into the shallows. Seconds later, the water rippled over Jenny's body, cooling her flushed skin, if not her embarrassment. Only Sam's shoulders and head were above the water and Jenny held on tight to keep from going under.

"Are you happy now?" she asked indignantly.

"Almost." He pulled her to him and found her mouth for a sizzling kiss.

"Sam..." she gasped when she finally could. "Th-there are people watching."

"No, they're not. Look." He turned and she peered over his shoulder.

What she saw was that Sam spoke the truth. Most of the luncheon activity was a good distance up the hill from them, and they were shielded from view by the hull of the sloop bobbing nearby. He'd snatched a moment of privacy for them.

Heading toward the ladder that hung over the stern, Sam settled Jenny on the bottom rung and moved into another kiss that left her breathless. The hard nubs of her breasts pressed into his chest, and he moved his hips against her in a heart-stopping rhythm.

"Sam," she whispered with what will she could. "Someone might come check on us."

"They know better," he growled, nibbling her neck. One hand insinuated itself beneath the fabric of her swimsuit, finding a place it knew so well.

Jenny moaned helplessly. Sam uttered a sound of sexual frustration.

"Sam, you wouldn't dare. Not here. Not now."

"I'd like to," he whispered in a seductive tone, then pulled away from her regretfully. "But I won't. Not this time."

His words set off a jumble of emotions. Should she prepare herself for a series of clandestine rendezvous? Sam certainly had ways to make her feel desired.

Jenny smiled mistily and bestowed a tender kiss on the side of his jaw.

"What was that in aid of?" He grinned crookedly.

"Oh, nothing," she said, not willing to share her thoughts.

But he must have had a good idea of what she was thinking, because he asked softly, "Having fun?"

She smiled. "Yes."

"Sorry you came?"

"No. Although I don't know how I'm going to face everybody when we go back up there."

"You think you've got problems." He guided her hand to his hard length.

She laughed. "You brought it on yourself, buster. Hauling me down here for puerile pleasures. I think you'd better take a swim."

She pushed him away, and he set off through the water with long, graceful strokes.

LATER, AS JENNY DOZED on the patio, she remembered the brief interlude. It seemed to set a seal of approval on the entire day.

Several members of the older generation had gone to the house to escape the blistering heat. The hammocks were full of napping bodies, and various guests were sprawled out on pallets. A few hardy souls were swimming their lunch off. And Sam, Andrew, Larry and Gary were out on the lake in a boat filled with an assorted miniature crew. Sam had sent Jenny a dark look as they cleared the docks, but the women shared conspiratorial smiles as they waved farewell.

Carol stopped to chat with Jenny before seeking air-conditioned comfort.

"Every time I get pregnant," she said, "I swear I'm going to time it better. In weather like this I feel like a hot-air balloon."

The implication of Carol's statement startled Jenny into asking, "Do you intend to go through this many more times?"

"I don't know." Carol's voice was dreamy. "I love big families, and Gary does, too. It's just mass-producing them I object to." She grunted as she pushed laboriously out of the chair. "You want to come in? I'll find you a spare bed."

Jenny shook her head. "I'll sit out here and roast for awhile."

Despite the goodwill and camaraderie Jenny was enjoying, she discovered she needed a moment alone.

Risa stopped by her chair to savor their strategy with the menfolk. "I love it when Sam gets that harried-uncle expression. Serves him right for not presenting Mom with his quota of grandkids." As she said this, Risa looked at Jenny with an interested eye.

"Sounds like Carol has cornered the market on grandkids," Jenny commented lightly. She wasn't about to fall into any traps.

Jenny succeeded in redirecting Risa's attention.

"My sister." Risa threw up her hands. "You'd think she never heard of the population explosion. I've had my three and that's enough. Four if you want to count Larry."

Jenny could hear the affection underlying the tart words.

After Risa left to manage the luncheon cleanup, Jenny realized that every member of the Grant family had individually welcomed her. The only one she hadn't had a private moment with was Sam's mother.

Jenny found she was apprehensive about such a meeting. Molly was so different from Annabelle. Warm, bosomy, looking after the needs of others, directing activities with the dispatch of a maternal MacArthur. She was very much the matriarch overseeing her brood.

Molly's children and husband seemed to take it with grace, although, as Sam mentioned, Risa was a younger version of her mom. Jenny was amused to see how two such similar women dealt with each other. Funny how the genes ebbed and flowed through a family. Risa and Carol looked like their father. But Tina, Carol's girl, could have been Sam's.

Sam. Molly's only son. Molly's beloved son.

How did Molly feel about his latest involvement? And how could Jenny measure up to a mother's expectations?

"Well, Risa ran me out of the kitchen."

Jenny looked up to find Molly settling herself in a chair close by.

"Did she?" Jenny asked a little faintly.

"Bossy, bossy, just like her mother."

Jenny smiled tentatively.

Molly grinned. "That's all right, dear, you're allowed to laugh. It's a standing family joke."

"Oh." *Wonderful. Brilliant repartee.*

"Actually—" Molly leaned close in a confidential manner "—I think she sent me out to talk to you. She must have decided we needed a chat."

"Oh."

"Don't worry." Molly patted her arm reassuringly. "I'll talk for both of us."

"You may have to," Jenny blurted out. "I can't seem to find anything to say."

Molly laughed. It was infectious laughter. Like Sam's. He'd gotten more than his coloring from his mother. There was also a knowing look Jenny recognized at once.

"I realize how brave you were to take us on like this," Molly said conversationally. "We can be pretty daunting. But I'm glad you came."

"I am, too." All at once, Jenny found the words simple to say.

"Good." Molly beamed as though Jenny had just eaten her spinach. "I thought it might be easier for you in a mob. You wouldn't feel like you were being dissected."

Molly was right. It had felt safe to meet the Grants on this kind of occasion, with a large crowd of people to camouflage her nerves. Jenny sensed she'd been gently but surely manipulated by Sam and his mother. If she hadn't felt so mellow she might have been incensed.

Instead, Jenny grinned, finding Molly amazingly comfortable to be with. "I might have known Sam had his reasons for insisting I come." She realized what she'd said and tried to back out of it.

But Molly wouldn't let her. She leaned close again. "Between you and me, we were anxious, too."

"Why?" Jenny asked, nonplussed by the confession.

"Well, everyone knew how important this meeting was when Sam gave us explicit instructions."

"He didn't." Jenny was horrified.

"He did." Molly nodded resignedly. "Isn't that just like a man. He might as well have waved a red flag in front of a bull. Although I have to say so far we've been on our best behavior." She said this last in the form of an anxious, amused question.

Jenny struggled with giggles. "Yes, you're right, so far you've all have been very well-behaved."

Both women broke into laughter. Jenny felt herself falling under Molly's spell.

They sat for a moment in companionable silence.

Jenny spoke first. "This is a lovely place. How long have you owned it?"

"Since Sam was a baby. We bought it with Drew's royalty money on the first textbook he wrote. Of course, that was when lakefront property was still reasonable. We remodeled and built the additions ourselves."

"I don't know how you stand going back to Austin. This stretch of lake is so peaceful."

"Sometimes it's hard. Of course, the children and their families use the cabin when they want to. You must get Sam to bring you up here one weekend. Take you sailing on his boat."

Jenny was confused by the implications of Molly's suggestion. "Yes, well..." She knew she was blushing. "It's kind of hard for me to get away. With the kennel and all."

"Sam'll find a way. I'm surprised he hasn't brought you here before. He's as pleased with that sailboat down at the dock as anything he owns. Designed it himself, had it built to specifications."

"He's ... very talented, isn't he?"

"Like his father." Molly smiled at Jenny with understanding lurking in her eyes. "For all that, they're just human. I was intimidated, too, when Drew and I started dating. But their needs are the same as other people's. You'll remember that, won't you?"

"Yes," Jenny said with some trepidation. "Yes, I'll remember that." Her voice was stronger.

Molly nodded with seeming content.

JENNY HAD ONE OTHER significant conversation. It came soon after her chat with Molly.

Sam's mother had gone inside to take the nap Risa insisted on, and Jenny was left alone with her thoughts. They were jumbled and incoherent and rather fantastical.

She and Sam were on his boat making love. People kept dropping in, nodding their approval and leaving again. No one seemed the least embarrassed. She must be dreaming. Yet she sensed she wasn't alone.

She opened her eyes and turned to find Nate in the chair Molly had vacated.

"I didn't mean to wake you."

"You didn't." She amended her statement with a drowsy smile. "At least not much."

"I saw you and Molly talking earlier and thought I'd come by to see how you were holding up."

Jenny caught his meaning immediately. "Pretty well." She laughed. "Mrs. Grant is charming."

"Molly Grant's the kindest woman alive. She can also be a little overwhelming. The whole family's overwhelming," Nate added. "Take it from an old hand. I've been in their clutches since I was ten."

"You don't seem to be hurting too badly."

"No," Nate said, laughing. "On the contrary. I probably devoured more of Molly's oatmeal raisin cookies than Sam ever did. But sometimes, being an only child with divorced parents, I get claustrophobic. All that love and affection."

He looked at her as if he sought understanding.

"I think I know what you mean," Jenny said.

"It's like being adopted by a king-size version of the Cleaver family. You wonder what you did to merit the honor."

"Except I don't think they see it that way."

"No, of course not," he agreed. "All this giving comes naturally to them. But sometimes it's hard, for me at least, to separate gratitude from my other emotions."

Something about their conversation, perhaps the fact Nate felt comfortable enough to confide in her, led Jenny to ask, "Why do you give Megan such a hard time?"

"Is it so obvious?"

"To me it is. You have to remember I'm, well, I'm interested in Sam's family."

"Then you must have noticed Megan returns the favor."

Jenny nodded.

"She didn't used to," he remembered with a crooked smile. "When Sam and I were teenagers Megan was our own personal mascot. She was like a little sister to me. I'm afraid I treated her as such. That could be why she's touchy now."

"Perhaps. It must be hard to establish your identity when you're the youngest member of a family."

"Well, she doesn't need to bring idiots like Michael around to prove she's an adult. He makes me wonder if Megan has the requisite number of brain cells. At least she'll get away from him on this trip she's insisting on taking."

"Don't you approve of that, either?"

"Megan tries her wings. Beautiful, pampered Megan on another harebrained adventure. Do you realize she's never had to make a hard decision in her life. Never had to sacrifice..." Nate caught himself abruptly. Laughed ruefully. "I guess I don't approve. But then what right do I have to pass judgment?"

"The right of an honorary big brother?"

"That's about the extent of it. You see what happens? Sometimes you forget you're only an honorary member of the family."

"No." Jenny somehow felt she had to protest. "I don't think what you say is true. It's plain they love you."

"Yeah?" He looked at Jenny levelly, and suddenly she felt included in his question. "But don't you sometimes wonder how long that can last?"

CHAPTER THIRTEEN

IT WAS A CROWD SCENE AGAIN, this time at the airport, where Megan's friends and relations were gathered. Jenny hadn't planned to be part of the farewell delegation. From conversations the previous Saturday, she had a fair idea of the numbers to be on hand. But Sam had come by the kennel to pick her up, leaving Jenny little choice in the matter.

And after all, Jenny thought, in the midst of the jostling people, a little jaded from the emotion around her, the leavetaking was a sight to behold. Megan's crowd of well-wishers dwarfed the other groups clustered in the waiting area, and her carry-on bag bulged alarmingly with care packages and presents.

The soon-to-be-world-traveler was radiant, receiving kisses and instructions with a regal grace.

Friends trooped by first.

"There's this charming hostel outside Perugio."

"Did you write down the address?"

"It's in your address book. Remember to ask for Mario."

"I'll be sure to."

"Don't forget the illuminated manuscripts in the British Museum," a fellow art major urged.

"I intend to live in the British Museum for at least a week."

"Be sure and drop me a postcard, sugar." This was Michael, who gave Megan a smacking kiss.

By this time her departure was fast approaching, and she moved into the circle of her family.

"Where are you sitting on the plane?" Molly asked nervously. "I hope it's near the front by an escape hatch."

"Mom," Megan assured her firmly. "Nothing's going to happen on the flight over."

Molly blinked rapidly and began to rearrange Megan's last-minute gifts.

"You be sure and call when you get to London, hon, so we won't worry."

"I promise I'll call as soon as I get to the bed and breakfast, Risa."

Risa gave her baby sister a hug.

"Have fun and find yourself a dark Italian." This was Carol, who was growing bigger by the day.

"And wind up like you? No, thanks, Carol sweetie. I intend to immerse myself in the cultural life."

Andrew was next in line. "Take care, have fun, live a little, daughter. And always remember, you're still my best girl."

"I'll remember, Daddy." Father and daughter shared a private moment.

Jenny had watched Andrew follow Megan's progress through the horde of well-wishers and detected the wistful look he wore.

Megan came to Sam. They hugged enthusiastically.

"Don't do anything I wouldn't do," Sam told her gruffly.

"Is that your final lecture?"

"Consider it a permission slip."

By this time, Megan's eyes held a hint of tears.

"Jenny." Megan embraced her. "I hope you're here when I get back. I'd like us to be friends." The next she said for Jenny alone. "No matter what happens."

"I'd like that, too," Jenny answered, her throat suddenly constricted.

Nate made up the end of the line. Interesting that he should show up for the final farewell.

Megan and he stood staring at one another as though they had nothing to say. Megan spoke first.

"Peace?" Smiling faintly, she held out her hand.

"Peace." Nate smiled crookedly. With an awkward movement he hauled her into his arms. "A year's a long time. Promise me you won't change too much."

"I make no promises. Except to come back."

"That'll have to do." Nate stared at her broodingly, then brushed her lips with a tender kiss.

By this time, Molly's cheeks were damp. She clasped her daughter to her again. "Promise you won't take any unnecessary risks."

"Mom, I promise. Nothing catastrophic is going to happen to me. Please don't worry. Dad?"

Andrew took both of them in his arms. "I'll do my best to make her behave, sweetheart."

"Mom?"

"I'll try not to worry." Molly made the effort to smile bravely.

"Now, I've given you an itinerary for the first few weeks. And I'll write from each place I visit, so you'll know how to keep in touch."

Just then, the announcement to board blared over the loudspeaker. Megan gathered her things, smiled one last smile that included everyone, waved and disappeared through the boarding gate. As Jenny watched the slim figure merge with the crowd of travelers, she finally grasped what Megan had tried to tell her. This wasn't a lark she'd embarked upon, as Nate imagined, it was a journey of exploration into herself.

Megan's smile and wave and a certain gallant expression stayed with Jenny all the way home.

LEIA MET HER as soon as they arrived at the kennel. "You have a message from Bob Ingram. He sounded upset. Asked you to call him at this number as soon as possible."

Sam had gotten out of the car and was walking around it. He and Jenny shared a look before she rushed inside with the scrap of paper Leia had given her.

"Southside Veterinary Clinic."

"This is Jenny Hunter. I was told I could reach Bob Ingram here."

"Yes. We were hoping you'd call. Arnie, Richard's dog, has been run over."

Jenny sucked in her breath, fighting a sudden sharp pain. "Is he dead?"

"No. But he's banged up pretty badly. There're bones broken and internal bleeding. Dr. Johnson's in surgery with him now. Wait, I'll get you Mr. Ingram."

Jenny held the phone tightly as the seconds ticked by. Sam started to come into the room but stopped in the doorway when he saw Jenny's expression.

"Jenny?" said a voice on the line.

"Bob."

"Did Dr. Johnson's assistant tell you?"

"Yes. She said it was bad. How is Richard holding up?"

"Richard's beside himself. He asked for you."

"I'll be right there." As soon as she hung up the phone Sam was beside her.

"What's wrong?"

"Arnie's been hit by a car. They don't know if he'll live." As she said the words she realized how grim they sounded. "I have to go there."

"I'll drive you."

She caught Sam's arm. "You don't have to. I heard you tell Nate you'd meet him at the office."

He cradled her shoulders. "I'd like to go with you. You might need me. I can call my office from the vet's."

Jenny imagined for a second the scene at the clinic, the dreadful possibilities ahead. She nodded shortly. "I'd like you to come."

As they drove to the clinic, Jenny reminded herself she knew Dr. Johnson and trusted him. He had as fine a surgical hand as any veterinarian in Austin.

But dogs and cars were unequal foes. She'd seen the grisly results of other clashes.

A dog's death was a part of the business Jenny hated, and she knew firsthand what Richard was going through.

"Freddy was run over by a car," she said bleakly.

"I remember you telling me."

"I was older than Richard, but it took months, years, for me to get over his death."

"I know. It may not come to that. Arnie's not gone yet."

He pulled into the clinic parking lot. Jenny rushed in the door ahead of him. Dr. Johnson's receptionist knew Jenny's face.

"They're in the first examining room."

"Any word on Arnie?"

"Not yet."

Jenny steeled herself and felt Sam's hand warm on the small of her back.

When she opened the door of the room where the Ingrams were waiting, Richard's blotchy face jerked up with dread. Bob's chalk-white features seemed to sag.

"Jenny!" Richard ran into her arms and began to cry. "A—Arnie's going to die. J-just like my m-mother. She was hit by a car, and he's going to die."

"Shh." Jenny cradled his head against her breast. "We don't know that. Dr. Johnson's a very good surgeon."

Deep sobs convulsed his body. "There...there was blood everywhere. He was crying with pain."

"I know. I know." She stroked his hair, fighting nausea. "It's hard to take. But he's not in pain now. The doctor's taken care of that."

"It's all my fault. I killed him."

Jenny's eyes flew to Bob. He lifted his hands in a mute gesture.

"What do you mean, Richard?"

"We were outside. Arnie was off his leash. He saw another dog and started up the street toward him. When I called him he turned and tha-that's when the car hit him."

"It was an accident, son." Bob started forward. "It wasn't your fault."

Richard turned and stared at him. "You said it was your fault when Mom died. You said...if you'd been with her...it wouldn't have happened."

Jenny saw Bob flinch at Richard's outburst, then he dropped on his haunches beside his son. "I know. I said a lot of foolish things after your mother died. It was so hard to comprehend what had happened. But it was a tragic accident, no one was to blame. Today was an accident, too. And nobody's fault."

Richard shook his head. "If it hadn't been for me, he wouldn't be hurt."

"Richard..." Bob struggled for words. "There are so many ifs in this life. We always say them when something bad happens. But we just have to face the bad things and go on."

Tears welled up in Richard's eyes. "I can't go on. Arnie's my friend. My very best friend. I need him." He turned to Jenny's shirtfront, weeping desolately.

Finally Jenny spoke. "Richard, I don't know if this will help, but I've been through what you're feeling. Remember, I told you about Freddy?"

Sam knew how hard it was for Jenny to scrape at an old wound.

Still crying, Richard peered into her face. "I—I remember."

"He was hit by a car like Arnie."

"Did he die?"

"Yes, he did." She smoothed a tear from Richard's cheek. "And he was my best friend, just like Arnie."

Richard swallowed hard. "Did it hurt bad? Did you...did you ever get over it?"

"It hurt very badly." Jenny took a deep breath. "You see, I lost my dad like you lost your mother. When Freddy died it reminded me of him. But eventually the hurt began to go away, and I got on with my life and made new friends. You know I love Hilde very much."

Jenny's revelations had widened Richard's eyes. But when she said the last, he vowed desperately, "Nobody will ever take Arnie's place."

"You're right. No friend can ever replace another. Whatever happens, Arnie will have a special place in your heart."

"No one can ever take Mom's place, either."

"No. But you have her memories."

"I know." Richard's voice was barely above a whisper. "I talk to Arnie about her all the time."

Sam had been watching Bob's face during this poignant exchange. He saw Bob's eyes close in immense pain.

Sam decided it was time to ask, "How long did Dr. Johnson say the operation would last?"

Bob pulled himself together. "He wasn't sure." Belatedly he offered Sam an awkward greeting. "It depended on whether he could...on the extent of the damage." Bob looked at his watch and had trouble reading it for a second. "He's ... he's been in well over an hour now."

"A good sign." Sam's assessment earned everyone's attention.

Jenny certainly understood what he meant. If Dr. Johnson had seen that Arnie's condition was hopeless, he wouldn't be working this long to mend him. Instead, out of mercy, he'd have put him to sleep.

Richard raised his head to question Sam. "You think he might live?"

Sam smiled at the boy. "I know Arnie's a fighter. If he has anything to say about it, he'll pull through."

The mood in the room lightened briefly. The tension, however, was a palpable force.

And then Richard began to talk, to ramble, really. About Arnie. As if saying his name could work a magic spell.

"Remember how small Arnie was?" he asked his dad. "You brought him home on my birthday. He must have grown over two feet."

"I remember." Bob seemed to glimpse the reason for Richard's chatter and he continued, "You know, when I walked into the pet store, I knew he was the one."

"Really?"

"Really. He told me, 'I belong to Richard.'"

Richard tried out a tentative grin. "Remember the first day we started wrestling on the carpet? Arnie tore my shirt."

Bob nodded. "The first of many. Remember how he couldn't get on your bed at first and he'd sit and howl until you picked him up and put him on it."

"Yeah." Richard's chuckle was watery, but it was a chuckle nonetheless. "Then when he was up he couldn't get down. And he'd howl some more."

Richard's look included Jenny. "You ought to see how Albert comes and sits between Arnie's paws. And Arnie licks and licks him till he's wet all over."

The door opened, Richard's voice faded and everyone turned. Dr. Johnson came in looking sober.

Richard stiffened inside the circle of Jenny's arms.

"He made it through surgery." Dr. Johnson spoke directly to Richard. "I've done everything I can for now. The next couple of days will tell the tale."

Richard's joy at the doctor's initial words vanished. "You mean he still may not make it?"

Dr. Johnson chose his words carefully. "I give him a little better than even chance."

Sam didn't envy him the performance of his duty.

Dr. Johnson tried to explain Arnie's condition in more detail. "He lost a lot of blood. I had to go in and patch up some internal organs, and his hip had multiple fractures from the impact. I put it in a cast. If Arnie does live he may have a permanent limp."

"I don't care about that," Richard declared vehemently.

"I know. I was just cautioning you. Would you like to see Arnie? He's still under the anesthetic."

Richard nodded. They all trooped into the surgery and found Arnie lying there, a distressing sight. His midriff was swathed in bandages, half his hindquarters was enveloped in a cast and an IV dripped into the vein of a front leg. But at least he was peaceful. Richard could remember him free of pain.

"There's nothing more to do, and he's not awake. The best thing for you folks now would be to go on home. We'll give you a call later and update you on his condition."

Richard looked up at the vet beseechingly. "Can't I stay with him tonight?"

"No, Richard." Bob spoke, glancing at the vet with an anxious look.

But the vet understood why Richard asked the question.

"That won't be necessary. We have a cot in the back. Either my assistant or I will be with Arnie all night. He won't be left alone."

Although the vet's assurance failed to mollify Richard completely, after several more minutes he allowed himself to be led away.

As soon as they left the building, Richard grabbed Jenny's hand. "Will you come home with us for a little while?"

Jenny and Sam exchanged looks. His arm encircled her. He said softly, "Go on over. Phone me at the office or at home when you feel you can get away, and I'll come by for you."

Bob cleared his throat. "I can take her home."

Sam shook his head. "That won't be necessary. You have enough to deal with." He kissed Jenny briefly and waved goodbye.

Little was said on the way to the Ingram home. All three passengers were engrossed in their own private thoughts. Richard leaned against Jenny's side and twisted his hands in nervous patterns, and Bob seemed to be pondering some idea of his own.

"Richard," he said, once they were inside, "let's go to the living room and talk awhile." Jenny headed for the kitchen. "No, Jenny, you come, too. Maybe you can help."

Albert, mewing loudly, brushed up against them. Richard reached for him and cradled him tightly, tears threatening again.

Jenny followed the Ingrams into the living room with some trepidation.

Yet Bob's first words were unexpected. "Richy, like Jenny said earlier, does today remind you of when your mother died?"

Richard, still clutching Albert, wiped at a tear. "Y-yes, a little. I remember we went to the hospital, only I couldn't see Mom. I had to sit and wait with Gran in the waiting room."

"Yes, I remember. Waiting for Arnie today must have been very hard."

"It still is."

Bob stroked his son's hair. "I know what you mean."

"Dad?"

"Yes, Richy?"

Richard hesitated a moment before he worked up his courage. "Did Mama hurt like Arnie did?" In spite of the tears, Richard's face was pale.

"No, son." Bob reached for Richard and pulled him closer. "Your mother was never in any pain. From the time of the impact she was unconscious."

"I heard someone crying at the hospital. I wondered."

Those two words wrung Jenny's heart. She could see the impact they had on Bob.

"I promise, Richy, it wasn't your mom. Why didn't you come and ask me about it?"

"I couldn't." Richard's face grew pinched.

"Why not?"

"You didn't want to talk about Mom. Ever. I thought...I mean, you said you killed her. I wondered..." He shrugged and shook his head.

They would probably never know all Richard wondered. Bob heaved a great sigh. "Oh, Richard, if only I'd known."

"I used to hear you crying late at night, and I was afraid to come to you. I cried, too, before I had Arnie."

"I wish you had come to me, Richard, we could have cried together. I loved your mother very, very much. Remember that. You and I both did. We shouldn't have grieved alone. I wish...I'd like us to talk about her now, when we feel like it. To share memories. Would you like that, too?"

Richard nodded and snuggled closer to his father. After a long while he spoke. "Dad?"

"Yes?"

"Why are you calling me Richy? You and Mom used to. Afterward—you never did."

"Because calling you Richy reminds me of her. You remind me of her, did you know that? You have her eyes and eyelashes."

"I do remind you of Mom?"

"Yes."

"I'm glad."

"I am, too, Richy. I am, too."

After another moment, Richard asked, "Will Albert die?"

The unexpected question startled Bob. "No. Of course not. I mean, why should he? Why do you ask?"

But Jenny knew.

"Richard, do you worry about people dying?"

Richard turned to her. "Yes. Sometimes."

"Who do you worry about?"

"Different people," he mumbled.

"Do you worry about your dad?"

"Yes." Richard's face began to crumble. "All the time."

The horror of Richard's confession struck Bob dumb before he protested, "But there's no reason to worry. I'm young and healthy. I intend to live a long time."

"Mom was young, too. Arnie's young. And he may not live."

"He's going to live. And I promise you I will. Oh, Richy, so many things we've been keeping from each other. We mustn't do that any more. Promise you'll come to me when anything worries you."

"If you want me to," Richard responded solemnly. "You didn't used to want me . . ."

"I want you very much. And I want us to share." He took Richard's hand and held it tightly. "I'm sorry for these last two years. I was so torn up when your mom died, I guess a little of me died with her. Maybe that's the reason you've been so scared. But I intend to live from now on. I promise."

He took Richard's other hand. "I'm also sorry I couldn't hear you crying. You heard me and you've taught me a lot. From now on if we need to cry, we'll do it together." Bob's voice trembled. He embraced his son and silent tears fell down his face.

Jenny rose quietly, went to the kitchen and phoned Sam's office. She left a message with his secretary that she was ready to leave. Then she drew herself a glass of water and sat at the table. Her fingers traced random doodles on a paper napkin she found.

She could hear the murmur of voices in the living room, and she sensed the miracle of healing that was taking place.

And she wished...how she wished...that at some time, long ago, she had had this conversation with her mother. That together the two of them had shared their tears.

She had no idea how much time had passed when Bob found her.

"Richard's fallen asleep on the sofa. He was exhausted."

"It's probably the best thing that could happen. I called Sam's office. He should be here soon."

"Jenny?"

"Yes?"

"What you shared at the clinic about your father, I think I understand why you and Richard have become so close."

Jenny nodded. "Richard does remind me of myself at that age. He's so vulnerable."

"I see that now. My eyes are finally opened. I feel I have you to thank for it." He smiled faintly. "And Arnie. I just hope the price isn't too high or the damage too great."

"Whatever happens, Bob, I feel you can handle it."

"I appreciate the confidence you have in me. I'll need it. I just wish you'd told me..."

"About my father?" Jenny folded her hands in a nervous gesture. "His death isn't something I talk about easily."

"Then I'm doubly grateful you shared it with Richard. But that's not what I was referring to."

"I don't understand."

"I wish you'd told me about you and Sam. The other night—if I'd known—it wouldn't have happened."

"Known what?" Jenny faltered.

"Known that you and he were more than friends."

"I—I would have told you. I should have told you. I know that now."

Bob grimaced. "Now you don't have to tell me. Sam's made what's between you perfectly clear."

Jenny started. "Did he? Has he talked to you about us?"

"He didn't have to. Today was enough to show me he's the man in your life."

"Bob, I'm sorry the other night happened also." Jenny held out her palms in a helpless gesture. "Quite honestly, I'm not sure what's between Sam and me. You're right, though. At this point, I couldn't think of another man."

"Except Richard. I'd better talk to him. I'm afraid he had high hopes for the two of us. I'm afraid I fostered them. It's up to me to undo the damage."

"No, don't. It'll be better if the words come from me. But I'll have to wait before I can explain my feelings. Right now I wouldn't know what to say. I'd only confuse him."

"Because you're confused."

"Very." Jenny sighed.

"I wish I could help you like you've helped me."

Jenny shrugged. It was a forlorn gesture.

"For what it's worth, Sam's a good man." A thought struck Bob and he asked anxiously, "He doesn't object to you and Richard?"

"Of course not. He's very fond of Richard. He understands how important our friendship is."

"Good. Because Richard still needs you. He really loves you."

"I love him, too. He . . . he came into my life at a critical time. Remember what you said to Richard, that he'd taught you a lot?"

Bob nodded.

"Well, I know what you mean. He's taught me, too."

"And a child shall lead them . . ."

CHAPTER FOURTEEN

THE NOONDAY SUN WAS DAZZLING, even through dark glasses and closed eyelids. The water lapped against the boat with a hypnotic rhythm, and the breeze was gentle as it rippled over Jenny's skin.

Too gentle. Sam had already enriched her vocabulary with a number of nautical idioms, most of them pungent, as he worked to angle the sails into the erratic puffs of wind.

Sam might be hard at work. Jenny, however, was feeling lazy. The heat was too enervating, the cushions too comfortable, her prone body too sated from sunning and swimming to care about any silly old wind.

Jenny decided that being on a sailboat in the middle of a lake on a summer Saturday constituted something of a miracle. Even more amazing was having the whole weekend to share with Sam. Jenny couldn't remember when she'd been away from the kennel for such an extended time. She hadn't realized till now how her business dictated her every move.

Sam had persuaded her to come with a combination of mysterious threats and tantalizing promises. And after all, arrangements had been surprisingly simple. Leia was more than happy to help out.

Jenny couldn't think of a single care in the world at this very moment. It was the oddest feeling. To be lying here utterly relaxed within touching distance of a very special man who'd explored her body and delved into her mind. Who knew her, perhaps, better than she knew herself. A troublesome thought if she followed it to its logical conclusion. She refused to do so, determined to dwell in the peace of the moment.

As if she'd tempted the fates, Sam's boat floundered in the waves and the rigging clattered as the sails whipped around. Sam let out a particularly salty epithet and Jenny chuckled throatily, not bothering to open her eyes.

"I had no idea sailing was such a frustrating hobby."

"I had no idea I'd signed on such an indolent crew."

"Mmm. What can you expect with the wages you pay me?"

"I see. Mutiny on Lake Travis. Being no Captain Bligh, however, I'm willing to negotiate terms."

Sam's voice was close. Jenny knew if she opened her eyes, she'd find his face just above hers, his mouth distractingly near.

Reveling in an intoxicating feeling, Jenny kept her eyes closed and tormented him with an enigmatic smile. "I don't know if I'm willing to negotiate anything. I may just lie here forever. Or until lunch, whichever comes first."

Without warning, Jenny felt one of her nipples tweaked through the wet halter of her swimsuit. Her eyes popped open as Sam whisked away her sunglasses.

"That's better," he announced. "I was wondering how I could get your attention. Turn over, cupcake, you're beginning to burn."

Jenny harrumphed but did as Sam instructed. In a moment, she felt her halter being unfastened and the straps smoothed away.

"Sam?"

"We wouldn't want that gorgeous back of yours to have a tan line."

"What about people in other boats?"

"You're decent as long as you lie there quietly. At my mercy."

"Whadda ya mean?" she mumbled.

He didn't bother to explain. In a moment, Jenny felt a cool, creamy lotion squeezed onto her back. Then his hands rubbed the cream over her shoulder blades, along the sides of her breasts, down the small of her back, to the line of her swim briefs. With silky strokes he repeated the procedure.

"Who's minding the tiller?" she asked groggily.

"I have it on automatic pilot."

"I didn't know sailboats had automatic pilots."

"I'd say," he murmured, "that you had a lot to learn."

He smoothed cream over her legs, skimming the insides of her thighs. His fingers moved to her ankles, her feet, and up again slowly.

By this time, Jenny was almost mindless. "I saw a scene like this in a movie once," she mumbled, barely resisting the urge to turn and take him into her arms.

"How did it end?" Sam whispered over her.

"With hundreds of violins and a slow fade-out. How's...this one going to end?"

He popped her smartly on the rear. "With lunch. The one thing you told me would get you vertical."

Jenny jerked up and realized her bathing suit was slipping. Sputtering, she lay down and tried to fasten it securely.

"Here," he offered, laughing wickedly. "Let me do that."

"Don't you touch me. You...you lech."

He backed away, his hands held high, a twinkle deep in his blue eyes.

She resumed her futile struggle.

Another minute or two went by before he asked with false meekness, "Are you sure you couldn't use some help?"

She sent him a sour look, but gave up on the offending garment in disgust. He settled it around her and deftly fastened it.

Jenny jumped up from the cushions she'd been forced to cling to and advanced on Sam in a menacing manner. "How dare you finagle me into a compromising position, drive me wild with a five-cent version of a seduction scene, then swat my rear and announce lunch?" By this time her breasts jutted against his bare chest.

"It was revenge," he explained, his hands sliding around her waist. "You've been driving me wild lying there like a peach, warm, pink, moist and ripe for eating. You made me hungry."

His lips came down on hers and his tongue dipped into her mouth. It was a kiss that tempted rather than satisfied. Jenny leaned into it greedily. Sam was the first to break away.

"But since I can't have you—" he sighed lustily "—at least not here in broad daylight, and since it's hot as hell in the cabin right now, I'll have to be content with a sandwich. And so, m'dear, will you."

Jenny's lips curved teasingly as she tried to control her pounding heart. "Did you know when you said that you sounded just like your father?"

"Did I?" He cocked a brow. "Well, I expect he, too, has his lecherous moments."

"I'm in love with your father." Jenny looked at Sam through her lashes.

"Are you?" He explored the dip in her waist. His fingers began an inventory of her rib cage.

She closed her eyes involuntarily. "Oh, Sam, I love it when you touch me."

He cupped her bottom and pulled her to him. "That's more like it. Just remember who you're supposed to be in love with around here."

Although Sam said the words in a mock menacing way, it was the words that made Jenny uneasy.

She broke away with a nervous smile. "I'd also love some lunch. I guess you're going to tell me I'm in charge of the galley."

He let her slip away, although his look narrowed briefly.

"Well, you'd better be good for something." He tossed out the warning as he hauled down the sails and threw over the anchor. Jenny looked around and discovered he'd found a sheltered cove in which they could enjoy their meal.

The tense moment passed. Together they explored the ice chest and sacks of groceries Sam had provided, then lingered over a simple but ample lunch.

Sam suggested a swim.

"Aren't you supposed to wait an hour?" Jenny asked, more in the mood to drowse like a lizard in the heat.

"Nonsense." He pushed her, protesting, over the side of the boat and followed with a whoop.

Later, Jenny climbed on board and stretched luxuriantly. "Mmm. Now I really need a nap." They were topside. Sam was right, the cabin was stifling. He was busy hoisting the sails and stopped what he was doing to turn and shake his head.

"No nap for you, m'hearty." He studied her for a moment. "Here, slip this on, you're starting to burn."

He tossed one of his shirts her way. She shrugged it on over her dripping swimsuit.

"Such a shame," Sam said in an editorial aside, his eyes sweeping over her obscured form. Then he turned to his previous topic. "You, my sweet, are about to learn what crewing's all about. You'd better hope for a steady breeze, because otherwise we're a good three hours from the dock."

"Three hours? It didn't take us that long to get here, did it?"

"Ah, you've hit upon one of the vagaries of sailing. We were tacking into the wind going down the lake. On the trip back we have to sail with it."

"If there's no wind, can't we just use the motor?"

He acted as if she'd shot him straight through the heart.

"Use the motor? I'll have you know this is a sailing vessel."

She covered her grin. "I see. A purist. Why then do you have an engine?"

"For close maneuvering and dire emergencies." Sam's voice was severe.

Jenny wondered what constituted a dire emergency, but decided not to press him on the issue. Instead she gave in gracefully. "I guess you'd better initiate me into the art of crewing, if I ever hope to see the shore."

She'd said the magic words. With a pleased smile, he proceeded to give her step-by-step instructions on handling the lines. In a short time she found she was getting a feel for the task.

She also discovered she was enjoying it. Sam was a patient and thorough teacher. And he so obviously knew what he was doing.

He gestured her over. "Take the tiller," he ordered, making room for her beside him.

"What?" Jenny backed away, deciding he'd lost his mind. "I don't think I'm ready for that."

"Sure you are. Come on. Come on," he repeated, with calm determination.

"Won't I turn us over or something?"

He laughed. "Not in this boat. And not in this breeze, you won't. Trust me. Now's the perfect time for you to get a feel for steering."

With great reluctance she squeezed between him and the tiller, took hold of it and pulled it to her jerkily. The sails flapped wildly.

"Sam!" She almost let go in horror.

"Don't panic," he instructed coolly. His arm reached around behind her, his hand covered hers and the delicate correction he made was communicated silently.

They sailed that way for several minutes, his tutorial wordless, touch to touch. Gradually relaxing, she began to focus on her senses. The pull of the hull through the water, the thrust of the wind into the sails. The feel of his hand over hers, coordinating the boat's momentum.

She began to anticipate his subtle corrections in her fingers. A kind of kinetic knowledge flowed up her arm. Gradually his hold loosened. Now she was dictating the movements of the boat.

She laughed delightedly. "I believe I've got the hang of it."

His laughter was a rumble against her back. "Yes, I think you have." She felt his lips lightly brush her neck.

Jenny shrugged him off. "Don't distract me," she admonished. Her face settled into a mask of concentration.

They must have sailed like that for close to an hour before she relinquished her place at the helm. Feeling very accomplished, she was content to sit in the curve of his arm, leaning back to scan the scene around her.

The sun was being tugged toward the horizon. But the sky was still an azure blue. The water sweeping by them was clear and green. Houses, some modest and some of baronial proportions, hugged the near and far shorelines. And all around, the limestone hills, dotted with juniper and scrub oak, formed a backdrop to the water, sky and scatter of white sails.

"It's beautiful." Jenny's tone was hushed. "Thank you for bringing me. I've lived in Austin two-thirds of my life, yet I've never been out on Lake Travis before."

"Haven't you?" Sam's fingers tightened around her companionably. "I'm glad I was the one to show it to you."

She drew closer. "I'm glad you were, too."

THEIR SENSE OF PEACE persisted over the course of the homeward sail. They docked at last as the sun was setting, presenting them with a glorious splash of color between the V of two hills.

"No wonder artists paint sunsets," Jenny breathed softly.

"Yet no painting I've ever seen can capture their beauty."

"Give me two miles of canvas and I'll give it a try."

Sam smiled. They fell into an easy silence as he began to secure the rigging and sails. She went below to clean the cabin, gathered their things and met him topside.

They started up the hill to the house, their conversation desultory. The peaceful feeling lingered, but underneath a sense of anticipation built.

In Jenny at least. All day long she'd been touched and stroked and petted and teased. All day long she'd watched Sam's movements. The play of muscles under his skin. The strong contours of his back. The glimpse of pale flesh beneath the waistband of his swim trunks. All day long she'd sat beside him and brushed against him and laughed with him and allowed her hands to make small, tentative forays over his arms and thighs and chest. All day long she'd been seduced by the complex scent of sweat, lake water, suntan lotion and male body.

Now as dusk settled around them, Jenny could admit she wanted Sam very badly. From the way his look played over her, he wanted Jenny, too. The only questions were when and where and how they'd satisfy desire.

Sam answered those questions when they entered the darkened cottage. The air conditioning had been on since morning and the gloom was chilly against their sun-heated skin.

Jenny shivered involuntarily. Sam pulled her into his arms, stared at her for a moment and proceeded to give her the kiss she craved.

"Mmm." He left her mouth to trail a line of kisses down the side of her neck. "I've been wanting to do that all day."

"Why didn't you?" she whispered.

"Because if I had, I'd have wanted to do this." One hand reached under her shirt to unfasten her halter.

"I thought you *had* done that."

"But then I'd have wanted to do this..." Now he cupped her breast and caught her nipple between his thumb and forefinger, rubbing it erotically.

"I seem to remember..."

"And this." His finger slid beneath her briefs and began to peel them off.

"You're right," she whispered, caught up in his teasing foreplay, "I don't remember that particular maneuver."

He dispensed with the bottom half of her suit, placed her arms around his neck and pulled her up so that she straddled him. He caught her thighs with his arms and began to walk down the hall, his hard length rubbing against her intimately.

"Where are we going?" she asked, not really caring, but noticing that they'd passed the first bedroom.

"To the shower."

"Oh." She found his earlobe with her mouth and amused herself in transit. "I do remember getting wet," she murmured when they entered the bathroom and Sam headed for the shower stall.

"Yes, but wet and wild is a whole other matter."

She began to see what he meant after he'd stripped them both, adjusted the spray of water and pulled her in beside him.

Was it the heat that steamed the glass or the love play between them, Jenny wondered, as Sam made an elaborate production of rinsing the lake and lotion and sun off various parts of her anatomy. She returned the favor and discovered what a sensual medium water was as it streamed over their sensitized skin.

Of course there was always time for a few kisses. Deep, searching kisses defined by thrust and tongue, leaving her pressed against him, moaning and pliant in his arms.

He dried them off and swung her into his arms, then carried her to the adjacent bedroom, laid her on the bed and switched on the nearby lamp. He allowed his eyes to feast on her. Sprawled on the spread, Jenny had no thought of modesty. All she could think was how magnificent he looked in the glow of lamplight.

"I've been hungry all day." His voice was a husky caress.

"So you mentioned." She lifted a shoulder provocatively and started to rise. "Shall we go cook supper?"

"Supper can wait." He stopped her with a palm between her breasts. "It's you I'm hungry for."

One knee bent on the bed as he leaned over her.

"I remember." She moistened her lips and saw his eyes darken. "You compared me to a ripe peach."

"So I did. Let's see how accurate the comparison was." Sam gently pressed her into the mattress and moved over her arms to her wrists, spreading them wide. As he did so he started to nibble at her lightly. Her earlobes, her nose, the corners of her eyes, her jaw, the hollow of her throat, the slope of her shoulder.

"Mmm. Tangier, I think. And more full-bodied." His voice was lazily sensual.

"Now you make me sound like a table wine." Jenny could hardly get the words out. He was driving her wild.

"No vin ordinaire, but a vintage year."

She would have laughed at the analogy, but his mouth and hands were taking her to a place beyond laughter. His fingers smoothed over her breasts, followed the contours of her waist, stroked over her hips and thighs, spreading her legs apart. He nudged his body between them.

His mouth found one of her nipples and suckled it to a hard nub. He gave the same thorough attention to the other breast. Jenny felt the sensation deep inside her, moaned and began to stir restlessly.

She reached for him.

"Not yet." He pinned her wrists again. His mouth continued its downward journey. "Not yet. I want to taste every inch of you."

"Sam . . ." she gasped, recognizing his intentions.

"Oh, yes, lover." Sam's voice drifted up from the concave of her stomach. His tongue dipped into her navel. His lips circled closer. His hands came first, tormenting, testing. "Oh, yes, lover, you want me."

She wanted him. Yes. She was hot and wet and ready for him. And when he sought and found her, his mouth and questing tongue started an exquisite ache that grew until she was twisting wildly beneath him. And his dark, explicit words of encouragement drove her on, higher, higher, until a deep, throbbing climax overtook her, leaving her limp.

"Oh . . . Sam . . ."

"Good, so good," he assured her hoarsely.

His body skimmed over hers. His tongue thrust into her mouth and he entered her deeply with a groan of guttural satisfaction.

"Oh . . . Sam . . ." she panted, their breaths mingling, her rhythmic contractions starting again as soon as his length fit inside her.

She was stunned with the surprise and pleasure of it.

"Oh, Jenny," he breathed, "how you do encourage me. I don't think I can wait much longer."

He moved, he filled her. He began the dance of love, renewing her aching need.

"Don't wait," she moaned urgently. "I want you."

He met her want and ache with deep, hard thrusts that sent her flying apart. Until with one last plunge he took them both over the edge into oblivion.

IT WAS SEVERAL MOMENTS before either of them spoke.

"You see." Sam's voice came first, laced with complacent satisfaction. "There are a hundred variations on the act of making love."

Jenny sprawled beneath him in an exquisite stupor. "You're beginning to convince me." Her voice was dazed.

He chuckled, scooted down until his head rested between her breasts. His breath was warm as it whispered over her. "Mmm, this is nice. I may never get up."

"I may not be able to." Her words were still stunned and a little slurred.

Drifting. She began to drift. Her eyelids grew heavy.

But her stomach was empty and expressed its dissatisfaction.

"Ah, another country heard from." He pushed up so he could gaze at her, a provocative glint coloring his grin. "As I recall, one of us hasn't eaten."

Jenny reddened furiously.

Sam's laughter was delighted. "Jenny, love, will I always be able to make you blush?"

"I don't know," she answered honestly. "If we keep carrying on like this, I expect you will."

"Well, come along, my tender morsel. I'm in the mood for a juicy steak."

Sam hauled her up, then pulled on a pair of cutoffs. Jenny rummaged around in her weekend bag for shorts and a shirt.

When she went into the kitchen Sam was on the patio, firing up the grill. Jenny mixed and tossed a salad and microwaved two potatoes. When the steaks were done to perfection, they took the fixings outside, ate and watched the stars come out.

Later he took her hand and led her to the water. As they stood on the shore, the night sounds rustled around them. Lights twinkled up and down the hills, setting up shimmering reflections. A light wind had sprung up.

"Come," Sam said softly. He helped her on to the boat. Went below and came back with a blanket. Spread it for them in the shelter of the hull.

He offered his hand to her as though requesting a waltz. His smile in the darkness held a touch of whimsy.

"Would you care to make love under a nighttime sky?"

"I'd care to very much," she answered softly.

Their hands touched and they sank down on the blanket together. And their clothes fell away as if by magic.

And Jenny was filled with a great generosity of desire. And a need to know Sam as he'd known her. And the dance they danced was yet another variation as she explored his body with her hands and mouth. And pleasured him as he'd pleasured her. And their mutual pleasure became a dazzling moment like shooting stars in the spangled night.

"I love you, Jenny. I'll always love you." Sam's voice was the barest whisper after they'd settled to earth.

They drowsed, holding each other closely, until the air cooled their bodies. Then they roused enough to walk to the house, to fall into bed and into a dreamless sleep.

—

JENNY WOKE FIRST the next morning and was disoriented for a moment. She felt Sam's arm slung across her stomach and realized where she was. Trying not to wake him, she slid out of bed, shrugged on her robe and padded to the kitchen.

Unease. Wariness. Those were the unsettling feelings she'd woken up to. Jenny tried to ignore them as she searched for coffee to perk.

She sensed rather than heard Sam behind her. His hands came around her waist to insinuate themselves between the lapels of her robe and his face burrowed into her disheveled curls.

"Now this is how I like to wake up in the morning," he murmured seductively. "With a warm body to hold and a hot cup of coffee."

She shrugged out of his embrace, trying to mask the movement by opening the refrigerator to peer inside.

But Sam was too sensitive to be fooled by the ploy. His look narrowed immediately and he leaned against the counter, studying her face.

"What's wrong?" he asked simply.

"Nothing." She glanced at him, smiling brightly. "Nothing at all. I was just wondering if you could survive one of my breakfasts. What did you have planned for the day?"

His grin was wry. "Well, I had intended on dragging you to bed to make mad, passionate love. Sex in the morning has a unique flavor. But I don't think that's called for. I have a feeling we need to talk."

"I don't want to talk." Jenny's words came too quickly. She tried to hide her wariness as her eyes met his.

"Jenny, love." His voice was very gentle. "What's the matter?"

"I—I don't know," she admitted finally. "I guess I'm just needing a little space. Don't make a big deal of it."

"Big deal or little, we have to talk. That's the way people work things out with each other."

"I don't want to talk," she repeated. "There's nothing to work out." Her tone grew shrill. "Look, don't crowd me, Sam. Remember, I'm not used to all this togetherness. I'm feeling claustrophobic. Like I felt that night at dinner with Bob. Only then it was because he was trying to fit me into a cubbyhole he'd created. This time, it's because..." She stopped, struggling to finish the thought.

"It's because I'd like to surround you with love." His quiet statement beat against her.

"Cage me, you mean," Jenny flung at him. Immediately she tried to snatch back her words. "Oh, please, please, Sam, don't let's argue and spoil the weekend."

But he wouldn't let her escape. Not this time.

"You know what's happening, don't you, Jenny?" he said patiently, as if he were prepared for this discussion to last the day. "I'm getting too close. I've made love to your body and exposed your soul. You need me. You want me. You're vulnerable to me." He paused significantly. "You love me."

"Don't use that word," Jenny snapped.

"Love?"

"Vulnerable. I hate being vulnerable."

"It scares you, you mean."

"I hate being scared." She faced him defiantly. "You want to talk. All right, we'll talk. But I don't think you're going to like what I say. I spent the entire first part of my life being frightened. I used to have panic attacks, but I don't any more. Because I've learned to conquer my fears. I've learned to stand alone. I've learned I don't need anybody to be a whole person."

"I thought you'd found needing me didn't diminish you as a person."

"Have I? Have I really, Sam? Then what the hell do you think this is all about?" Jenny stared at her hands and found they were shaking.

"I think," he said, seemingly unrattled by her outburst, "that it's about the painful process of discovery. All that's happening to you has brought out facets of yourself you had to suppress for survival. But sheer survival isn't enough for you now. You say you were a whole person when we met, Jenny. Yet your defenses with me were as brittle as glass. They weren't working any more. From the very beginning you were vulnerable to me.''

"No!"

"Yes. Listen to me, Jenny. Vulnerability doesn't have to be a dirty word. It can be a gift you share with someone equally vulnerable. It comes out of intimacy and friendship. It's created from moments of mutual joy.''

He sighed as he studied her bleak features. "Don't you think I realize how much you've needed your defenses? Don't you understand how much I admire and respect your courage?''

"Then why do you keep trying to break me down?''

"Oh, Jenny." His voice broke with anguish. "That's the very last thing I'd want to do." He reached for her, and because she needed his touch, longed for it, she jerked away from him.

"Don't keep saying you love me," she pleaded. "I'm not ready for that. I just wanted us to be together.''

"Where do you think being together leads if not to love? You may as well understand this now. I am passionately, eternally in love with you. I want to spend my life with you. I want us to be married.''

She laughed harshly. "And this declaration is supposed to relieve my fears? With Annabelle's marriage as an example?''

Sam sighed. "Don't you realize you're not seeing your mother and stepfather clearly?''

"I don't know what you mean." Jenny's spurt of anger relieved the pain. "And I sure as hell don't think we need to bring Annabelle and Lloyd into this.''

"You were the one who brought them up." Sam's face was lined, a little gray, but resolute. "And I do think, since they're part of the problem, we need to talk about them, too."

CHAPTER FIFTEEN

"SAM," JENNY WARNED, "I'm not in the mood to rake up the past or talk about my mother."

"It isn't past. You just showed me how it colors your feelings. You say you're caged by my love. But you were caged before I met you. Trapped by the walls you'd built on every side."

"I don't see what my mother's marriage has to do with what you're saying."

"It's a good marriage, you know," Sam stated flatly. "Filled with affection. I don't know how Lloyd and Annabelle felt about each other when they met. But they love each other now. You just can't see it. Just like you refuse to see how much Lloyd loves you."

"That's ridiculous!" Jenny gasped. "We fight constantly."

"I'm sure you both did, at one time. You're the only one doing the fighting now."

Jenny started to speak. Sam stopped her. "Wait. I realize Lloyd's not the easiest man to know. And he's controlled and rigid, as you say. I'm sure he was lost when it came to raising a child. Still, he waded in clumsily and did the best he could, and unfortunately made you feel like a burden. No wonder the relationship between you was a disaster. It doesn't have to stay that way."

Sam studied her expression as he went on, "Lloyd wants very badly to reach out to you. Yet you refuse to let him."

"So it's my fault we don't get along." Jenny glared at him, her head held high. But he saw what lay beneath the facade of defiance. He saw her rub her temples in an unconscious sign of stress.

"It's not a question of fault," he explained. "Or blame. It's a question of forgiveness."

"Whose forgiveness?"

"Yours. Because he wasn't and can never be your real father."

"Please don't bring my father into this." Jenny's anger deserted her. She felt tears threatening.

"Jenny..." Sam reached out to pull her into his arms.

"No. Don't touch me." Her lip trembled. She bit hard and tasted blood. "Just . . . say what you have to say."

"It all began with your father's death."

"What began?"

"The fear. The hurt. The anger. Only you can't be mad at a dead person."

"So I took it out on Annabelle instead. That's what you're implying."

"I'm sure your mother was angry, too. And bewildered. And very, very young."

"I know. I understand all that."

"But do you realize your mother's second marriage scarred her as much as you. Perhaps even more so. It stripped her of pride and self-worth. It led her to seek affection however she could find it. I imagine Lloyd did represent a lifeline when he came into her life."

"So I'm supposed to forgive my mother, also. I see where you're leading." She wiped at the wetness on her cheek. "What shall I forgive her for? My father's death? Gordon? The other men? Lloyd?"

"For being who she is. A rather weak, dependent, anxious woman. You can't change her, Jenny. You understand her better than she'll ever understand you. She does love you, however, the best she knows how. And you punish her each and every day you refuse that love."

She would not cry. She wouldn't!

"What's all this forgiveness supposed to get me?"

"It's going to set you free. To give me your love."

"Wow!" She laughed bitterly. "What a prize. I don't see how you can resist it."

"I can't," Sam said quietly, pain etched around his mouth. "And it is a prize. One that's very precious to me."

Jenny knew she was hurting him. But she couldn't stop herself from saying, "You may not have any choice in the matter."

"I won't let you run away."

"Dammit, don't you see? That's exactly what I'm doing. Running as fast and as far as I can." The sobs broke through. Jenny struggled to control them. "I can't handle this relationship. It's too unequal. You do all the giving. I do all the taking. I have nothing to offer you but pain. Can't you see that, at least? It's wrong to let this continue when I know it's no good."

Jenny's fingers covered her face. The tears trickled through them. "I—I didn't want it to end s-so soon. W-why couldn't we have had this weekend, at least?"

"Oh, Jenny, love, nothing's ended," Sam said with great tenderness.

This time she let him put his arms around her.

Still she said forlornly, "I think you'd better take me home."

He shook his head. "I'm not taking you home."

"I can't g-go on with this. It h-hurts too badly."

"I know." He led her to the sink. "Here. Take a drink of water. You have a headache, don't you?"

"How d-did you know?"

He smiled crookedly without bothering to answer. Instead, he searched a cabinet and found the aspirin bottle, opened it and shook two tablets into her palm.

"What are we going to do?" It was a bewildered question.

"You're going to lie down. And rest. This is a reaction to all the new emotions. I should have expected it."

At Sam's last statement, everything Jenny had been trying to say crystalized. "You should have expected it." She swung around so they were face-to-face and backed away from him. "*You* should have expected it? Who assigned you that duty? Who are you? Saint Samuel? All-wise, all-accepting, all-forgiving Sam."

Her voice mocked him. She mocked herself. "Jenny's just having another spell. Poor foolish, needy Jenny. Don't be angry with her. She can't help being an emotional cripple." Jenny presented Sam with an awful challenge. "Is that the way you want to spend the rest of your life? Playing the rescuer to a poor lost soul?"

At last she'd succeeded in cracking his patience.

"No, dammit. And I don't plan to." His face was set, but she saw anger flare in his eyes. "Because you, Jenny Hunter, are going to grow up. It might as well be today as any other."

While Sam spoke he didn't make a move to touch her, yet Jenny felt effectively pinned by his gaze. "You once said you hated feeling sorry for yourself. Well, don't start here with me, because I sure as hell don't feel pity. You're one of the strongest women I've ever met. And that's what life takes. Strength and courage. To love and hurt and lose and love and hurt again.''

He took a deep breath. ''And we're going to do all that together, sweetheart. So don't even think of running away. And for God's sake don't kid yourself you'd be doing me a favor. You're irreplaceable, Jenny, whether you believe it or not. I need you in ways you can't imagine. You give to me in ways you may never know.''

His anger had cooled. He smiled at her with faint irony. ''You might as well resign yourself to loving me, Jenny. Because I'm not going away.''

He headed for the door.

''Then where *are* you going?'' she asked, her eyes wide and her voice reedy.

''Out on the boat for a couple of hours. We both need a little space.'' He turned and pointed a finger at her. ''And don't you dare be gone when I get back.''

SHE MUST HAVE SLEPT for several hours, Jenny thought, as she slowly drifted to consciousness. The weeping spell she'd indulged in after Sam walked out had been like a last-round knockout in her emotional battle. She'd gone into a vacant bedroom, thrown herself on the bed, and when she'd cried her last tear, she'd fallen asleep like a baby.

She'd been overwhelmed. Sam was right. He was always right.

Jenny wrinkled her nose.

How disgusting.

But she might as well get used to it, Jenny decided. He'd made it quite plain he was here to stay. And as she lay in the darkened bedroom in that oddly relaxed state when all life's problems seem solvable, she knew, at last and for good, this was the way she wanted it.

Because Sam represented life. He posed possibilities that both frightened and entranced her.

If she ran away from this man who loved and accepted her, she wouldn't just be wrapping herself into a cocoon again. More than a cage would enclose and surround her. She'd have built a coffin and climbed right in. And Jenny didn't want to live the next fifty years as a dead person.

As Sam said, she might as well grow up and face some unpleasant truths about the way she'd conducted her life till now. She might as well learn to practice a little forgiveness. Not only with Annabelle and Lloyd, but with herself.

Oh, she'd talked big. About how she'd put herself together. About how independent she was. How satisfied she was with Jenny Hunter. But she knew something Sam hadn't mentioned this morning.

She knew she couldn't accept herself until she accepted everything that had gone into the making of her. That meant accepting the past. Accepting a frightened, lonely, angry child who'd spent years in hiding.

Jenny knew she still had a lot of growing up to do. But since she didn't plan on being the lesser part of an unequal marriage...

Marriage. Jenny circled the word for a minute as if she was judging a dog in a show. She studied it from an aesthetic viewpoint. Nice lines, good muscular definition, could probably handle childbearing.

Jenny felt her cheeks heating.

Talk about an entrancing possibility...

Where was she? Oh, yes. Since she didn't plan on remaining one of Sam's salvage operations, she meant to tackle the problem right away. After all, he'd called her a strong, courageous woman. A small grin drifted across Jenny's features. He hadn't mentioned tenacious.

Where was Sam, anyway? Jenny was awake enough to notice he'd come in and covered her with a light blanket. As she lay quietly, she could hear sounds in the other part of the house. She sniffed and smelled food cooking.

What a thoughtful man. Another grin flitted across her mouth. She'd have to find ways to return the favor.

She heard the faint ring of the telephone. A wrong number perhaps? For who could be calling them at the lake on Sunday? Unless there was a problem. At the kennel? Sam's work? One of Sam's family?

Jenny would forever remember her nebulous dread.

Sam entered the room.

The look on his face was terrible.

"Jenny?" His voice was anguished.

"I'm awake. What's wrong, Sam?"

He sank on the bed and covered his face with hands that trembled. "It's Megan. A ferry sank in the English Channel, and they think she was on it."

Jenny beat back the shock. "Is she . . . ?" Her throat constricted so she couldn't finish.

"They don't know. There are so many bodies. So many people hurt." His shoulders sagged. "Mom and Dad first heard it on the news. Mom got hysterical. Said that was the ferry Megan was on. Just when Dad calmed her, they were notified. Megan's name's on the passenger manifest. We have to go."

But he sat as though he'd been stunned by a blow.

"Of course . . . of course," Jenny murmured.

She wrapped her arms around him, holding him close. He grabbed her like a desperate man wanting sanctuary.

They stayed that way for an endless moment, between what was—and what would now be the terrible new reality they must face together.

Sam's chest heaved once. Twice. But when he finally dropped his hands his eyes were dry, his expression painfully blank.

"We must go to them," he said, his words slurring.

"I'll drive."

He looked at his fingers, watching them shaking. "I guess you'd better."

Jenny never wanted to repeat that trip. It was a thirty-minute journey into the teeth of tragedy.

At first Sam said nothing. He stared out the window distractedly, his breathing labored. Occasionally Jenny could hear a grunt of pain. At one point he took her hand in both of his and held it like a bewildered child would, facing an ordeal he couldn't comprehend.

He began to talk. "Mother knew. Remember how she was at the airport? She gets these goddamned feelings!" He broke off raggedly.

Began again. "Remember Megan's smile? How she looked when she waved goodbye? I don't think I've ever seen her more beautiful." This time his voice cracked.

Jenny forced back tears. She had to see to drive. She had to get them there for Sam's sake.

"I've got to be strong," Sam muttered. "For Mom and Dad's sake. Until we know something. The waiting..."

"I know."

"I've got to find strength." His words were a plea.

"You will." She squeezed his fingers. "You'll find strength for your family. And I'll find strength for you. We're in this together."

"To love and hurt and lose and love and hurt again. I hadn't thought it would come...so soon."

"Life's never civil about these matters."

"You know that, don't you? Better than I."

"I love you, Sam. If my saying it helps any."

"It helps. God, it does help." He drew her hand to his face to kiss it, and she felt the wetness on his cheek.

She drove to the Grant house. A number of cars were parked already. They were met at the door by Larry and Gary.

"There's still no word," they told Sam and Jenny as they led the couple into the family room.

Molly and Andrew were there. Both had obviously been crying, as had Risa and Carol, who each held a parent's hand. Risa's daughter Kelly hovered close, clutching her mother's shoulder. Nate sat hunched on the sofa, his face as blank as Sam's. Other relatives stood nearby, their expressions somber. A look outside explained where the younger children had been shuttled.

Friends and loved ones were gathered for the watch.

At Sam's appearance, Molly rose and began sobbing again as she went into his arms. "I knew something would happen. I had this awful feeling."

"Mom, nothing's for sure yet." His voice was infinitely gentle. "We still haven't heard."

"I hate this waiting."

"I know. I know." He led her to her chair. Laid his hand on his father's shoulder.

Andrew took hold of it convulsively. "I'm glad you're here," he said, his voice raspy with strain.

Sam went to his sisters. They clutched at him as his mother had done, and Jenny began to understand the role he must play.

Knowing this was no time to be self-conscious, she moved along in his wake, hugging each family member. She felt them drawing strength from her as they had from

Sam. She'd been accepted into the watch. Now she must learn the role she was to play.

Sam's brothers-in-law joined him and Jenny after the tearful greetings.

"Could you tell me exactly what they said over the phone? And who are they?" Sam asked.

"An executive for the ferry line," Larry said. "There's still a lot of confusion. But Megan's listed as a passenger." He stopped for a moment, fighting his emotions. "And the letter Molly got yesterday mentioned this was the ferry she planned to take."

"Did they say how soon we'd know something?"

Gary shook his head wearily. "They don't even have an accurate bod—they still don't know..." He couldn't continue. Jenny's arm went around Sam's waist as she felt him flinch.

One of the uncles spoke. "It's time for the news. Do you think we should watch it?"

There was dread in everyone's eyes as they exchanged glances. But of course there was no choice, really. Any scrap of information was better than the awful suspense.

"Mol, I don't think you should stay," Andrew cautioned, going to his wife and bending over her. "There may be pictures."

"I can't leave. I have to know..."

Andrew's look sought out his son. Sam went to stand beside them. Jenny followed instinctively.

"I don't think," Carol cried, "I can watch."

Gary helped her from the room.

Everyone else grimly gathered around the television. Jenny had never seen quieter spectators.

The ferry disaster, not surprisingly, was the lead story of the day. And Jenny knew as she grasped the tragedy unfolding that she'd never be able to watch the reporting of another disaster with the vague sorrow or horror or morbid curiosity she'd felt in the past.

Images flickered on the screen. Bodies floating in the water. People crying, dazed. The ambulances howling.

Somewhere in the midst of all that terror was Megan. Generous, eager, loving Megan.

Jenny covered her face. Sam watched every minute of the report, but his fingers were clawlike as they clung to hers.

"Ninety-four persons known dead. Approximately thirty-seven missing. Sixty-five passengers have been rushed to the hospital and another eighty-three escaped unharmed. Several Americans are known to have been on board the ferry, which commonly carries vacationers from England to France. With all the confusion, many of the bodies have not been identified, leaving next of kin to wait and hope and pray."

Molly broke into terrible weeping and was half-carried from the room. After a word with Sam, Jenny followed.

Molly, the strong one, the matriarch who held her family together, wasn't able to fill that function, and the other family members were breaking under the weight of her anticipatory grief. Jenny knew she had to try to help.

She found Sam's parents in their bedroom. Molly was on the bed, Andrew sitting beside her. A poignant silence filled the room.

"I thought maybe I could sit with you awhile, Molly." Jenny's voice broke the silence. "Perhaps you'd like someone to talk to."

Andrew rose, gave Jenny a look of heartfelt gratitude and left the two together.

Molly seemed to welcome her presence. "Thank you for coming. For being here with Sam."

"I wanted to be here."

"Andrew and I . . . we can't talk. It hurts too much for both of us."

"I understand."

"I. . . I keep trying to pull myself together. To hope. . ."

"There is still hope."

Molly shook her head. Her words became a maternal lamentation. "My baby might be dead!"

Jenny held her hand closely.

"I keep thinking I should have stopped her."

"I don't see how you could have," Jenny said quietly. "When we talked, she was determined to go."

Somehow Jenny's words seemed to pacify Molly. "You're right. Megan's independent. She thought I was being overprotective and told me so."

"You taught her to be independent."

Molly sighed. "I know." Jenny heard a hint of resignation. "She's always had a stubborn streak, as well."

"She and Sam both."

For the first time since Jenny arrived, she saw a ghost of a smile on Molly's face. "You found that out, did you?"

Jenny nodded.

There was silence for a moment before Molly spoke again. "Each of my children is different, you know. Risa's the practical one. Carol's the dreamer. Sam has vision. But Megan's the most in love with life." She broke off, tears spilling from her eyes. But this was a quiet, subdued weeping.

Jenny held Molly's hand, offering silent comfort.

Here in this room, Jenny understood her role in the unfolding drama. She could listen. Once removed from the brutal grief of the immediate family, Jenny could bear their tears as they could not bear each others'.

"She was a beautiful child," Molly said after a time.

"She's a beautiful woman."

"My prettiest girl, in spite of the fact she looks like me. Prettier than Sam, even."

Jenny chuckled as she knew Molly expected.

"Megan and Sam—" Molly was worried again "—have always been the closest. If she is...if she isn't...alive, he'll take it hard. You'll have to help him."

"I know. I promise to be here for him."

"I'm frightened." Molly caught her arm. "I can't say this to anyone else. Andrew's heart. He's had one attack already."

"Sam's watching him closely."

"Sam's a good son. We couldn't have asked for one better."

Several minutes passed.

"You should have seen her, Jenny, at her first prom. She was dressed in pink."

"She must have been lovely."

"Carol sewed her dress. My children...are good to each other."

"It's because of the mother and father they have."

Molly squeezed Jenny's hand. "Thank you." She paused. "Talking helps. Would you like to hear about the first birthday party we gave her?"

"I'd like to hear about that."

And Molly began to speak. She talked sometimes quietly, sometimes brokenly, for almost an hour, as if saying Megan's name could bring her into the room. She seemed to be gathering Megan's memory into her arms, protectively. It was the only thing she had to hold.

They both stiffened when the phone jangled. It had become an instrument of torture for everyone.

"Help me." Molly tried to rise, clumsy with fear. "I have to go. I have to know."

Jenny helped her through the hall. In the family room, Sam held the telephone receiver and listened silently. Everyone hovered nearby.

"I see. I see..." The other voice crackled over the wire. Sam answered tersely. "Yes, I can. Black hair, blue eyes. Five feet four, hundred and ten pounds. No distinguishing birthmarks." Another long silence. "Yes, please. We'll be waiting."

He hung up the phone and turned to the anxious faces, his features a mask. "There's little new information. However, they wanted us to know they've questioned the survivors who escaped injury. Megan wasn't among them."

Someone in the room breathed a heavy sigh.

Sam made himself go on. "They're now in the process of finding out who's hospitalized. Some of those passengers are injured too badly to identify themselves."

He didn't say what was on everyone's mind. That the authorities were going about the grim task of identifying the bodies. The other reason Sam had been asked for Megan's physical description.

Nobody could say it. But the knowledge was there in each person's eyes as he or she drifted out of the room or into small groups seeking comfort.

The next few hours were the longest Jenny had ever known. But at least she felt she was serving a purpose.

She spent time with Risa.

"Kelly's taking this hard." Risa stared at her twisting hands. "She adores her Aunt Megan. We all do." Risa's voice broke. It was several seconds before she continued. "We've all wanted so much good for her. I can't understand how..." She shook her head vaguely.

For the first time since Jenny had met her, Risa was at a loss for words. Larry came over, gave Jenny an appreciative look and put a protective arm around his wife's shoulders.

"Come on, hon, let's go lie down."

"The children..."

"The children are taken care of."

Risa let herself be led away.

Later, Jenny took a food tray to Carol's bedroom. She knocked softly.

"Come in," Carol said in a muffled voice.

"I've brought some supper."

Carol turned away with a shudder. "I don't think I can face it."

"Just a little—for the baby."

"Did Gary send you?"

Jenny smiled and nodded.

Carol sat resignedly on the bed and let Jenny coax her to eat.

Jenny's time with Andrew was perhaps the hardest.

"Thank you for staying with Molly."

"I wanted to."

"Mol's not usually this way. She's worried about me, isn't she?"

Jenny didn't know how she should respond.

Andrew covered her hand. "That's all right, m'dear. You don't have to answer. Mol and I can read each other after forty years. They've been good years. Very good years." A muscle twitched in his jaw. He blinked. A tear fell down his ruddy cheek.

"Grandpa?" It was Tina who came to pat him tenderly. Exquisite little Tina, a replica of Megan. "Don't cry, Grandpa. Aunt Meggie's okay."

Andrew hugged her tightly and smoothed her hair. "If you say so, sweetheart."

"I promise she is. Just like you promise me."

Andrew smiled at her earnest features. "You make me feel much better, m'dear. How about a kiss from my very best girl?"

Tina stretched to kiss him sweetly.

It was the closest Jenny came during the entire vigil to breaking down.

Later, she found Nate on the patio staring blindly into the deepening night.

"May I join you?" she asked quietly.

Nate looked at her, and the stunned anguish Jenny saw in his face drew her to his side.

"She promised to come back," he said harshly without preliminaries.

"I remember."

"I don't even have the right to be here."

"Of course, you do, Nate. You love her, too."

"Is it that simple? This feeling I have. Does it give me the right to wait and mourn? God, Jenny, nothing between Megan and me has ever been simple."

"That doesn't negate how you feel."

"I feel as if I'm being torn apart slowly. Drawn and quartered and twisting in the wind. If she's dead . . ."

"Don't give up hope, Nate."

"There are things I should have said to her."

"Maybe you'll get a chance to say them."

Nate began to pace. "But don't you see? I'm not even sure what the words would be. That's been the trouble between Megan and me. It was easy for us to say the things we didn't mean. But we could...can...can never say..."

He leaned his palm for a long moment on the side of the house and bowed his head.

"None of this counts," he muttered. "What I feel doesn't matter. As long as she's alive."

CHAPTER SIXTEEN

JENNY WAS CONCERNED. It had been too long since she'd talked with Sam. She'd glimpsed him over the evening. They'd kissed briefly. She'd taken note of his calm features and quiet voice. Since their arrival he'd been a bulwark of strength to the entire household. Yet Jenny sensed he needed her. She'd seen him as no one else had, struggling with dread. She knew more than anyone how he'd summoned his courage for the ordeal. A lover's prescience warned her his equilibrium was fragile.

She hunted for him in vain. Then Larry remembered seeing him climbing the stairs to the attic. It was the place Molly and Andrew had furnished him when he was growing up in this house. His male haven away from the girls.

She climbed the stairs into the gloom and stuffiness away from the air conditioner's cooling hum.

"Sam?" Jenny knocked on his door.

A moment later, he flung it open. "Has there been any word?"

"No." She laid her palm on his forearm placatingly. "I just couldn't find you. I was worried."

The wild look died out of Sam's eyes, and was replaced by an expression of extreme weariness. "I had to get away and be alone."

"Would you like me to leave?"

"No." He led her inside and shut the door. They were alone in the musty silence. "I want you with me. But I saw the good you were doing. You . . . you've been very necessary. I don't know what you said to Mom, but she's found new strength."

"Your mother was wondering how she might have kept Megan here. I let her talk out her feelings. By the end, she admitted there was nothing she could have done. As for me, I just listened."

"You've been the listener we needed. How do I say thank you?"

"You don't. I'm just glad to have been of use." Jenny walked into his arms and wrapped hers around him. "Saying thank you isn't necessary."

"You are."

Shudders rippled through him as she held him close.

"I keep thinking it's a bad dream." When Sam spoke, Jenny could hear his teeth chattering. "I guess that's the way it hits people. All the old clichés are true. I'll think I've come to grips with whatever's to come. And then suddenly I'll feel as though I'm shaking apart. It's sheer terror." He took a couple of long breaths. "And then I want to run and hide. Here, in your arms. Somewhere. I think of going out to the car, getting in it and driving away. Maybe if I drive fast enough and far enough none of this will have happened."

He bowed his head and rested it on Jenny's shoulder. "This is so hard to understand. How can it be happening? Megan represents everything that's good about life."

"Your mother said that of all her children Megan's the most in love with life."

"It's true. There's so much joy and laughter in her. She's young, but I look at her and know she has the makings of a beautiful woman. Not skin-deep beauty.

But beauty from the soul out. It's not fair we might lose her."

Jenny smoothed the bunched muscles of Sam's back. There were no words she could say. No answer to that particular cry.

"Oh, God, Jenny, it hurts so bad." He began to heave dry, wracking sobs. "What can I do to make it stop hurting?"

"Nothing." Jenny held him closer and kissed the line of his cheek. She poured comfort into the contact of her body with his. Although there were tears in her eyes, she didn't notice. All her attention was focused on him.

"Pain's like love, Sam, you can't run away from it...or deny it . . . or defy it. Sometimes you just have to endure. Don't expect too much of yourself. Your feelings are important, too." As she spoke, willing him strength, the heaving subsided. The muscles under her ministering touch began to relax.

"You're a wise woman," he whispered, after a long moment.

She grimaced wryly. "Yes, I guess, in this way, I am."

"And if not a hiding place, you are my refuge." His arms tightened around her. "I need you so much."

"I know." She smoothed his hair with trembling fingers. "I know you do."

They stood that way for a long time, holding one another.

When Sam spoke again, his voice had a detached quality. Perhaps what Jenny sensed was fatigue or resignation. Or perhaps it was the blessed numbness finally setting in.

"Weeks ago," he recalled, "after we'd first met, and I knew something of what you'd been through, I looked at my family and realized what a smug lot we were. As if we'd patented happiness. We had no idea it wasn't ours to own. Now suddenly we've lost it."

"Sam." Jenny pulled away enough to look at him. "Don't fault yourself for knowing what it means to be happy. Many people live all their lives and are never touched by tragedy. But they never understand what joy is, either. Your family has a rare gift."

He sighed wearily. "We've led a charmed life. If Megan's dead—" Jenny knew he'd purposely said the words "—do you think this family will ever recover?"

She held his face between her palms, her face reflecting the pain in his. "You don't recover. You just go on. And finally you reach a reconciliation with what has happened. When that time comes, the hurt's still there, but you're thankful for the memories."

THE CALL CAME right after midnight. The household was exhausted and numb with strain. The ringing of the telephone came as an awful release.

Once again, Sam answered, "This is Sam Grant speaking. Yes." He listened a moment, swayed and gripped the table. Although tears welled in his eyes, the spasm of relief on his face was self-explanatory. "Yes. I understand. Yes. I'm sure of it." Another long pause. Sam reached for paper and scribbled on it. "We're coming. We'll take the first available flight. No, there's no need to meet us. Just tell Megan... as soon as she's conscious, tell her we're on our way."

Sam turned as he hung up the phone and said simply, "She's alive."

His two words produced a babbling of voices. Andrew and Molly rushed into each other's arms. Relatives hugged on every side. Exclamations and questions came in equal measure. Yet for an instant, as Jenny watched,

Sam stood alone, within himself, assimilating the moment. Then the old Sam reappeared, cool, taking charge and sorting out the chaos.

"Did they say how badly she's hurt?" Molly had already moved beyond initial joy to the full implications of the conversation.

Sam cradled his mother's shoulders reassuringly as he held up a hand for quiet. "Megan's concussed. But they don't think badly. None of the tests shows brain damage. She's semiconscious, her vital signs are stable, and when they called her by name she responded. The doctors are hopeful that within twenty-four hours she'll be fully alert."

"What took them so long to make an identification?"

"She was picked up by a fishing boat. Got separated from the other injured. She wasn't included in the original count."

"Did she hit her head? How was she hurt?"

"They don't know. The fisherman who pulled her out of the water revived her." Sam thought for a moment before finishing. "Apparently she almost drowned."

"I have to go to her." Molly's voice was fierce.

"Of course, you do. You and Dad both. I'll fly over with you." He looked Jenny's way. She nodded slightly. "First I have to find a flight for us to take."

The task occupied Sam for quite some time. He contacted a number of airlines before he finally found three vacancies on a plane out of Austin the next afternoon. They'd make overseas connections in Dallas. The trip was going to take the better part of a day and night.

Everyone milled around, unwilling to leave. They'd shared the anguish, now they shared the happy ending.

Jenny felt limp and utterly exhausted. Later, after Sam had left on the plane, she would recall this time as a blur of happy, tearful faces, disconnected voices, a whirl of arrangements and last-minute plans, with bits of sleep occasionally wedged in.

Risa took charge of her parents' packing. Once more she was the practical, efficient daughter. Jenny had been relieved of duty.

Still, at some point, while Risa was organizing the next day's schedule, Molly dropped into a chair next to Jenny, giving in to temporary fatigue. They shared a small, serene moment in the eye of the whirlwind. Later, Andrew came by and hugged Jenny wordlessly, and she understood what he was trying to say.

Always, Sam kept her beside him. Jenny wasn't sure whether it was for his sake or hers. Because now when weariness sat lightly on his shoulders, as he finalized the arrangements with patient efficiency, Jenny was feeling more and more fragile.

Tears came easily, at the odd moments, and for no good reason. At one point, she came to and realized she'd dozed in the bend of his arm.

It was after 3:00 a.m. before the general exodus of neighbors and friends ended. Carol and Gary went home with their sleeping children. Risa and Larry took their brood away. Nate said goodbye, his face lined with exhaustion but his expression peaceful.

Finally only Andrew, Molly, Sam and Jenny were left in the house.

"Come on, Mol, we have to get some sleep."

"I don't think I'll be able to sleep until I see for myself that Megan's okay."

"I know. But we need to try. The next few days are going to be hectic."

"But not as rough as they might have been." Husband and wife shared a private look.

Sam stood. He seemed to unbend himself joint by joint, and for the first time, Jenny glimpsed his exhaustion. "I have to go home and pack. Jenny, did you get hold of Leia?"

Jenny had trouble for a moment remembering the phone call of a lifetime ago. She nodded finally. "When we first arrived. She'll stay until I get back to her."

"Then you're coming home with me." It was a statement of fact no one thought of disputing.

He hauled her off the couch and nestled her into his shoulder. The four of them walked slowly to the door they had entered eons ago, when the pain engulfing them had had no promise of ending. Now they could see the events of the day as a dreadful interlude bounded on either side by joy.

Although Andrew had aged ten years, he'd regained his humor. "This isn't how we planned to welcome you to the family, m'dear."

Jenny felt the rush of silly tears at his words and the endearment.

"Don't tease her, Drew," Molly scolded with a touch of her old spirit. "Can't you see she's exhausted? Jenny, dear." She gathered Jenny into a maternal embrace. "I can't tell you how much your being here meant to us."

Jenny nodded vaguely. She was having trouble keeping her emotions under control, touched beyond measure at their sparing for her this small moment at the end of an unutterably draining day.

As she and Sam walked from the house to his car, she really did feel welcomed to the family

JENNY WASN'T SURE how much later they arrived at Sam's house. By this time minutes and hours were equal. She leaned on him as they went inside. Groggily, she offered to help him pack.

He dismissed her offer with an indulgent kiss, and she lay on the bed watching as within minutes he accomplished the task. Of course, he was used to traveling at a moment's notice.

For the first time, Jenny faced the fact of his leaving. Her sleepiness vanished.

More silly tears threatened to undo her composure. She wiped at them hastily, determined Sam wouldn't see. More came in their place, and she turned to the wall, blinking rapidly.

The bed gave under Sam's weight and his hands came from behind her waist to pull her into his chest. His warmth spread the length of her body.

"You're crying." His soft breath teased her curls.

"I'm not really. Really I'm not." She dashed more wetness away, furious with her weakness.

"I have to go. You do understand." Sam's voice was low beside her ear. "Mom needs to take care of Megan. Dad needs to take care of Mom. And I'm there to take care of the three of them."

"Of course, you have to go! Please don't think..." Jenny made a disgusted sound. "Just ignore me, I'm being stupid."

"You're having a delayed reaction," he told her gently. "It affects people different ways."

She turned in his arms, clutching at him. "Oh, Sam, it's horrible. Now the waiting's over, and we know Megan's okay, terrible thoughts keep going through my head. I keep imagining what it would have been like if we'd really lost her. I can't stop wanting to cry. My tear ducts have permanently malfunctioned.'' She struggled again to contain herself. ''After what you've been through, and here I am weeping all over your shirt.''

''I can take care of that.'' Sam shrugged out of his clothes and dispensed with hers. ''Come,'' he said, after turning off the light and pulling down the covers. ''Get in. What we both need is a little bodily warmth.''

Jenny snuggled close to Sam, already feeling better.

But oh, how she was going to miss him. Miss being here like this. Love was so new and precious. She couldn't help feeling it was being snatched away.

''I'm going to miss you like hell,'' he muttered against her shoulder.

''I know.'' She gulped down a sob. ''You won't let anything happen, will you?''

''No, sweetheart. No premonitions. I'll be back.'' Sam hesitated. ''It may take awhile.''

''Don't you dare hurry on my account.''

Sam chuckled. ''It'll be on my account, lover, you can be sure.''

Jenny relaxed. And drifted. Sam had prescribed the right therapy. The aftermath of strain drained from her body as they lay heart to heart. She was almost asleep when she heard Sam whisper in her ear with a low urgency, ''Say it again, Jenny.''

Say what?

Jenny rummaged through her brain, trying to recall what magical words she'd spoken. A drowsy grin appeared when she realized what he wanted to hear.

''I love you, Sam.''

''That's nice,'' he responded with a contented sigh. ''I mean, it's one thing to be told in passing, so to speak. But I wanted a chance to savor the moment. Does this mean,'' he asked, ''that you'll marry me?''

"Is this a proposal?" she countered, dreamily.

"Of course not." Sam was indignant. "When I propose it'll be in the traditional manner. I'll have you know I'm a traditional guy. It certainly won't be at five in the morning after the worst day of my life when I feel like I've been run over by a tank."

Jenny dropped a kiss in the vicinity of his Adam's apple. "Then go to sleep, Sam. You have a plane to catch."

He muttered something, but did as she directed.

IT COULDN'T HAVE BEEN too many hours later that Jenny awoke to find Sam's hands roaming her body, as if he wanted to memorize every curve. The urgent message his hands relayed whirled her into passion.

Wordlessly, she sought his mouth. Her hands reached for him, clung to him. She communicated her need and the knowledge that this was their private parting.

He thrust into her with a driving hunger. She met his thrusts with a hunger of her own.

This was a different kind of lovemaking. With no tender foreplay. There was no time or need for it. There was only time for the dark desire that fit their desperate mood. After they both came with a gasping satisfaction, Sam stayed with her and held her as if he never wanted to part.

"I'll make coffee while you take a shower," she said at last, pulling away, keeping her voice even.

Sam grunted resignedly and let her escape.

Thirty minutes later he joined her in the kitchen, looking marvelous in slacks and a shirt, though somewhat haggard with stress and lack of sleep.

She offered him a steaming cup. "Coffee's one of the few things I do well."

He grunted again and sipped gingerly. After a moment he took a larger gulp and drank greedily, pleasing her inordinately.

Jenny sat across from Sam at the table. He ran a finger over her brow and around her jaw. "Have I told you how lovely you are in the morning?"

The last thing Jenny felt this particular morning was lovely. In Sam's robe and little else, she was unshowered, disheveled and as fatigued as he. She caught hold of his hand and settled it between hers on the tabletop.

"Sam," she said earnestly, "I'd like us to talk, just for a moment."

Immediate wariness entered his eyes. "Is this going to be a repeat of yesterday morning? Because if it is, I'll unpack, strip us both and haul you back to bed with me until we get this thing settled once and for all."

Jenny couldn't help grinning. "Is that how you handle all your arguments?"

"Is this going to be an argument?"

"Don't be silly," she chided. She stood and went around to his chair. She draped her hands over his shoulders and smoothed his chest with her fingers, dropped a kiss on his still damp hair and whispered in his ear.

"I just wanted to say thank you."

"For what?" he asked, his wariness waning.

"For yesterday."

Sam pulled her around, hauled over a chair with his foot and sat her directly in front of him.

"What about yesterday?" he asked.

"I learned something very important about myself."

"And what was that?"

"Well, really, it was about you and me...and my mother and your family...and people needing people."

He entwined their fingers and waited for her to continue.

"When my father died," she recalled, "I remember Mother crying at the funeral. And at night. For a long time after. I thought there was some way I needed to help her. Even something I might have done to keep Daddy from dying. You know the kinds of crazy thoughts children get. They blame themselves. Richard's had some of those same ideas."

Sam nodded. His fingers tightened.

"Then, of course, with the way Annabelle is . . . I do love her, you know."

"I know."

"But she makes me feel inadequate." Jenny felt she wasn't expressing herself very well, but she forced herself to continue. "Especially when I was growing up. I thought I could take care of her, yet nothing I did was ever enough. And then came all the men . . ."

"None of which was your fault," he interrupted. "You were a child with needs of your own. You couldn't be expected to meet your mother's needs. You were both in an unhealthy situation. It was a good thing Lloyd came along."

"I understand that now. I'm learning so much."

"What else are you learning?"

"That you need me."

"I need you very much."

"And it's okay, because I don't feel inadequate with you. I can meet your needs, or some of them, at least."

"The most important ones. Because—" Sam paused for a moment to kiss her palm "—what we have here is a healthy, adult relationship, made up of love and reciprocity. I love, you love, I need, you need, I give, you give. We are a symmetrical equation. There may be different elements on either side, but the balance is there."

"That's not all I learned, Sam."

"Isn't it?" He smiled tenderly.

"Yesterday," she said, "I learned I could be of use. It wasn't like when my father died. I knew there wasn't a damn thing I could do to save Megan. But I could be there for you and the people you loved. I could listen. There were lessons I've already learned that helped me make a difference."

"You made a great difference." Sam's quiet voice was absolutely sure.

"I know." Without warning Jenny lost her composure. "And . . . I—I just wanted to thank you for letting me make a difference. That's all I wanted to say."

She sniffed ingloriously, suspecting she'd made a hash of her speech. Still unsure if he understood exactly what she meant to say.

Sam hauled her into his lap.

"You're welcome." His voice was like velvet. He arranged her so she was cradled in his arms.

Jenny waited for him to continue. When he didn't, seemingly content to nuzzle her ear, she pulled away, vaguely discouraged.

"Is that all?"

"What else would you like me to say?"

"I—I don't know."

"Shall I tell you," he asked, his voice husky, "that you are everything I've ever dreamed of? That I'm madly in love with you? That the first time I saw you, I wanted you in my arms? Shall I tell you that you're gallant and courageous and very wise? That you are enchanting and bewitching and sexy as hell? That right now what I'd like more than anything else is to carry you into my bedroom and..."

Jenny jumped up and swayed precariously. "I think that'll do for a start. Sam..." She held out a warning hand when he looked ready to pounce. "We're running out of time, and I've got to take a shower, and I'm trying to be serious just for a minute."

"But don't you understand?" Sam asked, his voice and expression as serious as she could have asked for. "You won't let me thank you, as you've just thanked me. Besides, any words I come up with are woefully inadequate." He smiled. "You see my dilemma."

She smiled and after a moment murmured, "Point taken. You're welcome, Sam."

"That's more like it."

He lunged for her.

She sidestepped him neatly.

"*And* you have a plane to catch."

SAM AND JENNY didn't have another private moment. The airport scene was a repeat of the previous one, with a slight variation in the participants.

When everyone had gathered, Andrew announced they'd gotten through to Megan's hospital room before leaving for the airport and had spoken to her. She was alert enough to understand they were on their way.

After that, the leave-taking was joyous, but hectic. Everyone was punchy from lack of sleep. There were a million last-minute instructions to deliver. And Nate and Sam held a business conference while they were waiting in the lounge.

The last goodbyes came too soon.

Jenny was determined not to break down.

Still, when Sam took her in his arms for a last, lingering kiss she felt like one of those heroines in a forties movie, saying farewell to her star-crossed lover in a grimy railway station.

Molly must have sensed Jenny's mood. She hugged her lavishly. "Don't worry, we'll get him back to you, dear."

Andrew winked elaborately. Jenny giggled through her tears.

Then they were gone, and only the well-wishers were left, staring at each other with empty expressions.

Risa and Larry said their goodbyes. "Jenny, have supper with us one night this week. We'll compare news bulletins."

"I'd like that, Risa."

Gary and Carol came next. "Oh, Jenny, I don't know what I'm going to do."

"What do you mean, Carol?"

"If I have this baby while Mom's gone, she'll kill me."

Jenny grinned while she helped Carol negotiate the sloping concourse. "We'll have to think of some way to keep your mind off that terrible possibility."

"Please do."

Then Nate. "Sam's given me instructions to drive you home."

"What about Sam's car?"

"I'll pick it up later."

Jenny smiled at Nate, her look misty. "Wasn't that just like Sam to make arrangements? He knows I hate driving the Mercedes. It has too many gadgets."

"Engineers love gadgets. You might as well resign yourself to his toys. If you're planning to make it permanent." There was a question in Nate's voice.

Jenny's radiant expression answered it. Nate chuckled and shook his head. "Come on, we might as well get to know each other. On the way home, you can tell me about the beauty of love and how wonderful Sam is.''

"Oh, Nate, love *is* beautiful," she exclaimed expansively. "You ought to try it."

"Funny..." Nate grinned crookedly. "Those were almost Sam's exact words."

CHAPTER SEVENTEEN

"RICHARD," JENNY SAID, trying to gauge the mood of the boy skipping along beside her. "I'd like us to talk for a minute. Okay?"

Sam had been gone five days. Jenny was bereft, yet busy. And this was a moment she'd put off too long.

Richard's glance was wary. "Okay," he agreed. "But I already know what you want to say."

"Do you? Come on." Jenny put her hand on his back, "Let's sit on the porch out of the sun." She called Zeppo and Hilde to heel.

Richard followed, kicking dust in the air with the toes of his shoes. The dogs settled themselves by Richard on the step.

"You want some lemonade?"

Richard nodded, giving Jenny the silent treatment.

She went inside and returned five minutes later with two icy glasses. They drank thirstily, washing away the sweltering August heat.

"I'm glad Arnie's doing so well," Jenny began.

Richard smiled for the first time since she'd made her request. "Yeah. The vet says he's great. I would've brought him over, but Dad says he needs to stay home and rest. You gotta come see him, Jenny. He can already get around on his cast."

"I'll do that. With Sam gone—" she purposefully introduced his name "—I have extra time."

"Yeah." Richard's tone returned to being noncommittal. His face was set.

Jenny sighed inwardly. What had made her think this would be easy? "How are you and your father doing?" she asked, taking another tack.

"Good." Richard looked up at Jenny and then away. His facial muscles relaxed a little. "Real good. We've been talking about Mom a lot. How we both miss her. We've been going places, too. Dad promised he wasn't going to work so much, either."

"I'm glad to hear that."

A moment of silence.

"There's nothing going on between you and Dad, is there?" Richard asked abruptly, bringing up the forbidden subject on his own. "I mean, you're not seeing each other or anything."

"No, Richard," Jenny answered gently. "Your dad and I are just good friends."

"I guess I figured that out." Richard's tone was grudgingly resigned. A flicker of fear crossed his features. "We're still friends, too, aren't we? You're not mad at me for, well, you know..." His voice dwindled as he watched her expression.

"We're the best of friends, I hope, and I have no reason to be angry with you. We all get ideas in our heads about how we'd like things to be. A lot of times they don't turn out that way. It's usually for the best."

"I guess." Richard sighed, giving up a dream. He glanced at her sharply. "Just as long as we don't change."

"We won't."

"I can keep coming out and helping you?"

"As much as you want." Jenny put her arm around him. "I would be very sad if you stopped helping me. In fact, maybe later, you could train to assist me when I give my classes.''

"Oh, wow! That'd be neat." At last Richard gave her a genuine smile. "I guess, then, it's okay about you and Dad. Anyway, Dad told me he wanted us to get to know each other better, before we started looking for someone else to bring into the family. He said I should consult him before matchmaking again."

Jenny hid a grin and nodded wisely. "I think that's very sound advice."

"So." Richard's look grew impish. "You getting married to Sam?"

"Richard." Jenny's voice was aggrieved. "Remember what your dad told you about matchmaking? Besides, that's a highly personal question."

"Come on, Jenny." He poked her in the ribs. "You can tell me."

"Oh, I can, can I?"

"Yeah. I kinda like Sam."

Jenny gave him an ironic look. "Sam will be very glad to know you've given your consent to the union."

"So, you are getting married. I knew it."

"Richard..." To her great chagrin, Jenny blushed.

Richard giggled gleefully. "Sam loves Jenny. Jenny loves Sam." He backed out of her reach as he repeated the taunt, the very picture of a mischievous ten-year-old.

Jenny laughed and began chasing him through the yard, Hilde and Zeppo trailing them eagerly.

"You can't catch me!"

"Don't bet on it, kiddo!"

She lunged for him and they fell on the ground. The dogs took the opportunity to lick them profusely.

"Zeppo! Hilde! Get off!"

Everyone was rather breathless.

Jenny found a place under a tree, and Richard rested beside her.

"Richard..."

"What?" His face was red from exertion and giggling. He grinned at her and leaned his head against her arm offhandedly.

"I really am glad to have you for my friend."

"Yeah. Sure." Richard's voice was nonchalant. Then he caught her serious undertone and turned so they faced each other.

"I think we both needed one this summer."

He met her gaze with an earnest expression.

"I had a lot of things to straighten out in my head, and you helped me with them."

"Yeah?"

"Yeah. You know it's not only children who get mixed up. Grown-ups do, too."

Richard nodded sagely. "That's what my dad says."

"Anyway, what I'm trying to say is, this friendship we have is a two-way street. You'll always be special. Sam's not the only male who's stolen my heart." She grinned at him teasingly. "Have I told you what a really neat kid you are?"

"Nope." Richard flushed, but he couldn't keep a beaming smile from emerging. "Didn't have to. I knew it already."

Jenny broke into laughter, and Richard joined her.

SAM HAD BEEN GONE TOO LONG. Jenny's days were full but her bed was empty. Only his nightly calls sustained her through the lonely hours. Those calls were informative, though frustrating, consisting as they did of mutual progress reports, whispered endearments and charged silences. Besides her talk with Richard, Jenny had another major accomplishment to share with Sam.

She'd found a home for the brute who was terrorizing Mrs. Wakefield. A good old boy with a pickup truck needed a guard dog and "wanted a mutt with guts." More importantly, Mrs. Wakefield had been persuaded to buy a place in the country. Her neighbors had finally risen up in arms.

The son had located a house with acreage and a caretaker so Mrs. Wakefield wouldn't be alone. Jenny knew that by moving her out of town, the son hoped no more strays would find her door.

Sam reported that Megan was doing beautifully and convalescing in a London flat. Molly and Andrew were trying to persuade her to come home with them, but she was resisting the idea, determined to put the tragedy behind her.

Supper with Risa's family came and went and produced another invitation. Carol met Jenny for lunch one day, and the topics were babies and general family gossip. If she wasn't careful, Jenny realized amusedly, the Grant family would take over her life.

THERE WAS ONE MORE THING Jenny needed to do. As the days dragged by she kept putting it off, not sure how she would work up the courage. But when Sam called to say he had plane reservations into Austin the following week, Jenny knew she had to act.

She called her mother.

"What are you and Lloyd doing this Sunday?"

Annabelle was nonplussed by the unexpected phone call. "Why...why, nothing, dear. Would you like to come by and have lunch with us?"

"Yes. There's something I want to tell you."

There was a prolonged silence at the other end of the wire as Annabelle assimilated this surprising statement. Jenny hadn't voluntarily discussed anything with her mother in over ten years.

"I hope it's nothing bad." Annabelle's tardy response was a familiar one. "You're not ill, are you, dear? I knew you weren't eating right."

"Annabelle..." Jenny's first response was familiar, too. She reined herself in determinedly. "It's nothing like that. I promise. I'm as healthy as a horse. I just want to see you."

"Oh. Well." Annabelle regrouped. "Why don't you bring Sam along? Lloyd enjoyed meeting him. He says Sam has a lot on the ball."

"Sam's not in town." Jenny's tone was unconsciously bleak.

"That's what's wrong, isn't it?" Annabelle reacted instantly. "You and Sam aren't seeing each other any more. Oh, Jenny, I liked him so much. I've been so worried you wouldn't meet someone..."

"Mother," Jenny wailed. Then she laughed and realized why. The conversation between them was so predictable and ridiculous.

"Mother," she repeated more calmly, "will you stop overreacting. Your only child is doing fine. More than fine. If you can control yourself and not try to wheedle it out of me, I'll explain everything Sunday."

Another long silence.

"You called me Mother," Annabelle said haltingly. "You haven't called me Mother in twenty years."

Jenny felt goose bumps rising at the tone of her voice. "Do you mind?"

"Oh, no, honey. I just...are you sure you're not sick?"

Jenny laughed shakily. "I'm okay. And you are my mother. At least you were the last time I checked."

"Yes, yes, of course, I am." She seemed to take Jenny's teasing literally. "I can hardly wait until Sunday, darling," she finally got out. "You must have something very important to say."

The important words came more easily than Jenny expected.

She was helping her mother clear the dishes after an unlikely meal. Conversation had been strained but divergent from the old patterns. Everyone was venturing into the unknown. Because Jenny had changed.

Strange, Jenny thought, but seeing the three of them through Sam's eyes had given her a salutary perspective. Now the affection between her mother and Lloyd was obvious. As was the protectiveness they felt for each other. Because of her.

Had she really tyrannized them for so long with her anger? Jenny was glad to slough off that anger like a layer of old, constricting skin.

Lloyd came into the kitchen, monitoring the proceedings, and Jenny decided the time was right. She put down the plate she was rinsing and took a deep breath.

"I—the reason I wanted to come today—Mother, Lloyd—I wanted to tell you Sam and I are getting married."

"Oh, Jenny! That's wonderful!" Annabelle immediately broke into tears. She embraced her daughter. "I'm so happy for you! How did it happen? When did he propose?"

Jenny laughed. "He hasn't, yet. Don't worry, a proposal at this point is a technicality." She said this last to placate Annabelle when the older woman drew back in momentary panic.

"Oh, Jenny," Annabelle repeated, starry-eyed. "I liked Sam from the minute I saw him. I told Lloyd what a nice young man he was. The day you brought him here, well, we talked later, Lloyd and I, and we decided he was perfect for you."

Jenny smiled indulgently at her mother. "This time, Mother, I have to agree."

"Jenny." Lloyd stepped forward stiffly. "I'm very pleased, and I hope you'll be happy. Sam Grant seems to be a fine young man."

"He thinks highly of you, too, Lloyd."

Jenny moved out of her mother's embrace and gazed at him for a small moment. It seemed so simple to walk over and hug him. After a stunned moment, Lloyd's arms closed around her awkwardly.

"Thank you for giving me your approval," she said. Their eyes met. Astonishingly she saw tears. "I believe," she went on quietly, "that if he's as fine a man as you, Lloyd, I'll be as happy as you could wish."

Jenny would treasure forever the look of genuinely amazed gratitude that appeared on Lloyd's face. She'd presented him with a unique gift, one only she could give.

By this time, Annabelle was weeping openly.

"Now, Mother, you're going to have to stop crying. How can you plan a wedding when you can't see to make a list?"

"A wedding?" Jenny's words stopped Annabelle's tears in mid-drop. "You're going to let me plan your wedding?" She stared at Jenny in damp astonishment.

Jenny decided she was getting the hang of this gift giving. Her eyes met Lloyd's, and they shared a look.

"Of course, I am. You'd do it so much better than I."

Immediately, Annabelle got down to business, as if she was afraid Jenny would change her mind. "There's so much to do. The rehearsal dinner. The reception. Have you set the date?''

"Not yet. With Megan and everything that's happened, Sam and I haven't had a chance to talk."

Jenny's statement necessitated an explanation, and she managed to include a fair amount of general information about the Grants.

"I'm so pleased they like you, dear. That makes it even more important that the wedding be perfect. Give me enough time to do it justice."

"Mother," Jenny interrupted hurriedly. "There is one problem . . ."

Jenny had one last present in mind to give.

"What is it?"

"I want a small wedding. I thought I'd ask Megan to be my only attendant."

"Of course, darling," Annabelle said, relieved. "I'll plan it however you say."

"But even a small wedding costs money." Jenny assumed a worried expression. "The kennel isn't bringing in much extra income. I guess somehow we'll manage, but we'll have to be . . . very careful about how much we spend."

"Jenny," Lloyd intervened hesitantly, "as far as I'm concerned, money's no object. I'd like to give you your wedding, as a present. If you'll let me? You are my stepdaughter, and I haven't been able to help you very much till now."

Annabelle fairly beamed with pleasure. "Oh, Lloyd, that would solve all our problems." She halted when she saw him waiting for Jenny's approval.

Jenny turned to him with a serene smile.

Lloyd thought as he looked at her that she was as beautiful as Annie.

"Thank you, Lloyd," she said and kissed him on the cheek. "What a wonderful wedding present. And, you know, it's your duty to give the bride away."

He looked deeply touched by Jenny's words, but he surprised both women by saying, "I don't know if I can do that."

"What do you mean?" Annabelle asked, horrified.

Lloyd's arm encircled Jenny's waist. He was still awkward with the act. "I feel like I just got her. I'm not sure I want to give her away."

NOT BAD, JENNY THOUGHT, surveying herself in the mirror. And certainly surprising for those who knew her. This was a new Jenny Hunter, who'd taken a flight of fancy.

She wore a silken dress that shimmered with her every movement. Its fine material adorned her curves. Around her shoulders she'd draped a shawl fringed with golden satin. The individual strands brushed against her skin like a lover's caress. Golden hooped earrings swung from her ears. Her pointed face was made up with delicate perfection.

The gypsy who stared at Jenny looked exotic and mysterious.

Sam had been home two weeks, his parents one. Sam and she were gloriously happy. There was just one item unresolved between them. And that, Jenny decided firmly, would be settled as soon as he arrived.

After all, this celebration at the Grants this evening was in honor of their supposed engagement. The two families were meeting for the first time. Over the course of the party, they would be asked a hundred questions. Questions for which Jenny had no answers.

Yes, Sam had some explaining to do.

Jenny heard him approach the house.

A flock of butterflies took flight in her stomach. Would it always be that way? No matter how long their life together? Would she always feel this giddy anticipation when he came near? She devoutly hoped so.

A small smile appeared as she went to meet him.

Sam's stunned look was all Jenny could have hoped for. He approached her slowly, his hands took hold of her shoulders and he brushed her lips with the most delicate of kisses.

"You know," he said huskily, "the first time I saw you, you reminded me of a water sprite. Tonight you're Titania, queen of the fairies."

"You are so extravagant, Sam. You certainly know how to turn a girl's head. Though you could still take lessons from your father."

"Leave Dad out of this," he growled. "I thought I made it clear who you were supposed to love around here."

"Why, yes, I believe you did." Jenny offered him a demure smile and slipped from his grasp. "I'm afraid—" she wrinkled her brow in elaborate distress "—I'm not very clear on a few other things."

"Oh?" There was a glint in his eyes as he watched her performance.

"Yes. A girl doesn't like to presume too much. I mean—" she glanced at him through her lashes "—she doesn't like to feel she's railroading a man."

A speculative smile played around his mobile lips. "I see. Could you be more specific?"

"Well—" Jenny gave a tiny shrug with a delectably bare shoulder "—Mother's ordered champagne. We've visited three bridal boutiques. Lloyd's already shelled out a couple of hundred dollars, and I've written Megan asking her to be my maid of honor. Yet, I am reminded of the fact you haven't actually proposed." She sent him her most wistful look.

"Sit down."

"What?"

"Sit down," he ordered.

She sat, a trifle disgruntled that he'd curtailed her theatrics.

"You couldn't wait."

"What do you mean?"

"You had to nag."

"I do *not* nag."

"Shh." Sam sealed her lips with his own. After a long moment, he pulled back and gazed at her, pleased with his efforts. Jenny's eyes were sultry, her skin was flushed and her lips were moist from his kisses.

"Jenny Hunter, will you marry me?"

Jenny's eyes popped wide for a second, then her lashes fell. "I don't know." She tried to control the tilt of her lips. "I'd hate to saddle you with a nagging wife."

"You have to marry me." His voice was a seductive murmur.

"Oh?"

"Think about the champagne your mother's ordered, and Lloyd's pocketbook and your letter to Megan. Not only that..." He stopped for a moment, deciding the slope of Jenny's shoulder hadn't had enough attention.

"Not only what?" Jenny said faintly a few moments later.

"I just signed an earnest money contract on some lakefront property. Five acres. I'll take you out there tomorrow."

"Sam." Jenny drew back. "What do you mean? Lake Travis property is too expensive."

He pulled her into his arms. "I knew you'd go stir crazy in the town house. And while this place—" he waved his hand "—has a quaint charm, it lacks certain creature comforts and amenities."

Jenny had a sudden vision of their home-to-be. Nate had warned her.

For a brief moment Sam looked uncharacteristically nervous. "I didn't mean to sign this contract without your say-so. But when I saw the land, I had to act. It's perfect for a house and kennel. If you don't like it we'll look around some more."

"Sam." She took his face between her palms. "I'm sure I'll love the place. You just shouldn't have been so extravagant."

"I am—" he looked slighted offended "—a man of some means."

"Yes, dear," Jenny said, kissing him on the cheek.

"Jenny..."

A long moment passed.

"You haven't given me an answer."

"Haven't I?" Her eyes when she gazed at Sam were full of laughter and so much more.

"No. You haven't," he grumbled, "and I'm getting impatient."

"Yes, I'll marry you."

They sealed her acceptance with another kiss.

"Sam...people are waiting for us."

"Let 'em wait," he whispered, his lips brushing the swell of her breasts.

"Sam! You're—you're wrinkling my dress."

"We could take care of that problem." His hands moved around to her zipper.

"Sam..." Her voice was a sigh rather than a reprimand.

Reluctantly he pulled away. "Okay. I'll restrain myself until later in the evening."

"Is that a promise?"

"That I'll restrain myself?"

"No," she said softly, "later in the evening."

He smiled. She smiled at him, her heart fluttering. Oh, how she adored this man!

"I love you," she told him with sudden urgency.

"And I love you." His voice was calm and very sure. "There is one other thing..."

Jenny looked questioning as Sam dug in his pocket. Her eyes widened when he pulled out the jeweler's box. Tucked in the velvet was an emerald nestled in a cluster of diamonds set on a golden band.

"Sam, you shouldn't have." Jenny was genuinely flustered. "A ring wasn't necessary."

"I told you I'm a traditional kind of guy."

He slipped it on her finger while she stared in wonder.

"And that—" he nudged her chin up with a finger so he could drop a kiss on the end of her nose "—is what I was waiting for. The ring had to be custom made."

"Are you sure this isn't a dream? I'm afraid I'll wake up and find you gone. I don't ever want to go back to the way I was living."

"I don't, either. I can't imagine my life without you." Sam stood and pulled her into his arms. They held each other in affirmation of all the promises that had been made. And all the gifts that had been given.

"I have the feeling things have changed between you and Annabelle and Lloyd," he said finally.

"Lloyd's paying for the wedding. Annabelle's planning it and playing mother of the bride. It might be one of her finest hours."

"That was generous of you," he said quietly.

"It's easy to be generous when you've been given so much."

"Speaking of generous, we have people waiting. Since you won't let me ravish you, we'd better go."

Twenty minutes later they arrived at Sam's parents' house. Cars lined the street in both directions. The entire crowd was assembled.

Somebody must have been watching for the couple's arrival, because as they walked up the steps, a rousing if wildly original rendition of the wedding march from *A Midsummer's Night Dream* drifted out to them.

Jenny and Sam shared a last private look, joined hands and went in to face the music.

Harlequin Superromance®

COMING NEXT MONTH

Harlequin Superromance®

A powerful restaurant conglomerate that draws the best and brightest to its executive ranks. Now almost eighty years old, Vanessa Hamilton, the founder of Hamilton House, must choose a successor. Who will it be?

Matt Logan: He's always been the company man, the quintessential team player. But tragedy in his daughter's life and a passionate love affair made him make some hard choices....

Paula Steele: Thoroughly accomplished, with a sharp mind, perfect breeding and looks to die for, Paula thrives on challenges and wants to have it all ... but is this right for her?

Grady O'Connor: Working for Hamilton House was his salvation after Vietnam. The war had messed him up but good and had killed his storybook marriage. He's been given a second chance—only he doesn't know what the hell he's supposed to do with it....

Harlequin Superromance invites you to enjoy Barbara Kaye's dramatic and emotionally resonant miniseries about mature men and women making life-changing decisions. Don't miss:

- CHOICE OF A LIFETIME—a July 1990 release.
- CHALLENGE OF A LIFETIME —a December 1990 release.
- CHANCE OF A LIFETIME—an April 1991 release.

You'll flip . . . your pages won't!
Read paperbacks *hands-free* with

Book Mate • I

The perfect "mate" for all your romance paperbacks

Traveling • Vacationing • At Work • In Bed • Studying • Cooking • Eating

Perfect size for all standard paperbacks, this wonderful invention makes reading a pure pleasure! Ingenious design holds paperback books OPEN and FLAT so even wind can't ruffle pages— leaves your hands free to do other things. Reinforced, wipe-clean vinyl-covered holder flexes to let you turn pages without undoing the strap...supports paperbacks so well, they have the strength of hardcovers!

Pages turn WITHOUT opening the strap

SEE-THROUGH STRAP

Reinforced back stays flat

Built in bookmark

BOOK MARK

BACK COVER HOLDING STRIP

10 x 7¼ opened
Snaps closed for easy carrying, too

Available now. Send your name, address, and zip code, along with a check or money order for just $5.95 + .75¢ for postage & handling (for a total of $6.70) payable to Reader Service to:

Reader Service
Bookmate Offer
901 Fuhrmann Blvd.
P.O. Box 1396
Buffalo, N.Y. 14269-1396

Offer not available in Canada
*New York and Iowa residents add appropriate sales tax.

BM-G

COMING SOON

In September, two worlds will collide in four very special romance titles. Somewhere between first meeting and happy ending, Dreamscape Romance will sweep you to the very edge of reality where everyday reason cannot conquer unlimited imagination—or the power of love. The timeless mysteries of reincarnation, telepathy, psychic visions and earthbound spirits intensify the modern lives and passion of ordinary men and women with an extraordinary alluring force.

Available in September!

EARTHBOUND—Rebecca Flanders
THIS TIME FOREVER—Margaret Chittenden
MOONSPELL—Regan Forest
PRINCE OF DREAMS—Carly Bishop

DRSC-RR